As she shook her head the auburn hair fell about her shoulders, and although he could not see the woman's full face, there was no doubt about that profile, at almost the same angle as she had assumed for the artist Jacques Louis David. He knew the face so well, for David's portrait – painted for her dead husband and later captured by Drinkwater – now inexplicably lay rolled under the desk of the Prince of Eckmühl.

In his distraction Drinkwater resisted the tug of his guard so that the soldier became angry, stepped behind him and thrust his ported musket into the small of his prisoner's back with a sharp exclamation. Drinkwater stumbled forward, losing his balance and attracting the attention of Lieutenant Dieudonné and the woman. Gilham caught Drinkwater's arm; recovering himself, Drinkwater looked back. Beyond the menacing guard the woman was staring after him, her face in the full light of the leaping candles on the staff officer's desk.

There was no doubt about her identity: she was Hortense Santhonax and she knew Nathaniel Drinkwater to be an officer in the Royal Navy of Great Britain.

*Also by Richard Woodman:*

*In the Nathaniel Drinkwater series*

AN EYE OF THE FLEET

A KING'S CUTTER

A BRIG OF WAR

THE BOMB VESSEL

THE CORVETTE

1805

BALTIC MISSION

IN DISTANT WATERS

A PRIVATE REVENGE

THE FLYING SQUADRON

THE DARKENING SEA

ENDANGERED SPECIES

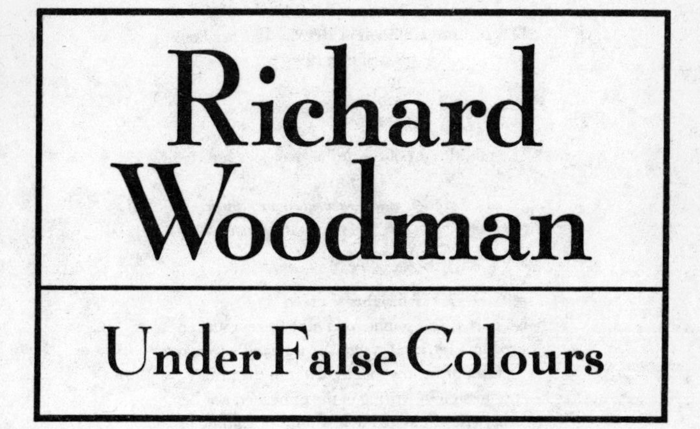

# Richard Woodman

# Under False Colours

A *Warner* Book

First published in Great Britain in 1991
by John Murray (Publishers) Ltd
This edition published in 1992 by Warner Books
Reprinted 1996



A CIP catalogue record for this book
is available from the British Library.

ISBN 0 7515 0023 2

Printed in England by Clays Ltd, St Ives plc

UK companies, institutions and other organisations wishing
to make bulk purchases of this or any other books
published by Little, Brown, should contact their local
bookshop or the special sales department at the address below.
Tel 0171 911 8000. Fax 0171 911 8100.

Warner Books
A Division of
Little, Brown and Company (UK)
Brettenham House
Lancaster Place
London WC2E 7EN

# Contents

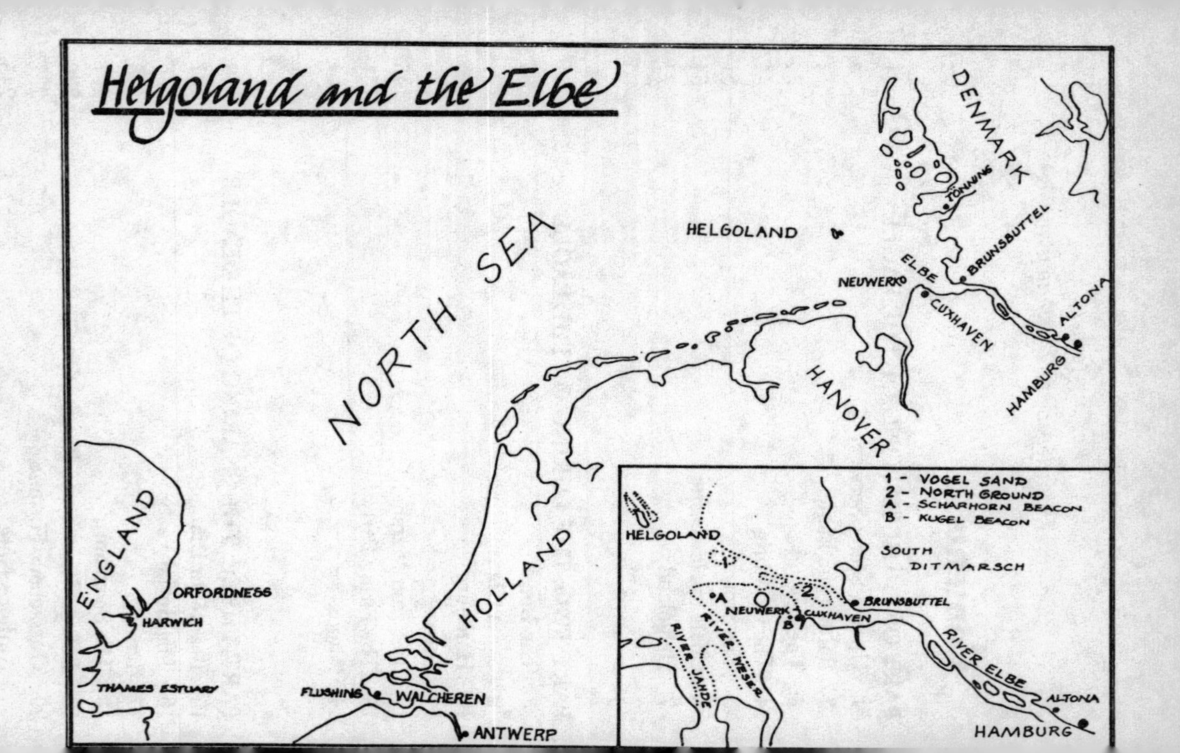

Helgoland and the Elbe
DENMARK
TÖNNING
BRUNSBUTTEL
HELGOLAND
ELBE
NEUWERK
CUXHAVEN
ALTONA
HAMBURG
NORTH SEA
HANOVER
HOLLAND
ENGLAND
ORFORDNESS
HARWICH
THAMES ESTUARY
FLUSHING
WALCHEREN
ANTWERP
1 - VOGEL SAND
2 - NORTH GROUND
A - SCHARHORN BEACON
B - KUGEL BEACON
HELGOLAND
SOUTH
DITMARSCH
BRUNSBUTTEL
NEUWERK
CUXHAVEN
RIVER WESER
RIVER JANDE
RIVER ELBE
ALTONA
HAMBURG

*For my father,*
*who first mentioned the Northampton boots.*

PART ONE

# The Baiting of the Eagle

'The British Islands are declared to be in a state of blockade.
All commerce and all correspondence with the British Isles are prohibited.
Every . . . English subject . . . found in countries occupied by our troops . . . shall be made prisoners of war.
The trade in English commodities is prohibited . . .'

NAPOLEON
Articles 1, 2, 4 and 6,
The Berlin Decree,
21 November 1806

CHAPTER 1 August 1809

# Upon a Secret Service

'God's bones!'

Nathaniel Drinkwater swallowed the watered gin with a shudder of revulsion. His disgust was not entirely attributable to the loathsome drink: it had become his sole consolation in the weary week he had just passed. Apart from making the water palatable the gin was intended as an anodyne, pressed into service to combat the black depression of his spirits, but instead of soothing, it had had the effect of rousing a maddeningly futile anger.

He pressed his face against the begrimed glass of the window, deriving a small comfort from its coolness on his flushed forehead and unshaven cheek. The first floor window commanded a view of the filthy alley below. From the grey overcast sky – but making no impression upon the dirty glass – a slanting rain drove down, turning the unpaved ginnel into a quagmire of runnels and slime which gave off a foul stench. Opposite, across the narrow gutway between the smoke-blackened brick walls, a pie shop confronted him.

'God's bones,' Drinkwater swore again. Never in all his long years of sea service had an attack of the megrims afflicted him so damnably; but never before had he been so idle, waiting, as he was, above a ship's chandler's store in an obscure and foetid alley off Wapping's Ratcliffe Highway.

Waiting . . .

And constantly nagging away at the back of his mind was

the knowledge that he had so little time, that the summer was nearly past, had *already* passed, judging by the wind that drove the sleet and smoke back down the chimney pots of the surrounding huddled buildings.

Yet still he was compelled to wait, a God-forsaken week of it now, stuck in this squalid room with its spartan truckle bed and soiled, damp linen. He glared angrily round the place. A few days, he had been told, at the most . . . He had been gulled, by God!

He had brought only a single change of small clothes, stuffed into a borrowed valise with his shaving tackle; and that was not all that was borrowed. There were the boots and his coat, a plain, dark grey broadcloth. He had refused the proffered hat. He was damned if he would be seen dead in a beaver!

'You should cut your hair, Drinkwater, the queue is no longer *de rigueur*.'

He had avoided *that* humiliation, at least.

He turned from the window and sat down, both elbows on the none-too-clean deal table. Before him, beside the jug and tumbler of watered gin, lay a heavy pistol. Staring at the cold gleam of its double barrels he reflected that he could be out of this mess in an instant, for the thing was primed and loaded. He shied bitterly away from the thought. He had traversed that bleak road once before. He would have to endure the gristle-filled pies, the cheap gin and the choked privy until he had done his duty. He swung back to the window.

The rain had almost emptied the alley. He watched an old woman, a pure-finder, her head covered by a shawl, her black skirt dragging on the ground where amid the slime, she sought dog turds to fill the sack she bore. Two urchins ran past her, throwing a ball playfully between them, apparently oblivious of the rain. Drinkwater was not deceived; he had observed the ruse many times in the past week. He could see their victim now, a plainly dressed man with obvious pretensions to gentility, picking his way with the delicacy of the unfamiliar, and searching the signs that jutted out from the adjacent walls. He might be something to do with the shipping lying in the Thames, Drinkwater mused, for his like did not patronize the establishment next door until after dark. He was certainly not the man for whom Drinkwater was waiting.

'You'll recognize him well enough,' Lord Dungarth had said, 'he has the look of a pugilist, a tall man, dark and well set up, though his larboard lug is a trifle curled.'

There had been some odd coves in the alley below, but no one to answer that description.

Drinkwater watched the two boys jostle the stranger from opposite sides, saw one pocket the ball and thumb his nose, saw the stranger raise his cane, and watched as the second boy drew out the man's handkerchief with consummate skill, so that the white flutter of its purloining was so sudden and so swift that it had vanished almost before the senses had registered the act. The two petty felons, their snot-hauling successful, capered away with a gleeful dido, the proceeds of their robbery sufficient to buy them a beef pie or a jigger of gin. The stranger stared after them, tapped his wallet and looked relieved. As the man cast a glance back at the trade signs, Drinkwater withdrew his face. A moment later the bell on the ship's chandler's door jangled and the stranger was lost to view. In the narrow ginnel a vicious squall lashed the scavenging pure-finder, finally driving her into shelter.

Drinkwater tossed off the last of the gin and water, shuddered again and contemplated the pistol. He picked it up, his thumb drawing back each of the two hammers to half cock. The click echoed in the bare room, a small but deliberately malevolent sound. He swung the barrels round towards him and stared at the twin muzzles. The dark orifices seemed like close-set and accusing eyes. His hand shook and the heavy, blued steel jarred against his lower teeth. He jerked his thumb, drawing back the right hammer to full cock. Its frizzen lifted in mechanical response. It would be *so* easy, so very easy, a gentle squeezing of the trigger, perhaps a momentary sensation, then the repose of eternal oblivion.

He sat thus for a long time. His hand no longer shook and the twin muzzles warmed in his breath. He could taste the vestiges of gunpowder on his tongue. But he did not squeeze the trigger, and would ever afterwards debate with himself if it was cowardice or courage that made him desist, for he had become a man who could not live with himself.

In the months since the terrible events in the rain forest of Borneo, his duty had kept him busy. The passage home from Penang had been happily uneventful, blessed with fair winds and something of a sense of purpose, for Lord Dungarth had written especially to Admiral Pellew – then commanding the East Indies station – that Captain Drinkwater and his frigate were to be sent home the moment they made their appearance in the China Sea. The importance of such an instruction seemed impressive at a distance. His Britannic Majesty's frigate *Patrician* had arrived at Plymouth ten days earlier and Drinkwater had been met with an order to turn his ship over to a stranger and come ashore at once. Taking post, he had reported to the Admiralty. Lord Dungarth, head of the Secret Department, had not been available and Drinkwater's reception had been disappointingly frosty. The urgency and importance with which his imagination had invested his return to England proved mistaken. Captain Drinkwater's report and books were received, he was given receipts and told to wait upon their Lordships 'on a more convenient occasion'.

Angry and dejected he had walked to Lord North Street to remonstrate with Dungarth. He had long ago angered the authorities – in the person of John Barrow, the powerful Second Secretary – but had hoped that his destruction of the Russian line-of-battle ship *Suvorov* with a mere frigate would have mollified his detractor. Apparently he remained in bad odour.

There had been more to fuel Captain Drinkwater's ire than official disapprobation. In a sense he had been relieved to have been summoned so peremptorily to London. He did not want to go home to Petersfield, though he was longing to see his children and to hold his wife Elizabeth in his arms again. To go home meant confronting Susan Tregembo, and admitting to her the awful fact that in the distant jungle of Borneo he had been compelled to dispatch his loyal coxswain Tregembo, whose tortured body had been past all aid, with the very pistol that he now held. The fact that the killing of the old Cornishman had been an act of mercy brought no relief to Drinkwater's tormented spirit. He remained inconsolable, aware that the event would haunt him to his own death, and that in the meantime he could not burden his wife with either himself or his confession.*

In such a state of turmoil and self-loathing, Drinkwater had arrived at Lord Dungarth's London house. A servant had shown him into a room he remembered, a room adorned with Romney's full length portrait of Dungarth's long-dead countess. The image of the beautiful young woman's cool gaze seemed full of omniscient accusation and he turned sharply away.

'Nathaniel, my dear fellow, a delight, a delight . . .'

His obsessive preoccupation had been interrupted by the entry of Lord Dungarth. Drinkwater had thought himself ready for the altered appearance of his lordship, for Admiral Pellew, sending him home from Penang, had told him Dungarth had lost a leg after an attempt had been made to assassinate him. But Dungarth had been changed by more than the loss of a limb. He swung into the room through the double doors on a crutch and peg-leg, monstrously fat, his head wigless and almost bald. The few wisps of hair remaining to him conferred an unkempt air, emphasized by the disarray and untidiness of his dress. Caught unprepared, shock was evident on Drinkwater's face.

'I know, I know,' Dungarth said wearily, lowering himself into a winged armchair, 'I am an unprepossessing hulk, damn it, a dropsical pilgarlic of a cove; my only consolation that obesity is considered by the *ton* a most distinguished accomplishment.'

'My Lord . . . ?' Drinkwater's embarrassment was compounded by incomprehension.

'The Prince of Wales, Nathaniel, the Prince of Wales; a somewhat portly adornment to the Court of St James.'

'I see, my Lord, I had not meant to . . .'

'Sit down, my dear fellow, sit down.' Dungarth motioned to a second chair and regarded the drawn features, the shadowed

* See *A Private Revenge*.

eyes and the thin seam of the old sword cut down Drinkwater's hollow cheek. 'You are altered yourself; we can none of us escape the ravages of time.' He pointed to the Romney portrait: 'I sometimes think the dead are more fortunate. Now, come sir, a drink? Be a good fellow and help yourself, I find it confounded awkward.'

'Of course.' Drinkwater turned to the side table and filled two glasses.

'At least our imbroglio in the Peninsula has assured a regular supply of *oporto*,' Dungarth said, raising his glass and regarding Drinkwater over its rim, his hazel eyes as keen as they ever were. 'Your health, Nathaniel.'

'And yours, my Lord.'

'Ah, mine is pretty well done in, I fear, though the brain ain't as distempered as the belly, which brings me in an orotund way,' Dungarth chuckled, 'to my reasons for sending for you.' His lordship heaved his bulk upright. 'I'll come directly to the point, Nathaniel, and the point is Antwerp.

'We've forty thousand men on Walcheren investing Flushing; forty thousand men intended to take Antwerp, but bogged down under the command of that dilatory fellow Chatham.'

'The *late* earl,' Drinkwater joked bleakly, referring to Chatham's well-known indolence.

'You've heard the jest.' Dungarth smiled as he rang for his servant. 'Where are your traps? We'll have them brought round here. And William,' he said as he turned to his valet, 'send word to Mr Solomon that he is expected to dine with us tonight.'

'The point is,' Dungarth went on when the man had withdrawn, 'we are no nearer securing Antwerp than when we went to war over it back in 'ninety three, unless I am much mistaken. The expedition seems set to miscarry! We have expended millions on our allies and it has gained us nothing. We bungle affairs everywhere – I will not bore you with details, for their recounting does no one credit, but our fat prince is but a symptom of the disease . . .'

Dungarth's tone of exasperation, even desperation, touched Drinkwater. He had sensed in the earl's voice a war weariness, and the fear that all his services were to come to nothing.

'Between us, Nathaniel, I am driven almost mad by blunders and folly. Furthermore, Canning holds the purse for my work at the Secret Department, and I fear to cross Canning at this delicate juncture.' Dungarth paused.

'And this delicate juncture touches me, my Lord?'

'Yes, most assuredly. D'you command a following on that frigate of yours? A lieutenant who can be trusted?'

'I have a lieutenant who is dependent upon me, and a midshipman with an acting commission whom I would see advanced.'

'You can depend upon the lieutenant, utterly?'

'I can depend upon them both.'

'Who are they?'

'Lieutenant Quilhampton . . .'

'The cove with a wooden hand?'

'The same, my Lord, and a man recently displaced by my removal from the ship.'

'And the other?'

'Mr Frey, an able fellow, well enough used to doing his duty now.'

'How would they fare doing duty in a gun-brig on special service?'

'Admirably, I shouldn't wonder.'

Dungarth seemed to consider some secret design, then he looked up. 'Very well, since there seems no impediment . . .'

'Ah,' Drinkwater broke in, 'there is one matter to be taken into account: Mr Quilhampton is anxious to marry. The affair has been deferred before and I doubt his *fiancée* will consent to further delay.'

Dungarth frowned. 'Then let him marry at once, or wait . . .'

'Wait, my Lord, for how long?'

'How long is a rat's tail? Be assured this service will not last long. It must be accomplished before the ice forms in the Baltic –'

'The Baltic . . . ?' Drinkwater interrupted, but a distant bell diverted Dungarth's attention.

'That will be Solomon, Nathaniel,' he said, ponderously drawing himself to his feet. 'He is to be trusted, despite appearances.'

Dungarth's man announced the visitor and Dungarth performed the introductions. 'My dear Solomon, may I present Captain Nathaniel Drinkwater, lately arrived from the Pacific; Nathaniel, Mr Isaac Solomon, of Solomon and Dyer.'

'Y'r servant, Mr Solomon,' Drinkwater said, taking the Jew's hand. He wore the shawl and skull cap of Orthodoxy and had a fine-boned, palely handsome face framed by long, dark hair.

'Yours, Captain Drinkwater,' Solomon said, bowing slightly and regarding Drinkwater with an appraising eye.

'You will not refuse a slice or two of cold mutton, Isaac?' Wielding his crutch, Dungarth led them into an adjacent room and they settled before the earl resumed. 'What we propose,' Dungarth said, drawing Drinkwater into the web of intrigue and indicating that the mysterious Jew was party to the plot, 'is to send you to Russia.'

'To Russia!' Drinkwater frowned. ''Tis late in the year, my Lord . . .' He began to protest but Dungarth leaned forward, his knife pointedly silencing the criticism.

'A single cargo, Nathaniel,' he began, then threw himself back in his creaking chair, 'but Isaac, you elucidate the matter.'

'I have no need to extol the effects of the blockade of the European coastline by our naval forces, Captain,' Solomon said in a low, cultured voice, 'it is our chief weapon. But to oppose it the Emperor Napoleon has proclaimed a "Continental System", an economic interdiction of any British imports upon the mainland of Europe and Russia. Such a declaration was first thought to have been the phantasm of a disordered mind; alas it has proved remarkably successful.'

Drinkwater watched the eloquent gestures of the Jew's hands, accurately guessing the man belonged to that international mercantile confraternity that overcame political boundaries and evaded belligerent obstacles whenever possible.

'Two years ago we took Helgoland, both as a listening post with its ear close to the old independent Hanse city of Hamburg, and as an entrepôt for our trade . . .'

'But a wider breach must be cut in Napoleon's wall of *douaniers*, Nathaniel,' Dungarth broke in suddenly, 'something that does more than merely discredit his policy but *destroys* it! A cargo to Russia, a cargo to Russia as one of many cargoes! Such a cargo, widely advertised in Paris, could not fail to sow seeds of mistrust between Napoleon and his vacillating ally, Tsar Alexander.'

'You seek, if I understand aright,' Drinkwater said, 'to detach the Russian Tsar from his present alliance and reunite him with Great Britain?'

'Exactly! And it is our only chance, Nathaniel, before we are ruined, our last chance.'

'And this cargo, my Lord, has something to do with me, and Lieutenant Quilhampton?'

'It does.'

'Well, what is this cargo?'

'A quantity of Northampton boots, Nathaniel.'

'*Boots?*' Drinkwater's astonishment was unfeigned.

Dungarth nodded, his face a mask of serious intent, adding, 'and yourself, of course, to be employed upon a most secret service.'

CHAPTER 2 August 1809

# Baiting the Eagle

Below him the jangle of the chandler's door bell recalled Drinkwater to the present. The stranger emerged, settling his tricorne hat on his head and holding it there against the wind. The man turned away with his coat tails flapping, leaving the alley to the sleet and a solitary mongrel, which urinated purposefully against the wall of the pie shop opposite. The grey overcast was drawing the day to a premature close, but still Drinkwater sat on, recalling the twilight of that dawn, eight days earlier, when at the end of a night of planning he had sat at Lord Dungarth's escritoire. Apart from the servants, Drinkwater had been alone in the house, Isaac Solomon having departed an hour earlier, his lordship following, bound in his coach for the Admiralty.

'Do you write to your protégés, Nathaniel,' he ordered, 'and I will have orders drawn up for the expeditious preparation of a gun-brig for your escort. Deliver your letters by seven and I will have them carried by Admiralty messenger.' He had been about to depart then added, as an afterthought, 'If you wish to leave word for your wife, I will have it sent after your departure. It would be best if few people know your whereabouts.'

Few people, Drinkwater ruminated savagely, would think of looking for him here, even if they knew him to be in London; and the fact that his Lordship's proposal fell in with his private desires did nothing to assuage his sense of guilt. To this was added an extreme distaste for his task. It was perfectly logical when expounded in Lord Dungarth's withdrawing room, but it was a far cry from his proper occupation, commanding one of His Britannic Majesty's ships of war.

'You will assume the character of a shipmaster of the merchant marine,' Dungarth had instructed. 'Here are a coat and *surtout*,' he had said as his servant brought the garments in, 'and a pair of hessian boots.'

Drinkwater regarded them now; they had once been elegant boots, a tassel adorning the scalloped tops of their dark green leather.

'I don't need more than one at a time, these days,' he recalled Dungarth joking with bitter irony. 'I'll have your sea kit shipped aboard Quilhampton's brig . . .'

Drinkwater had slipped into Wapping feeling like a spy.

And he felt worse now, worn by the tedious days of idle waiting, trying to sustain his spirits with the assurances of Dungarth and Solomon that his part in lying low in Wapping was crucial to the success of the mission, but unable to stop worrying whether or not Elizabeth knew of *Patrician*'s arrival home, or how Quilhampton, the matter of his marriage pressing, had viewed his secret orders.

But over and over again, as he waited interminably, it seemed, his thoughts came round to the secret service to which he was now irrevocably committed.

'Isaac has provided the capital and made arrangements for a large consignment of boots and greatcoats to be loaded aboard a barque lying in the Pool of London. To all outward appearances the whole transaction is a commercial one, a speculative venture that contents the manufacturers,' Dungarth had explained.

That much Drinkwater had guessed. Mr Solomon was clearly a cut above the Jewish usurers, slop-sellers and hawkers who supplied credit, cash and personal necessities to His Majesty's fleet. Solomon had alluded to a considerable illicit trade run through Helgoland and Hamburg, actively encouraged by Bourrienne, once Napoleon's private secretary, but then the Governor of Hamburg.

'M'sieur Bourrienne,' Solomon had explained, 'suffered from a sense of grievance at the loss of his influential position with the Emperor; his co-operation was not difficult to secure.' Solomon had smiled. 'And, of course, Captain, every cargo sold to Hamburg or Russia is of benefit to England . . .'

Staring down into the rain-lashed ginnel, Drinkwater thought of the snatches of rumour and news he had gleaned in his brief period back on English soil. There were scandals in both the army and the navy, in addition to the fiasco that seemed inevitable at Walcheren. More disturbing were the riots in the north and the increasingly desperate need for markets for manufactured goods. Doubtless Solomon would profit privately from this venture, for Dungarth's remarks concerning Canning suggested his alliance with the Jew was a bold stroke, but if a trade could be opened with Russia, it might ameliorate the sufferings of the labouring poor as well as achieve the object Dungarth had in view.

But would a consignment of boots succeed in disrupting a solemn alliance between the two most powerful individuals on earth? True, there were a few other titbits. 'A few hundred stand of arms,' Dungarth had enthused, 'and a brace or two of horse pistols in the consignment, sufficient to equip a squadron or two of cavalry. Given the usual cupidity of the tier-rangers and the other waterside thieves, word of the nature of the consignment will become common knowledge along the Wapping waterfront.'

And that was the crux of the affair, that was why he, Captain Nathaniel Drinkwater of the Royal Navy, was detached upon a secret service, why he occupied this squalid, rented room and played the character of a merchant shipmaster, perpetually drunk, cantankerous and misanthropic. Sadly, it was all too easy in his present state of mind.

'Among that waterside riff-raff, you have only to find Fagan,' Lord Dungarth had finally said, 'and spread this tittle-tattle to him. He's a man known to us, d'you see, Nathaniel, a courier who passes regularly between London and Paris carrying gossip and the odd, planted message. You have merely to indicate the value, content and destination of your cargo, for its departure to be reported to Paris. We are expecting Fagan daily; he keeps rooms above a pie shop in Wapping . . .'

Drinkwater peered across the alley. It was almost dark. He struck flint on steel and coaxed a stump of candle into life.

'We want you to bait the eagle,' Dungarth had said as they rose to disperse, 'see that the Emperor takes the lure . . .'

It was not quite that easy, of course, his instructions went much further. He had to ship with the cargo, to play the charade to the last scene, to see that it reached Russia safely.

Drinkwater stood stiffly and stretched. If Fagan did not arrive soon the enterprise would have to be scrapped. Perhaps he had already arrived, and was engaged elsewhere; how did one trust or predict the movements of a double agent?

Drinkwater threw himself on the narrow bed and considered Dungarth's warning of the burden of the war, his consuming conviction that only an alliance with Russia would break the stalemate between Great Britain's superiority at sea and France's hold on the continent of Europe.

Drinkwater remembered the Russian army in its bivouacs around Tilsit. The sheer size of that patient multitude was impressive and the cogent fact that the Tsar's ill-trained levies had inflicted upon Napoleon's veterans the near defeat of Eylau and the Pyrrhic victory of Friedland argued in favour of Dungarth's ambitious policy.

'We *must* have Russia as a continental reinforcement,' Dungarth had reiterated with characteristically single-minded vehemence. 'Without her almost inexhaustible resources of manpower, there is nothing on earth to oppose France . . .'

That was true. Prussia had long ago succumbed, Austria was beaten, Germans, Poles and Danes all bowed to the imperial will. Apart from the British, only the isolated Swedes and the erratic Spaniards defied Paris . . .

'And it's such a fragile thing, Nathaniel,' Dungarth's voice echoed in Drinkwater's memory, 'this alliance between Alexander and Napoleon, so flimsy, based as it is upon a mutual regard by two vain and selfish men. The one is utterly unreliable, the other determined, wilful, but fickle . . . we have only to interpose a *doubt*, the one about the other and . . .'

He woke with a start, aware that he had dozed off. It was quite dark in the room, for the candle had gone out. From the alley came the noise of a few passers-by, seamen bound for the neighbouring knocking shop, he guessed, noting the rain had stopped. From within the house came the dull buzz of conversation and domestic activity. The ship's chandler had shut up his store to take his evening meal with his wife and mother-in-law. Later, when he had finished, he would come and attend to his uninvited guest. He was in the pay of the government, a gleaner of news who talked freely to masters and mates in want of necessaries for their ships, seamen requiring outfits and slops and all those associated with the huge volume of merchant trade which flourished despite Napoleon's Continental System.

The gin had left Drinkwater thirsty and with a foul taste in his mouth. He got up and peered into the jug. The stale smell revolted him and he found he was in want of the privy.

'God's bones,' he swore, putting off the distasteful moment and standing by the window scratching the bites of the vermin which infested his mattress. Overhead the cloud was shredding itself to leeward. 'Wind veered nor' west,' he muttered to himself. Neither the westerly gale nor the veering wind would allow a boat to slip across the Strait of Dover. Fagan would not come tonight, nor tomorrow. Not unless he was a man of uncommon energy and sailed from Cherbourg, or some other port well to the westward.

Drinkwater went back to the bed and, hands behind his head, stared up at the pale rectangle of the ceiling. Where were Quilhampton and Frey now? Had James Quilhampton caught the mail coach and raced to Edinburgh to marry Mistress MacEwan? Drinkwater had sent him a draught to be drawn on his own prize agent to finance the wedding; but there was the troublesome person of the girl's aunt and the matter of the banns.

And had Frey done as instructed, and seen the bulk of Captain Drinkwater's personal effects into safe-keeping aboard his gun-brig?

The thoughts chased themselves round and round Drinkwater's brain. He longed for a book to read, but Solomon's clerk had conducted him to the vacant room above Mr Davey's chandlery with such circumspection that Drinkwater, eager not to lose a moment and expecting the mysterious Fagan to appear within hours of his taking post, had not thought of it for himself. Mr Davey's store had yielded up a copy of Hamilton Moore, but Drinkwater had spent too many hours conning its diagrams of the celestial spheroid in his youth to derive much satisfaction from it now.

Lying still, the urge to defecate subsided. How long would he have to wait before he confronted Fagan? And how would he accomplish that most subtle of tasks, the giving away of the game in a manner calculated to inform without raising the slightest suspicion?

A scratching at the door roused him from his lethargy. He opened the door upon Mr Davey's rubicund face.

'A bite to eat, Cap'n?'

'Aye, thank you, Mr Davey, and I'd be obliged for a new candle.'

'Of course . . . if you'll bide a moment . . .'

Davey slipped away to return a few moments later. 'Here you are, sir. There's no news I'm afraid, Cap'n . . .'

'And not likely to be with this wind,' Drinkwater said morosely as Davey struggled with flint and steel.

'I wouldn't say that, Cap'n. Mr Fagan has a way of poppin' up, as it were. Like jack-in-the-box, if you take my meaning.'

'D'you know him well, then?'

'Well enough, Cap'n,' replied Davey, coaxing the candle into life. 'He takes his lodging in the room yonder. When I gets word I tell the one-legged gennelman.'

'I see. And the customer you received late this afternoon? What was his business?'

Davey winked and tapped the side of his nose. 'A gennelman in a spot o' trouble, Cap'n Waters,' he said, using Drinkwater's assumed name. 'Word gets round, d'ye see, that I sell paregoric elixir . . .' Davey enunciated the words with a certain proprietorial hauteur. 'He's afeared o' visiting a quack or a 'pothecary, but mostly o' Job's Dock.'

'*Who's* dock?' asked Drinkwater, biting into the gristle that seemed the chief constituent of the meat pie Davey had brought him.

'Job's Dock, Cap'n, the venereal ward at St Bartholomew's. He's got himself burnt, d'ye see . . .'

'Yes, yes . . .' Drinkwater was losing his appetite.

'I stock a supply for the benefit of the seamen . . .'

'I understand, Mr Davey, though I did not know tincture of opium was effective against the pox.'

'Ah, but it clears the distemper of the mind, Cap'n, it relieves the conscience . . .'

When a man has a bad conscience, Drinkwater thought, the most trivial remarks and events serve to remind him of it. Perhaps Davey's paregoric elixir would remove the distemper of his own mind. He visited the privy and turned instead to the replenished jug of gin. An hour later he fell asleep.

He had no idea how long he had slept when he felt himself being shaken violently.

'Cap'n, sir! Cap'n! Wake ye up, d'ye hear! Wake up!'

Snatched from the depths of slumber Drinkwater was at first uncertain of his whereabouts, but then, suddenly alarmed, he thrust Davey aside to reach for his pistol. 'What the devil is it, Davey? Damn it, take your hands off me!'

''Tis him, sir, Fagan . . . !'

Drinkwater was on his feet in an instant and had crossed the room to stare out over the dark gutway of the alley. No light betrayed any new arrival over the pie shop opposite. There were noises from the ginnel below, but there always were as the patrons of the adjacent bordello came and went.

'He's next door, sir, in Mrs Hockley's establishment, Cap'n.'

'How the deuce d'you know?' asked Drinkwater, drawing on the borrowed boots.

'She sent word, Cap'n. She keeps her ears and eyes open when I asks her.'

'You didn't mention me?' Drinkwater asked, relieved when Davey shook his head.

He wondered how many other people knew that Fagan was expected in the Alsatia of Wapping. It was too late for speculation now. His moment had come and he must act without hesitation. He pulled on his coat and took a swig of the watered gin, swilling it round his mouth and spitting it out again, allowing some of it to dribble on to his soiled neckcloth.

'I wouldn't take your pistol, Cap'n, Ma Hockley don't allow even the gentry to carry arms in her house . . . here, take the cane.'

Drinkwater took the proffered malacca, twisted the silver knob to check the blade was loose inside, clapped his hat on his head and left the darkened room. 'Obliged to you, Mr Davey,' he said over his shoulder as he clattered down the stairs with Davey behind him. Davey pushed past him at their foot and led him through the store, opening the street door with a jangle of keys and tumbling of locks.

To Drinkwater, even the air of the alley smelled sweet after the stifling confinement of his room. Despite the slime beneath his feet and the sulphurous stink of sea-coal smoke, the wind brought with it a tang of salt, blown from the exposed mudflats of the Thames. He caught himself from marching along the alley and walked slowly towards the door of Mrs Hockley's. It was open, and spilled a lozenge of welcoming yellow lamplight on to the ground.

He turned into the doorway to be confronted by a tall ugly man.

'Yeah? What d'you want then?'

Drinkwater leaned heavily on his cane. He hoped his nervousness gave some credibility to his attempt to act drunk. He chose to speak with deliberate care rather than risk exposure by a poor attempt to slur his words.

'A little pleasure . . . a little escape . . . a desire to make the acquaintance of Mistress Hockley . . .' He eased his weight against the wall.

''Eard of 'er, 'ave you?'

'In the most favourable terms.' Drinkwater leaned against the wall while Mrs Hockley's pimp and protector half turned and thrust his head through a door leading off the hall.

'Got a nob here, Dolly, a-wishin' to make your hacquaintance . . .'

Mrs Hockley appeared and Drinkwater doffed his hat and, still leaning on the wall, made a bow.

'Madam . . . at your service . . .' He straightened up. She was a voluptuously blowsy woman in her forties, her soiled gown cut low to reveal an ample bosom which she animated by shrugging her shoulders forward. 'Charmed, Madam,' Drinkwater added for good effect, admittedly stirred by the unrestrained flesh after so long an abstinence. 'I am in search of a little convivial company, Madam . . .'

'Oh, you 'ave come to the right place, Mr . . . ?'

'Waters, Madam, Captain Waters . . . in the Baltic trade . . .'

'Oh, ain't that nice. Let the Captain in, Jem.' She smiled, an insincere stretching of her carmined lips, and took his arm. 'What does the Captain fancy, then? I 'ave a new mulatto girl an' a peachy little virgin as might have just bin specially ordered for your very pleasure.'

Drinkwater followed her into a brightly lit room. It was newly papered and an India carpet covered the floor. Over the fireplace hung a large oil painting, an obscene rendering of the Judgement of Paris.

Four of Mrs Hockley's 'girls' lounged in various states of erotic undress on *chaises-longues* and sofas with which the room seemed overcrowded. The light was provided by an incongruously elaborate candelabra which threw a cunningly contrived side-light upon the bodies and faces of the waiting whores. Of the mysterious Fagan there was no sign.

'A little drink for the Captain,' Mrs Hockley ordered, 'while he makes his choice.'

Drinkwater grinned. 'No, thank you, I did not come here to drink, Mrs Hockley . . .'

'My, the Captain's a wit, to be sure, ain't 'e girls?'

The whores stared back or smiled joylessly, according to

their inclination. Drinkwater swiftly cast an eye over them. He was going to have to choose damned carefully and he was aware that his knowledge of the female character was wanting.

'This is Chloë, Captain, the mulatto girl of whom I spoke.' She had been handsome once, if you had a taste for the negro, Drinkwater thought, her dark eyes still contained a fire that suggested a real passion might be stirred by even the most routine of couplings. She would be dangerous for his purpose, a view confirmed by her sullen pout as he turned his attention away.

'And this is Clorinda . . .' Bored and tired, Clorinda stared back at him through lacklustre eyes, her pseudo-classical trade name sitting ill upon her naked shoulders. 'And this is Zenobia . . .'

Mixed blood had produced a skin the colour of *café au lait* and a luxurious profusion of raven hair. Zenobia was not handsome, her face was heavily pocked, but she had a lasciviously small waist and she met his stare with a steady gaze. She held his eyes a moment longer than prudence dictated, but the twitch of pure lust that ran through Drinkwater was masked mercifully by a heavy thud from the floor above. It prompted a self-conscious giggle from Chloë and the fourth girl as Mrs Hockley, growing impatient with her vacillating customer, played her ace. 'And this, Captain, offered to you at a special price, is Psyche.' Mrs Hockley drew the girl forward and, like a trained bear, the giggling bawd assumed a demure, downcast pose, as though reluctantly offering herself. 'A virgin, Captain . . . certified so by Mr Gosse, the chirurgeon.'

Psyche's shoulders twitched and Drinkwater caught the inelegant snort of a suppressed laugh. The means by which Mr Gosse established Psyche's intact status were not in doubt.

'Really?' he said, trying to show interest while he made up his mind. There was a strong reek of gin on Psyche's breath. Clorinda was poking an index finger between the bare toes of her right foot and Chloë had turned away. Only Zenobia watched him, a look of hunger in her eyes. She turned slightly, cocking a hip at him in a small, intimate gesture of invitation.

He looked again at her waist and the riot of black hair that tumbled over her shoulders and down her back, curling over the breasts elevated by her tight corsage. From overhead, the bumps indicated someone was having a riotous time. He hoped its originator was Mr Fagan.

'How much, Mrs Hockley, are you asking for this quartern of bliss?' He gestured to Psyche with the head of his cane.

'Two guineas, Captain,' Mrs Hockley said, placing an intimate hand on Drinkwater's arm as if implying some kind of guarantee.

'And she is truly a virgin?'

'Would I lie, sir?' she asked, her hand abruptly transferred to her bosom, her red lips an outraged circle and her false lashes fluttering. 'She is fresh as a daisy, Captain, as I live and breathe . . .'

'As she lives and breathes, Madam, there is an excess of gin! I'll take Zenobia.'

'Oh, sir, you *are* a wit, Zenobia is two guineas . . .'

'Ten shillings, Madam, and for as long as I want pleasuring.' He was sickening of the charade, eager to be out of the heavily perfumed stink of the room.

'In advance, Captain, if you please.'

He drew the coins from his waistcoat pocket, dropped them into Mrs Hockley's eager palm and abruptly gestured Zenobia to lead him to her chamber. Upstairs, the false luxury of Mrs Hockley's *salon* gave way to a bare-boarded landing with half a dozen unpainted deal doors leading from it.

Zenobia, whose given name was more certainly Meg or Polly, entered one of them and closed the door behind them. The room had a small square of carpet, an upright chair and a bed. The sheets were stained and rumpled. The window had been bricked up, Drinkwater noticed, as Zenobia went round the room, lighting a trio of candle stumps from the single one she had brought upstairs. The air was filled with the strong scent of urine as Zenobia pulled a drab screen to one side. Instead of a commode a cracked china jordan stood on a stool.

''Ave a piss, Capt'in, I'll get undressed.'

'No, wait . . . how much will you be paid for this, Zenobia?'

'Five shillin' plus me board and lodgin', why?' She had paused and was looking at him.

'Because I want you to do something special for me.'

She turned away and made to unhook her stays, her face uninterested. 'You'll still have to piss . . . I'm a clean girl . . .'

Drinkwater blushed, aware that, for all his bravado, he was not used to this sort of thing, was unfamiliar with the rituals of what passed for love, and of what exotic treats might be available to him.

'You don't understand, I'll give you two guineas . . .'

The woman looked up sharply, throwing her skirt over the back of the chair and drawing her stays from her body. Her breasts, still tip-tilted, swung free, catching the light of the candles.

'You pay me what you like. I'll do what you want, but no beating. If you beat me, I'll scream for Jem. An' I wants to see yer 'and-spike . . .'

'For God's sake, *be quiet*. Here . . .' Drinkwater fished the coins from his pocket and held them out to her. She seized them and bit them.

'Is a man called Fagan in the house?' he asked, before she could say more.

She looked at him through narrowed eyes. Her hand reached out for her skirt and she drew it to cover her breasts as though he had asked her a most improper question. 'What's yer game?' She backed towards the door.

'It's all right Zenobia, I mean you no harm. Just tell me if a man called Fagan is in the house. If you help me I'll pay you another guinea.' He knew it was a mistake, the moment the words were out of his mouth. He saw the quick movement of her eyes to his waistcoat pocket, gauging how many more guineas reposed there. If she summoned Jem they might roll him for the contents of his pockets and that would be disastrous. He took a small step forward and she fell back towards the door.

'You ain't 'ere for a fuck, are you?' she asked, edging towards the door, her voice rising wildly. He raised his cane and stabbed its point into the door, preventing her from opening it. His left hand reached out and caught her black tresses. He gave a quick tug and pulled the wig from her head. With a sharp whimper she shrunk back into the room, crouching in her humiliation. He knelt quickly beside her, putting an arm about her shoulders. Strands of hair clung to her skull and suddenly he felt sorry for her.

'Please, Zenobia,' he hissed insistently into her ear, '*trust* me. You will come to no harm and I will not forget you. Is the man Fagan here, now? A big man, like a prize fighter, with a thick left ear? Tell me.'

She looked up. 'You won't tell Mrs Hockley?' Her eyes were imploring.

'What? That I didn't bed you?'

'No, about my 'air. If she knows about my 'air, she'll chuck me out. I've a boy to feed, a good boy . . .'

'No, of course not. I'll give you something for the boy if you help me . . .'

'Will ya? Honest?'

'Yes, now come, I haven't much time . . .' He stood and held out his hand. She took it and gave him a shy smile, sitting herself on the bed.

''E's 'ere,' she jerked her head, 'next door, wiv Annie, I means Lucinda. It was 'im, the pig, as was making all the bleedin' noise.'

'Will he stay all night?'

'No, not 'im. 'E'll be at it for an hour or so, then 'e'll sleep orf 'is drunkenness, then 'e'll give 'er another turkin' afore he leaves. 'E likes 'is money's worth, does Mr Fagan.'

'Does he just leave? He doesn't stop below, for a drink or a chat with Mrs Hockley?'

'What you askin' all these questions for? Are you a runner, or a magistrate's man or somefink?'

'No . . .' He fell silent, trying to think out his next move. He had to come upon Fagan in a situation of the most contrived casualness . . .

'Have you ever been with him?'

'Fagan? No. 'e's the kind who gives a girl a rough time.'

'How d'you know?' Drinkwater asked.

'We talk, Mister,' Zenobia said, a note of contempt in her voice. 'We don't spend all our lives on our bleedin' backs. Annie, I means Lu, told me.'

'You mean you don't offer yourself to him because of . . .' He picked up the wig and held it out to her.

'Yeah, 'e'd soon find out, then 'e'd tell Ma Hockley and I'd be in the gutter.'

'D'you have a bottle of gin or anything here?'

'I got a bit.' She held up her skirt questioningly. 'You ain't going to . . . ?'

He shook his head and said, 'Where's the bottle?'

Fastening her skirt she reached on to a shelf. The bottle was only a quarter full. 'It ain't free.'

'I'll give you tuppence for it. Now listen,' he dug for the pennies, 'I want you to be a very good girl. I want you to tell me the moment Mr Fagan comes out of the room next door . . .'

'You ain't going to . . .' she made a lunging and twisting movement with her right hand, 'give 'im one wiv that rum degen of yours, are ya?' She nodded at the sword-stick. 'I don't want nuffink to do wiv you –'

'I only want to talk to him.'

She stared at him, weighing him up, her head cocked on one side. ''E's a dangerous bugger. If 'e gets wind I helped you . . .'

'Look,' said Drinkwater urgently, exasperation creeping into his voice, 'if you do exactly what I ask, I'll leave another two guineas with the chandler next door. For your boy . . .'

'How do I know . . . ?'

He did not blame her for her suspicions, but he could now hear the noise of voices from the adjacent room. All the indications were that Fagan had finished with the obliging Annie. He had no time to lose. 'Do as I say,' he said sharply, keeping his voice low, 'or I'll have that wig off again and I'll be on that landing screaming for Mrs Hockley that you've poxed me!'

The words struck her like a whip. Her face blanched. She

turned and put her hand out to a framed print on the wall. Lifting it off its hook she jerked her head at the hole hidden behind it. 'See for yerself.'

He put an eye to the hole and peered through into the next room. The white body of a voluptuous girl lay spread in total abandonment on the bed. Her hands were tucked behind her head, her tawny hair fanned out across the pillow. She was laughing at some remark her companion was making. Then the bulk of a man came into view. He was almost dressed, his hands busy with his neckcloth. Drinkwater needed to see no more. He turned back into the room, took the print from Zenobia's hand and replaced it.

''E gets a bit rough sometimes,' she said, nodding at the erotic print, 'Ma Hockley sometimes keeps an eye on 'im. All the rough ones get that room.'

Her tone suggested a pathetic attempt to palliate what she had taken for anger on Drinkwater's part. The poor creature must be desperate for money.

'Get into bed, pull the sheets up . . .'

She did as she was bid while he pulled off his coat and tugged at his own neckcloth until it hung loosely about his neck. He threw his coat over his arm and picked up his hat and cane. Hoping to look as if he had just risen from a bed of illicit love he stood beside the door, his right hand on the knob. He turned to Zenobia. 'I'll leave the money with Mr Davey next door. I've some business to transact with him.'

He opened the door a crack. Outside the landing was lit by a single lantern. From below came loud male laughter, more customers, Drinkwater guessed, which might make his task easier. He strove to catch the noise of the latch of the adjacent door, but Zenobia was saying something.

Angrily he turned. 'Quiet,' he hissed.

'Don't ya want it then?' She was holding out the nearly empty gin bottle.

'Damn!' he muttered, crossed to the bed and grabbed it from her. As he reached the door again he saw the light from Annie's opening door, and the shadow of a man's figure. The sound of his voice rolled along the bare passage.

'Let me go, you wanton bitch.'

On tip-toe, Drinkwater stepped out on to the landing, closing the door behind him. Fagan stood in the adjacent doorway. Annie was clinging to him, stark naked. Fagan was pulling her arms from about his neck.

'Upon my soul, you've been riding a fine horse, sir,' Drinkwater said in a loud voice. Fagan looked round at him and finally disengaged himself as Annie slipped back into her room. 'Heard you thrown a few times as you went over the fences.'

'What's it to you?' Fagan turned, his expression darkly belligerent.

'Nothing sir, nothing, except it puts a fellow off his own gallop. Have a drink,' Drinkwater held out the bottle. 'Cool yourself . . .'

Fagan stared at Drinkwater, frowning. 'Who the hell are you?'

'Captain Waters at your service, sir. Master of a barque lying in the stream. Waiting for a wind.' Drinkwater stepped towards Fagan, putting up his left arm with its coat, cane and hat to catch Fagan's elbow in a gesture of assumed friendship. 'Got a damned good rate for my freight, if I can run it,' he rattled on. 'If I can persuade those jacks-in-office of the Custom House that it's for Sweden.' He threw back his head and laughed, feeling the resistance in Fagan's demeanour relax. They made their way to the head of the stairs.

Fagan paused at the top and turned to his accoster. Drinkwater smiled to cover his anxiety; Fagan's next remark would show Drinkwater whether he had the slightest chance of success in this mad enterprise.

Fagan's irritation at the untimely encounter appeared to have gone. He affected a degree of casual interest in Drinkwater's drunken gossip.

'But it ain't for Sweden, eh, Cap'n? That your drift?' There was the trace of a brogue there, Drinkwater noted as he nodded. He held out the gin bottle again. 'Here,' he said, 'drink to my good fortune,' and he finished the sentence with a laugh.

'So where are you taking it? Somewhere the Custom House men wouldn't like, eh?'

'Drink,' Drinkwater repeated, boldly banging the bottle into Fagan's barrel chest. The big Irishman continued to regard him through shrewd eyes. 'Go on, drink, wash that woman out of your mouth . . . Customs Officers? God damn you, no, I'm on to bigger game than running a cargo to the damned French or the Dutch.' Drinkwater stopped suddenly and stared hard at Fagan, as though recovering his wits and regretting his free tongue.

'So where would you be taking your cargo, Cap'n, if not to the French?'

Drinkwater made to push past Fagan. He drew his mouth into a mirthless grin, as though suddenly nervously anxious. 'Ah, that'd be telling. 'Tis a secret . . . a damned good secret . . .' He was almost past Fagan, had his right foot on the top stair when he delivered the Parthian shot. 'And one the damned French would love to know . . .'

Fagan's paw shot out and jerked Drinkwater's left shoulder back so that he struck the bannisters. 'Hey, damn you!'

'Don't push, Cap'n . . . I'll have the drink you were kind enough to offer me, and then we should take a bite to eat. Rogering makes a man hungry, eh?' Fagan began to descend the stairs, his powerful fist digging into the scarred muscle of Drinkwater's right shoulder. Drinkwater felt himself propelled downwards. At the foot of the stairs he twisted free. 'I have a boat to catch . . .'

'And what ship would you be going to?'

'That's my business, sir.'

'Oh, come now, Cap'n. All men are brothers in a house of pleasure. I'm only after a little light conversation. You were civil enough to be sure, when that wench upstairs had left you in a good humour. You're not mean enough to deny a fellow a companion over his breakfast.'

Fagan slapped him amiably on the back and Drinkwater was ironically aware that they had exactly reversed roles.

'I can easily find out your ship. I know your name and I

can soon bribe a Customs man to show me your inward jerque note . . . if I had a mind for such foolishness. But d'you see I'm a trifle out o' luck myself at the moment and, taking you for a man o' spirit, I was wondering if we might strike a deal. An investment in your cargo, perhaps, with a decent return on it, might set me up and save you a guinea or two of your own.' Fagan paused and Drinkwater pretended to consider the matter. Hearing their voices, Mrs Hockley had emerged from her salon to see if her customers were satisfied.

'I didn't know you gennelmen was acquainted,' she said, but Fagan took no notice and with his arm across Drinkwater's shoulders, thrust him out of the street door. 'Come,' he said, 'we'll discuss the matter over a bottle of porter and a decent beef pie.'

They had crossed the alley and Fagan was hammering on the locked door of the pie shop. Drinkwater looked up at the narrow strip of starlit sky above their heads. The wind was dying to a breeze.

A boy, woken by the noise, let them in and Fagan sent him back to his bed with a cuff. Moving with the ease of familiarity, Fagan led Drinkwater into a back kitchen where a large table and a black iron stove stood. The stove had a banked fire and Fagan, kicking it open, soon had a stump of candle guttering on the table. Then he drew half a pie from a meat-safe and cut two slices with a pocket knife. Turning aside he found two horn beakers and set them down.

'Come now, Cap'n, sit yerself down. Where's that bottle o' yours?'

Drinkwater meekly did as he was bid. 'How much were you thinking of risking, Mr . . . ?'

'Gorman, Cap'n, Michael Gorman . . . well now, how would, say, two hundred pound do; say at a five per cent return on completion o' the voyage, to be remitted by . . . when would it be remitted?'

'It would be a single voyage, Mr Gorman. I'm not expecting a homeward freight. That depreciates my chance of profit, and there are risks, Mr Gorman, very great risks, and five per cent on two hundred, well . . .' Drinkwater broke off and shrugged. Affecting lack of interest he took a bite at his slice of pie.

'Well, just supposing, and I'm not saying I will, but think of what it means to reducing your own capital risk . . . you are risking your own capital in the venture, ain't you?'

'Would I take such risks for another?' Drinkwater asked, his mouth full.

'No, no, of course not. But just supposing I was to invest *four* hundred pounds, could I expect a return of five per cent?' Fagan leaned forward and Drinkwater met his eyes. 'I'm not saying I can raise the money, but if I could, would you shake on the deal?'

'I might.'

'Well what is the cargo? I must know . . .'

'Of course, Mr Gorman,' Drinkwater said reasonably. 'A few stand of arms, greatcoats and military boots . . .' Drinkwater watched the tiny, reactive muscles round Fagan's eyes. Leaning forward over the candle they showed clearly, twitching even as Fagan lowered his eyes in dissimulation.

'You'd be wanting something on account?' Fagan did not wait for an answer. 'I'll give you ten guineas now, against your written receipt, I've pen and paper to hand . . .' Fagan rose and disappeared up a narrow staircase hidden behind a door. In a few minutes he was back. He threw the guineas on to the table and produced a pen and inkwell. The gold gleamed dully in the candle light. Drinkwater stared at it. It was a bribe, designed to disarm him for the next question. He took up the pen and dipped it.

'And where would these military boots be bound, Cap'n Waters?'

Drinkwater did not look up as he carefully wrote the receipt. 'To Russia, Mr Gorman. There's a great demand for English armaments and military stores in Russia.' He passed the receipt across the table and laid down the pen, looking directly at Fagan. 'I shouldn't wonder if the Tsar ain't considering some trouble, but that's no concern for the likes of us, is it now, Mr Gorman?' He stood and took up his cane. 'Do you bring the balance to Davey's chandlery at noon and I'll have a deed made out in your favour.' He put his hat on and held out his hand. 'I hope you profit from the venture, Mr Gorman.'

Fagan rose and took Drinkwater's hand. The Irishman seemed withdrawn, as though inwardly meditating. 'Until noon then . . .'

In the alley Drinkwater gave his cane a half-twist, ensuring the blade was ready for use against footpads; then he turned and made his way past Davey's chandlery. Fagan would be watching him, and he must not betray his intimacy with the chandler, though to use his premises as a rendezvous would not excite suspicion. He had until noon and before then he had to meet Solomon.

Again the air in the alley was wonderfully fresh, and he walked with a lighter step. He was not gratified merely at being out of doors again, nor of having, as Dungarth had eloquently put it, baited the eagle, but because he no longer had to dissimulate. Nathaniel Drinkwater was not cut out to play games in brothels, nor to be a spy.

CHAPTER 3 August 1809

# The Jew

It was not, Drinkwater reflected as he waited for an answer, a duty normally expected of a senior post-captain, to be waking up Jewish merchants in the middle of the night, notwithstanding the usefulness of the race both to the officers and the men of His Majesty's navy, or, in the matter of high finance, to His Majesty's government. However, in the event, there were mitigating and somewhat personal circumstances that encouraged him.

He had made the journey from Wapping to Spitalfields without mishap or interference, if one excepted the invitations of the score or so of raddled drabs too caried to work under the roof of a respectable house. He had passed a few roistering jacks, a brace of kill-bucks slumming it down from St James's, two decrepit parish Charlies and the sentinels outside the Royal Mint.

Drinkwater heard the heavy bolts withdrawn and the door opened a trifle.

'Captain Waters, Mr Solomon.'

'Come in, come in.' Drinkwater felt the Jew pluck his sleeve. A lamp illuminated the hall and a faint odour of unfamiliar cooking filled the air.

'I apologize for the lateness of the hour, Mr Solomon.'

'There is no need, Captain, it is as arranged. Pray follow me.'

Solomon's study lay off the hall, a comfortable, book lined

room, with a large desk on which sat piles of ledgers, and an exotic landscape in oils above a fire of sea-coal.

'As you see,' Solomon said, indicating a chair, 'I was working. Please be seated. You will find a glass and decanter beside you.' He held up his pale hand at Drinkwater's query. 'No, I do not indulge.'

Drinkwater sipped the claret. After the raw rasp of gin, the rich Bordeaux was revivifying. 'You have no idea how excellent this is, Mr Solomon,' he said.

'Would you like a bath, Captain? It will not take long to arrange. You will want hot water for a shave and his lordship has sent fresh clothes for you.'

'I fear I stink a trifle.'

'A trifle, Captain, but you have been successful, yes?'

'Indeed. The bait was well swallowed. If I mistake not, the news will be in Paris within the week. And you and the ship?'

'They expect you to arrive at any moment. You are to sail as a supercargo, sent, I have told the master, by the consigners. He is aware that certain high placed individuals have an interest in his cargo,' Solomon smiled. 'So prevalent is the practice of revenue evasion that the matter was easily arranged, as was your assumed status. The master, Captain Littlewood, has accepted the fact that the ship is cleared outwards at the Custom House in your name. You may make such private arrangements as you require once at sea.'

'That seems satisfactory. What news of the gun-brig?'

'Your man joined her at Harwich two days ago. She will be at the rendezvous by now. Will you sleep an hour while the water heats?'

'A moment more of your time, Mr Solomon . . .'

'Of course, how can I be of service?'

Drinkwater stood and undid his waistcoat. 'Forgive me a moment . . .' He turned away and drew from within his breeches a small baize bundle. 'I would appreciate your opinion, Mr Solomon, as to the value of this.'

He rolled the heavy nuggets of unrefined gold on to Solomon's desk where the light sparkled on the gritty irregularities of their surfaces. Drinkwater watched the Jew as he bent over the gold. His sensitive fingers reached out and he cupped them speculatively in one hand.

'Where did you acquire these?'

'From a dead man in California.'*

'California?'

'A province of Spanish America.'

'What is your title to it, Captain?'

'A spoil of war, I imagine, though doubtless a law-broker would argue differently. It was found by an American citizen in a land claimed by Spain, Russia and Great Britain, somewhere beyond the rule of all but the most natural law – that of possession. I am not a greedy man, Mr Solomon, but I have obligations beyond my means, dependants I have collected in the course of my duties and for which the state bears the moral burden but which it has abandoned to my ingenuity. I offer you ten per cent of the value if you can dispose of them without fuss.'

From a drawer Solomon drew a small box and lifted out a set of hand held scales. He weighed the nuggets, nodding with quiet satisfaction.

'I think this *avoirdupois* will make your burden considerably lighter, Captain,' Solomon said wryly. 'It would be premature of me to mislead you, but upwards of two thousand pounds would seem possible. I see that surprises you, well, well.'

Drinkwater shut his foolishly gaping mouth. Solomon smiled.

'Now, an hour's rest, and then a bath.'

Drinkwater slept well, luxuriating in clean linen and down pillows. Later he broke his fast in Solomon's study. The Jew's quiet manner gave the impression that while his guest slept he had been busy, and, even as Drinkwater drank his fourth cup of coffee, Solomon bent industriously over papers and ledgers on his desk. From within the house came the noise of a banging door, a snatch of children's laughter and the sound of a family. The noises shocked Drinkwater with the pain of nostalgia and he tore his mind from the contemplation of such things. Beyond the windows, the raucous bedlam of

* See *In Distant Waters*.

Spitalfields market intruded. Drinkwater watched Solomon. He was deeply touched by the man's solicitude, the clean linen for his soiled body, the hip bath, warm towels and an apparently copious supply of hot water. Dungarth might have suggested the clean underdrawers, the starched shirt, breeches and stockings, but Solomon had attended to the details and Drinkwater was vaguely ashamed of his suspicion of the Jew.

From time to time a confidential clerk, a Hebrew like his master, came and went upon errands concerned with Solomon's business interests. After one of these Solomon looked up and, seeing Drinkwater had finished his breakfast, smiled and removed the spectacles from his nose.

'I trust you have had sufficient, Captain?'

'To the point of over-indulgence, Mr Solomon, but I think the bath the kinder thought on your part.'

Solomon inclined his head, then pulled out his watch. 'You will be wanting to leave shortly . . .'

'There is one small matter that has just occurred to me.'

'Please . . . ?'

'Would you be kind enough to advance a small sum against the gold?'

'Of course, but I have yet to advance you the money for contingent expenses.'

'No, this is a private request. Say twenty sovereigns?'

'Of course, Captain.' Solomon rose and from a fold in his robe, produced a ring of keys. Bending to a safe behind his desk, he drew out two purses. From the larger he took a handful of coins and placed twenty pounds on the table. The other he held out to Drinkwater. 'Two hundred and fifty Maria Theresa *thalers*, Captain, on account.'

Drinkwater took the purse and pocketed the coins.

'They have not the value of your specimen, Captain, but they are more readily negotiable.'

'Indeed they make me the more apprehensive, though I confess to a fit of nerves when confronted with the pimp last night. He would have had rich pickings even if he undervalued the sale. You wish me to sign a receipt?'

Solomon shook his head. 'It is better there is no record of such a transaction, Captain. A nosy clerk, a ledger left open carelessly . . .' Solomon shrugged and waved his hand, 'you understand?'

'I think so.' Drinkwater paused, then asked, 'The man Fagan, he took the bait well enough. Will he report to Talleyrand?'

Solomon nodded. 'Yes, and Fouché too, that is why your disguise was necessary. Fouché might have smelt a rat had we not dissembled, now he will bring the matter to the Emperor's notice if Talleyrand does not.'

'So Fouché is also betraying his master?'

Solomon smiled again, a curiously knowing smile, like an adult distantly watching the tantrums of children. 'Napoleon has taught them all that ambition knows no boundaries. Do you recall Aristotle's epigram on the state of mind of revolutionaries? That inferiors revolt in order that they may be equal, but equals that they may be superior.'

'He had a point,' Drinkwater agreed. 'So Lord Dungarth concludes Napoleon himself ordered the attempt on his life in which he lost his leg, and that this was intended not merely to destroy his lordship and to damage our Secret Service, but to serve as a warning to Talleyrand and perhaps Fouché?'

Solomon shrugged, spreading his hands palms upwards. 'To *discourage les autres*, perhaps . . . but you are inclined to doubt the assumption, yes?'

Drinkwater's mouth twisted in a wry expression. 'I am not convinced. We blame Napoleon as the head of the body, but the cause may be elsewhere. Mayhap the heart . . .'

Solomon's intelligent eyes watched his guest, though he did not press the point. Drinkwater's grey eyes were introspective.

'Well,' Solomon broke in on Drinkwater's thoughts, 'it is true that men are not always moved by logic in these matters, Captain, though the French can generally be expected to employ reason more than most; but passions and desires, even distempers, are powerful motives in all human activities. Napoleon is, after all, a Corsican.'

Drinkwater gave a short laugh. 'A follower of the vendetta,

yes! So Dungarth *did* go into France to arrange for some such "accident" to befall the Emperor; well, well . . .' Drinkwater recalled earlier attempts to dislodge Bonaparte. He remembered picking up the mysterious and half-mad Lord Camelford from a French fishing boat in the wake of the Pichegru conspiracy. A *quid pro quo* might also account for Dungarth's detached lack of vindictiveness.

'Who can say, Captain? I am not in his lordship's full confidence, but many things are possible among these shadows.'

The metaphor, intended by Solomon to turn the conversation away from speculation, failed in its purpose. Instead, it uncannily echoed Drinkwater's own theory, developed in the long months since he had first heard of the explosion of the fougasse beneath the earl's carriage.

'It is the shadow world to which I allude, Mr Solomon. That the Emperor himself, with all his preoccupations, made so clumsy and obvious an attack is unlikely, but perhaps it was done by someone wishing to incriminate Bonaparte.' He paused, catching Solomon's interest again. 'Like you, I flatter myself that I enjoy a measure of his lordship's esteem and confidence. Like you I see some corner of the affair. But unlike you here in London, I have been at a more personal risk, and if I am correct, the matter touches me.' Drinkwater caught the Jew's eyes. Solomon showed no reaction to the oblique and gentle goading. 'Did his lordship never mention a woman?'

Solomon's narrowed eyes betrayed the whetting of his interest. His stock in trade was not simply gold, nor bills of exchange, to say nothing of Northampton boots. Isaac Solomon traded as much in news, gossip and informed opinion; his was a business that turned on channels of intercourse denied to others, more obscure than those of diplomacy, but they were far more robust. They withstood the blasts of war, the impostures of envoys and the imposition of military frontiers with their *douaniers* and tariffs.

'You imply *dux femina facti*, Captain? That a woman was leader of the deed?'

Drinkwater smiled and nodded. 'Just so. 'Tis a theory, no more.' He did not admit that after the past week's almost unendurably squalid inactivity he felt himself electrified by the speed and stimulation of events overnight; nor that his theory, viewed objectively, was insubstantial as air. He too was as devoid of logic as Solomon's hypothetical protagonists. Besides, how did one explain to a man of Solomon's obvious intelligence, a hunch that had matured to conviction?

'Tell his lordship, when next you speak, that I am of the opinion that he fell victim to the malignance of a widow.'

Solomon raised his dark eyebrows. 'Whose widow?' he asked softly.

'The widow of Edouard Santhonax, Mr Solomon, née Hortense de Montholon; Dungarth is acquainted with the lady.' He held out his hand. 'Good day to you, sir. I am much obliged to you for your kindness and courtesy, and hope we meet again.'

They shook hands. The Jew's grip was firm and strong. Drinkwater felt a strange kinship with the man that was as hard to explain as it was to deny; rather like his belief that it had been Hortense Santhonax who had been influential in the placing of the infernal device beneath Dungarth's carriage, he thought.

'I will tell his lordship what you have said, Captain. He has never mentioned her in my hearing.'

'She was an *emigrée* we rescued after the revolution, but she had her head turned by Edouard Santhonax and soon afterwards turned her coat. She was in this country during the naval mutinies of 'ninety-seven. In a fit of weakness Lord Dungarth let her return to France, where she married. Her husband was one of the Emperor's personal aides-de-camp . . . he fell in an action with the frigate *Antigone*.'

'Which was under your command?'

'Yes. That was just over two years ago. It was our fate to cross swords several times and I earned his wife's displeasure long before I made her a widow. So did Dungarth. The last I heard she was sharing Talleyrand's bed.'

Solomon nodded gravely, as though lodging the facts precisely in his astute mind. 'I will tell his lordship what you say.'

'Obliged sir. Now I must be off.'

Drinkwater was back in Davey's chandlery by noon. He still wore the borrowed hessian boots and the soiled waistcoat, but clean breeches, shirt and neckcloth combined with a dark blue coat with plain gilt buttons to proclaim him a shipmaster. Davey produced his valise from the room above and shook his head when asked if Fagan had been enquiring after Captain Waters.

'I saw him leave this morning,' Davey said, nodding in the direction of the pie shop opposite, 'but I ain't seen him since.'

'It don't surprise me,' said Drinkwater turning his attention to another matter. 'There is something personal I would be obliged to you for attending to, something entirely unconnected with this affair. There is a woman next door in Mrs Hockley's establishment who hawks herself under the name of Zenobia . . .'

Davey frowned with concern. 'I know her; the black-haired trull.'

'Just so, but 'tis a wig . . .'

'Did ye make that discovery before or after you . . . ?'

'A fool could see it at pistol shot, Mr Davey!'

'You've saved yourself . . .'

'Job's Dock, I know it, but do you persuade her to get herself to a physician. She wants none of your paregoric elixir. Take her boy on as an apprentice and here is twenty pounds to see to the matter. You would oblige me greatly, Mr Davey.'

'You be careful of a soft heart in your line o' work, Cap'n. She will lose her living . . .'

'She will lose her life else. Just oblige me, sir,' he said curtly.

Davey took the money reluctantly and Drinkwater had turned for the door when a scruffy boy burst into the shop with a jangle of the bell, thrust a piece of paper on the counter and ran out again, being gathered up by a gang of ne'er-do-wells who promptly ran off. Davey caught the paper from fluttering to the floor, cast an eye over it and handed it to Drinkwater.

*Mr Gorman regrets he is unable to raise the necessary funds for the transaction with Capn. Waters, but begs the Capn. leave his deposit with Mr Davey.*

'I thought as much,' Drinkwater said, adding Fagan's guineas to the money laid out for Zenobia. 'There Mr Davey, you are become a banker *and* a philanthropist in a single forenoon.'

Drinkwater had no difficulty hailing a waterman's boat at Wapping Stairs and having himself pulled off to the barque *Galliwasp*, whose name Solomon had given him. He noted as the waterman's skiff rounded her stern that she was pierced for eighteen guns. He wondered how many she actually mounted. More gratifying, given the frustrating week of delay he had suffered, was the fact that her topsails and courses hung ready in their buntlines, lifting and billowing in the westerly breeze. A young ebb bubbled around her creaking rudder stock and, as he looked upward before seizing the manropes and ascending her rounded side, he sighted a welcoming party that gave every appearance of wishing to be away.

'Captain Littlewood at your service, sir . . .' The master was a small, rubicund man with a mop of white hair tied under his cocked hat in an unruly queue. He had, despite a regal paunch, a restless energy that soon became apparent the moment the formalities of welcome were over. 'I had word from Solomon and Dyer that you would want to leave the moment the ebb was away; my boy will see you below,' and he turned, speaking trumpet to his mouth, bellowing to let the topsails fall and to sheet home. Drinkwater was hardly below before, through the stern windows, he saw the distant prospect of London bridge receding as they slipped downstream. Mr Solomon had arranged things to a most efficient nicety.

'Built for the West India trade, sir,' Littlewood explained when Drinkwater joined him on the deck. 'Gives her the look of a sloop o' war. Hellum down a point . . . 'midships . . . meet her . . . steady . . . steer so . . . Mind you she don't mount so many guns . . . Lee braces there, look lively now! Only a dozen carronades . . . Haul taut that fore-tack, Mister, God! What's the matter with you? Had your brains dished up in a whore's bedpan? You'll have us spliced to the King's Yard at Deptford and the whole damned crew of you pressed before you can say "Lucifer", deuce take you! Mind you we've a quaker or two to fill the empty ports . . .'

Drinkwater noticed the dummy gun barrels just then being dismounted and rolled out of the way.

'. . . And she's been doubled round her cut-water, though I apprehend the ice will be late in the Baltic this year. Stand by the braces! Make a show of it passing their Lordships' palace now. Let 'em see what fine jacks the press missed . . . Easy larboard wheel now . . .'

They slid past Greenwich Hospital and Littlewood kept up the commentary, goading and cajoling his crew, dodging sprit-sailed barges, a post office packet and a large East Indiaman off Gravesend. His crew, few in number compared to a naval complement, seemed agile and able enough. Drinkwater was content to relax for the first time in weeks. He realized, as someone else accepted the responsibility for a ship's navigation, that he enjoyed the freedom of merely overseeing which, with a man of Littlewood's stamp to hand, would be an easy task. He realized, too, that the mental fencing with Fagan and Solomon had driven all thoughts of his obsessive guilt from his mind.

He watched a red kite wheel back over the marshes below Tilbury, and a flight of avocets stream in to settle on the emerging mudflats of the Lower Hope. Soon, he thought, staring down river, the pelagic gannets would glide past them, for already the air was sharp with the salt tang of open water.

'Captain Littlewood . . .'

'Captain Waters.'

'A word with you, sir.'

Littlewood took a look at the set of the sails and crossed the slightly heeling deck. 'I don't know what orders your charter party gave you, Captain, but are you aware we have to rendezvous with a naval escort?' Drinkwater asked.

'I was instructed, sir, to wait upon your pleasure and that you would acquaint me with such instructions as were necessary.'

Dungarth or Solomon had done their work well. It was damnably unusual to find a master in the merchant service so willing to relinquish his much cherished independence.

'I was told you were a seafaring man, Captain Waters,' Littlewood went on, partially explaining his acquiescence, 'and that our cargo is for Riga. I command, but under your direction as the charter party's supercargo.'

'Quite so, Captain Littlewood; you seem to understand the situation thoroughly. I trust that you are satisfied with your own remuneration?'

Littlewood laughed. 'Tolerably well,' he admitted. 'The ship had been taken up for the Walcheren business but, thank the Lord, this other matter came up . . .'

'Ah, yes,' Drinkwater hedged, wondering how much Littlewood already knew, and trying to recall what Solomon had told him. It was probable, he concluded, that having been requisitioned by the Transport Board, Littlewood guessed the authorities were behind the present charter. When he better knew the man, Drinkwater resolved, he would be frank with him, but not yet.

'Don't worry, Captain Waters,' Littlewood said as if divining Drinkwater's train of thought, 'honest men never profit. Who am I to query one transport engaged in a little trading on the side, eh? In the last war I was once master's mate and I know there ain't an admiral, nor a post-captain neither, that don't keep a few widows' men on his books to feather his own nest! Why, love a duck, what's one old barque missing from two or three hundred sail o' transports, eh?' Littlewood grinned and edged closer to Drinkwater who was wondering whether the allusion to naval graft was a sly reference to himself. 'Lord love you, Captain,' Littlewood added with a nudge and a wink, ''tis to most Englishmen's inclination to sacrifice their principles to profit, and, when a *lord* tosses the purse, why damn me, sir, 'tis a *command*!'

# The Gun-brig

'Pray mind your head, sir. Take a seat . . . perhaps a glass?'

Bent double under the deck beams in the cramped cabin, Drinkwater eased himself into a rickety chair. Opposite him, across the table, Lieutenant James Quilhampton seated his tall, spare frame on to a second chair, splayed his legs and propelled himself dextrously across the cabin to a side shelf where a trio of glasses and a chipped decanter nestled in fiddles.

The small, one-hundred-ton vessel lifted easily to a low swell rolling down from the northward. With just sufficient wind to give them steerage, James Quilhampton's twelve-gun command in company with the *Galliwasp*, stemmed the flood tide sweeping south round Orfordness.

'Welcome to His Britannic Majesty's gun-brig *Tracker*, sir,' Quilhampton said as he poured two glasses of blackstrap with his sound hand. 'My predecessor was a tall fellow. He had this chair fitted with castors.' He swivelled round and propelled himself back towards the table whose once-polished top bore the stains of ancient wine rings, assorted blemishes and idly carved notches in its rim. 'A becket allows me half a fathom traverse centrical upon the ring bolt below.'

Quilhampton leaned forward with a full glass held in his wooden fist. Drinkwater disengaged it from the painted fingers, conscious that the young man's awkwardness was due to more than his old disability.

Drinkwater raised the glass of what looked like a villainous concoction. 'Your good health, my dear James, and to that of your wife.' Drinkwater sipped and suppressed the strong instinct to wince at the acidulous wine. 'I am sorry to be the cause of you having to part so soon.'

Drinkwater saw the flush of embarrassment mount to Quilhampton's face.

'I am . . . that is to say, I am not . . .' Quilhampton spluttered, 'damn it, sir, she is not my wife. In short, I'm not married!'

Drinkwater frowned, staring at his friend with unconcealed concern. 'Is it the odious aunt?'

Quilhampton shook his head vigorously.

'She refused you?'

'No, damn it, she did not refuse me.' Quilhampton tossed off his glass, suddenly shot sideways with a rumble of castors, refilled it and trundled back to the table. He took a mouthful of the second glass and slammed it, slopping, down on the table. A blood-red drop of spilled wine reflected the light from the skylight above them.

'I put it off, sir, delayed the thing . . . it didn't seem fair . . .'

Quilhampton stared at the spilled wine, his expression one of extreme anguish. He dabbed at the escaped droplet with his forefinger, dragged it so that its form became elongated round his fingertip and formed the shape used in the tangent tables to express infinity; then it broke and Quilhampton raised his finger and looked up. Two separate droplets of wine now gleamed on the neglected polish of the table top.

'It was better, sir . . .'

'But you regret it now, eh?'

Their eyes met. 'Of course I do.'

'Is the situation irreversible?'

'I expect so, by now.'

'Damn it James, the poor young woman has waited six years! What has she done to be spurned?' Drinkwater bit his lip. He wanted James Quilhampton's mind uncluttered by such preoccupations, and was aware that he was increasing the young man's misery. 'I'm sorry James, 'tis none of my affair. I assume she was otherwise attached?'

'I wish she had been,' interrupted Quilhampton hastily. 'It is my fault, my fault entirely. The fact is I came up all standing and jibbed it.' The swiftly swallowed wine began to unlock Quilhampton's tongue. 'I've no money, sir . . . oh, I'm deeply grateful for your influence in securing this command, but I've little in the way of expectations and my mother . . .'

'But you do still feel something in the way of affection for Mistress MacEwan?' Drinkwater asked sharply, a trifle exasperated and anxious to get on to the reason for his visit.

'More than ever.'

'And she for you?' Quilhampton's dejected nod revealed the true state of affairs.

'For God's sake, man, write to her, hail a fishing boat and get a letter to the post-master at Harwich. I need your undivided attention on our service, James; I cannot support a bleeding heart.'

'Of course not, sir. I'm sorry. Had you not pressed me . . .'

'Very well. Let the matter rest. Assure the young woman of your affections and that I shall have you home again before the ice forms in the Baltic.'

'Thank you, sir. I am indebted to you. Another glass?'

Drinkwater stared down at the half-finished blackstrap. 'Thank you, no. Now, James, to the business in hand . . .'

He outlined their task, amplifying Quilhampton's orders and explaining the reason for his own disguised appearance, already intimated in Quilhampton's instructions.

'I fear it is an open secret now, sir. I have several of the old Patricians aboard, Derrick, for instance.'

The news that a few hands from their former ship had been transferred with Quilhampton and Frey did not surprise Drinkwater. Quilhampton went on to explain that the brig had been undermanned, his predecessor being frequently compelled to relinquish hands to frigates and sloops desperate for men and under orders for foreign service. The dry-docking of the old *Patrician* at Plymouth had released her company and

Drinkwater was rather pleased that the eccentric Quaker who had served as his own clerk was aboard.

'He's rated servant,' Quilhampton said, 'though I employ him as a purser's clerk.'

'If I ever command again, I should not be sorry to have him back.' Drinkwater smiled at Quilhampton's look of surprise. 'I am not entirely in good odour at the Admiralty, James. I once crossed Mr Barrow. That is why I wanted you to have this command: I cannot guarantee you preferment by your personal attachment to my person.'

'But this special service, sir, surely 'tis important enough to warrant some recognition?'

'It is precisely because it must only be recognized by the intended party that it is unlikely to merit attention elsewhere. It is inimical to secret operations that they should be trumpeted. For your own part an efficient execution of your duty will earn my warmest approbation, and therefore,' Drinkwater was about to say 'Lord Dungarth's', but thought better of it. His Lordship's department was not commonly known about in the sea service. It was sufficient for Quilhampton to know he sailed under secret Admiralty orders.

They were just then interrupted by a knock at the cabin door. Mr Frey's head peered round.

'Beg pardon, sir, but the wind's freshening and the merchantman's jolly boat crew are a trifle anxious about the delay.'

'Don't disparage a merchant seaman, Mr Frey,' said Drinkwater rising cautiously. 'Captain Littlewood would only man his boat on my strictest promise that you would not press any of them.'

Frey grinned. 'The thought did occur to me, sir.'

'I'm sure it did.' Drinkwater picked up his hat and went on deck. The tiny ship with her stumpy carronades ranged along her deck was neat and well ordered, even if she did show all the signs of hard service and lack of fresh paint. Drinkwater had exaggerated Quilhampton's chances of preferment. It was frequently the fate of lieutenants-in-command to discover that being posted into a gun-brig was a cul-de-sac to ambition.

'Why is Captain Drinkwater incognito, sir?' Frey asked Quilhampton, alluding to Drinkwater's plain coat, as they watched their former captain being pulled away from *Tracker*'s side in the *Galliwasp*'s boat. 'And why is he aboard that barque?'

Quilhampton turned abruptly. 'I'll explain later, Mr Frey. At the moment I would be obliged if you'd lay me a course to intercept that bawley. I've a letter to write.'

From the deck of the *Galliwasp* Drinkwater watched Quilhampton's little brig run down towards a fishing bawley, heave-to and pass the fateful letter. He sighed with relief and hoped the affair, if not settled, would cease to weigh on Quilhampton's mind. As for himself, he felt depressed by the interview with his friend, not so much on account of James Quilhampton's amorous miscarriage, as by the wider implications of their meeting. In the stinking room above Davey's chandlery, fortified by gin and a sense of purpose inculcated by Lord Dungarth, and afterwards – misgivings soothed by Solomon's confident assurance – the mission assumed a vital character. As long as he remained detached from the Service it was possible to maintain this assumption; but the sight of Quilhampton's puny little gun-brig with its dozen bird-scaring carronades made him doubt the wisdom or importance of Dungarth's cherished plan. On the one hand the sight and smells of even so small a man o' war were powerfully nostalgic to a sea-officer, on the other the very size of the brig seemed totally inadequate as an instrument of defiance to the French Empire. Moreover, the sight of his old friends had awakened other, more personal memories; the dark preoccupations he had managed to shake off for a while. Frey's report that he had Drinkwater's personal effects aboard *Galliwasp* for safe-keeping, reminded Drinkwater of the painful reasons why he could not have them conveyed home. The death of Tregembo hung over him like a spectre, and continued to do so in the subsequent days as they headed for the Skaw. The ambivalence of his position aboard the *Galliwasp* confined him to his cabin and denied him the occupations he was used to, though Littlewood was an amiable host and allowed him the freedom of his deck. But at that moment of parting from Quilhampton, as he watched *Tracker* swing and her sails fill as she sought to catch up with her consort, Drinkwater's gaze stretched beyond the filling canvas of the gun-brig, taking in the long shingle spit and the twin lighthouses at Orfordness. It was hereabouts that he had fought the Dutch frigate *Zaandam* whose magazine had been blown up by the intrepidity of James Quilhampton while he himself had given the death wound to Edouard Santhonax. It was odd, if not fateful, the way his path had crossed that of the French officer. Providential, he admitted privately, a manifestation of what he held to be a spiritual truth. It had been a desperate fight as Drinkwater sought to bring out of Russia a state secret, and Santhonax attempted to thwart him.

Now Drinkwater was going back, and the thought struck him that perhaps he was still bound to Santhonax, even in death, for the moment of his fall from grace at the Admiralty had concerned the preservation of the secret, and its consequences continued to affect him and those close to him.*

'Damn this wind!' bellowed Littlewood, clapping a hand over his hat. 'Why don't it back a point, or even fly to the sou'west.'

It was not a question, merely an explosion of frustration as the northerly wind forced them tc lay a course to the eastward of their intended track, driving them towards the Bight of Helgoland rather than north east for the Skagerrak. They had already made a long board to avoid the Texel, and reached the latitude of Whitby with every prospect of fetching the Skagerrak, but the wind had veered a point and obliged them to lay a course of east-north-east, directly for the Horns Reef.

'The season for the equinoctials will be upon us soon,' Drinkwater said consolingly, though he no more liked the delay than Littlewood, for both men were worried about the cold northerly wind hastening the formation of ice in the Baltic.

''Tis too much to ask for a fair wind,' Littlewood said

* See *Baltic Mission*

irritably, turning to follow Drinkwater's stare. Astern of them *Tracker* buried her bow, then lifted it, the water streaming from her knightheads and the spray tearing to leeward in a cloud.

'She's about as weatherly as my hat!'

Drinkwater grunted agreement. Even in this wind, which was no more than a near gale, conditions on the gun-brig would be appalling. He recalled his own service in a cutter: it had been wet and gruelling, but at least they had had the satisfaction of going to windward like a witch. Poor Quilhampton was going to have to exert himself to the utmost to carry out his orders. The thought made Drinkwater smile grimly.

'You are amused, Captain?' Littlewood asked.

Drinkwater nodded. 'A little,' he admitted. 'The young fellow in command over there had his head filled with romantic notions the other day. I daresay he has other things on his mind just now.'

Littlewood laughed. 'I'll shorten down for him, if you wish; there's no point in outrunning him.'

'I'd be obliged to you, Captain Littlewood,' Drinkwater nodded, acutely conscious that it was the gun-brig that was to afford them protection, rather than the reverse.

'It's bound to back soon,' said Littlewood, turning away to give orders to his crew, 'bound to . . .'

But Littlewood's optimism was misplaced. Nightfall found them shortened to triple reefed topsails and the clew of a brailed spanker as the wind increased to gale force.

CHAPTER 5 September 1809

# The Storm

Drinkwater was unable to sleep. Although *Galliwasp* was not his personal responsibility the habits of command were too deeply ingrained to be swept easily aside. Besides, the moral burden for the former West Indiaman and her mission were laid squarely upon his lop-sided shoulders, so at midnight, wrapped in a tarpaulin, he sought Littlewood and found him at his post on deck.

'There are times, Captain Waters, when the temptation to suck on a bottle in one's bunk and leave the deck to one's mates and the devil are well-nigh irresistible,' Littlewood shouted, staggering across his wildly lurching poop to grab a backstay somewhere behind Drinkwater's right shoulder.

'You don't fool me, sir,' Drinkwater shouted back, grinning in the darkness despite his discomfort. Littlewood's black humour suggested he would be a good man in a tight corner. 'Though I imagine a snug anchorage in the Scheldt seems more attractive than our present position.'

Littlewood leaned towards Drinkwater. 'It's getting no better, Captain,' he said, the confidence imparted in a loud voice to sound above the mounting roar of the rising wind. 'By my reckoning we can let her go 'til morning, but at first light we will have to put about . . .'

'You'll have to wear ship . . .'

'Aye,' Littlewood agreed, 'she'll not tack in this . . .'

Both men stared to windward thinking the same thoughts

simultaneously. The *Galliwasp* heeled under the wind's weight, rolling further to starboard as grey seas reared out of the darkness to larboard and bore down upon her. Some broke to windward and the spray from their collapsing crests streamed across their exposed deck with a sibilant hiss. Some she rode over, groaning and creaking in protest as the roaring gale plucked new, higher pitched notes from the strained weather stays and a curious resonant vibration from the slacker, lee-ward rigging. Others broke on board, sluicing with a roar across the deck and filling the scuppers and waterways of the starboard waist, while some broke against the hull with Titanic hammer blows that shook the *Galliwasp* from keel to truck. Then the thwarted wave threw itself into the air where, level with the rail, the wind caught it and drove it downwind with the force of buckshot; an icy assault that struck exposed cheeks with a painful impact and left the wet skin to the worse agony of the wind-ache that followed.

The duty watch huddled from the hazard in odd corners, only the mate on watch and the helmsmen weathering it behind a scrap of canvas dodger. Even Drinkwater and the bare-headed Littlewood could not avoid the stinging, lancing spume bursting upon them out of the black and howling darkness.

Ineffectively dodging one such explosion, Drinkwater re-covered his balance and dashed the streaming water from his eyes, to stare astern and to leeward.

'What the devil's that?' he asked.

'Bengal fire?' queried Littlewood beside him.

The thrust of the wind sent both men down the deck to leeward. They cannoned into the lee rail, aware that the deep red flare had gone, either extinguished or obscured by an intervening wave crest.

'There's another!' Littlewood pointed, though Drinkwater had already marked the sudden glow.

'Signal of distress from the brig, sir.' The *Galliwasp*'s second mate staggered from handhold to handhold to make his report.

'We see it, Mr Munsden, thank you.'

'It'll be the brig, sir.'

'So we apprehend,' replied Littlewood, turning to Drinkwater. 'That young fellow in command, the lovesick one, what stamp of man is he, Captain?'

'Not one to prove craven,' snapped Drinkwater with mounting anxiety. Straining his eyes into the impenetrable darkness that followed the dousing of the second flare, his brain raced as he thought of Quilhampton and Frey struggling, perhaps for their very lives, less than a mile away.

'Captain Littlewood! You'd oblige me if you'd put up your helm and wear ship now, sir! We should fall off sufficiently to catch a sight of the *Tracker* and you've enough men on deck to see to it.'

Drinkwater sensed Littlewood hesitated, then with relief saw his white head nod agreement and heard his shout. 'Mr Munsden . . . !'

But from above their heads came a thunderous crack and then the whole ship shook violently as the main topsail blew out.

Littlewood spun round and with a bull-roar galvanized his crew. 'Away aloft there you lubbers, and secure that raffle! Call all hands, Mr Munsden!'

Drinkwater swore with frustration, turning from the flogging canvas to stare again into the darkness on the starboard quarter, praying that on the beleaguered deck of the *Tracker* they would light another Bengal fire. But there was no sign of the flare of red orpiment and Drinkwater succumbed to a sensation of blazing anger as another stinging deluge swept the *Galliwasp*'s deck.

'By your leave, sir,' he shouted at Littlewood, shoving past the captain and climbing into the main shrouds, suddenly glad to do something, even if the work in hand was not what was expected of a post-captain in His Majesty's Navy.

He reached the futtock shrouds before he felt the folly of his action come with a shortness of breath and a weakness in the knotted muscles of his mangled shoulder. The power of the wind aloft was frightening. Gritting his teeth, the tail of his tarpaulin blowing half way up his back, he struggled into the top. Here, he found himself face to face with one of the

*Galliwasp*'s men who recognized him and made no secret of his astonishment.

'Jesus, what the bloody hell . . . ?'

'Up . . . you . . . go . . . man,' Drinkwater gasped, 'there's work to be done.'

The mast trembled and the flailing of the torn canvas lashed about them. The air was filled with the taste of salt spray and the noise of the wind was deafening, a terrifying howl that was compounded of shrieks and roars as the gale played on the differing thickness of standing and running rigging, plucking from them notes that varied according to their tension. Each responded with its own beat, whipping and thrumming, tattooing the mast timbers and their ironwork in sympathy, while the indisciplined, random thunder of the rent canvas beat about them.

The men of *Galliwasp*'s duty watch scrambled up beside Drinkwater, huddling in the top until they saw their moment to lay out on the trembling yard. Drinkwater found himself shuddering shamefully, regretting the foolhardy impulse that had driven him aloft. It had been a complex nervous reaction prompted initially by the need to do *something* for Quilhampton and his brig. Denied of the familiar catharsis of bawling orders to achieve results, he had sought to influence the *Galliwasp*'s small civilian crew by this foolhardy gesture. There had also been the realization that from aloft he might obtain a better view, might indeed be able to see the *Tracker* and direct some means of alleviating his friend's plight from such a vantage point. But neither of these rational if extreme reasons were what truly motivated him: what he sought in the wildness of that night was the oblivion of action, the overwhelming desire to court death or to cheat it, to invite fate to deal with him as it saw fit, to submit himself to the jurisprudence of providence, for the truth of the matter was that he could no longer bear the burden of his guilt for the death of old Tregembo.

The folly of his ill-considered action came to him now as he panted in the gyrating top, clinging with difficulty to the mast as his body was flung backwards and forwards and the thudding of his heart failed to arrest the pitiful weakness that made jelly of his leg muscles, so that he quivered from within as he was buffeted from without.

Littlewood was shouting from below, 'Lay out, lay out!' and Drinkwater realized the master had ordered the barque's helm put up so that she eased off the wind and ran before it, taking the flogging remnants of the topsail clear of the yard. The men around him were suddenly gone, their feet scrabbling for the footrope, one hand clinging to the robands, the other reaching for the stinging lashes of the wild strips of canvas. Now they were mere ghosts, grey and insubstantial shapes in the gloom, laying out along the yard that seemed to lead into the very heart of the gale.

Drinkwater stood immobilized, unaware that he was the victim of mental and physical exhaustion. Not since the day more than two years earlier, when he had hidden in an attic in Tilsit observing the meeting of Tsar Alexander and the Emperor of the French, had he known a moment to call his own. The strain of bringing home the secret intelligence; the fight with the *Zaandam*; the killing of Santhonax, and the damage to *Antigone*; the row with Barrow at the Admiralty; the hanging of a seaman and the blight it had thrown on the outward voyage of His Majesty's frigate *Patrician*; the killing of the deserters beneath the waterfall on the island of Más-a-Fuera; the loss and recovery of his ship and the consequences of their finally reaching Canton to make the fateful rendezvous with Morris – all seemed to have led inexorably to the terrifying necessity of murdering his oldest and most loyal friend. And to add to his guilt was the knowledge that Tregembo had sacrificed everything out of a sense of obligation to himself, Nathaniel Drinkwater.

While he could drown in gin the memory of what had happened, and play the agent at Lord Dungarth's behest; while he could avoid confronting the truth by dicing fortunes with Fagan or veil his soul with the mercantile intrigues of Isaac Solomon, his self-esteem clung to this outward appearance from habit. But now the gale had laid his nerves bare and drawn him up into the top by playing upon his anxiety, pride and weakness. Now it held him fast, exhausted, robbed of the energy or courage to lay out upon the yard and serve as an exemplar to the merchant seamen even now pummelling the torn topsail into bundles and passing gaskets to secure it. He wondered if they could guess at his fearful inertia as he clung to the reeling mast for his very life.

Why had he not reached the yard before this torpor overcame him? Why had he not dropped into the sea and the death he longed for? Why did some instinct keep his hands clenched to the cold ironwork of the doubling?

Quilhampton . . .

The thought came to him dully, so that afterwards he thought that he must have swooned and lost consciousness for a few seconds, saved only by the seaman's habit of holding fast in moments of overwhelming crisis. Quilhampton's plight and his own deeply engrained and ineluctable sense of duty brought him from the brink of what was both a physical and a spiritual nadir.

Reeling, Drinkwater stared out to starboard where he thought *Tracker* might be seen, and he was suddenly no longer the supine victim of his own fears. The wind that had desolated him now returned to him his vigour, for he was abruptly recalled to the present with the sinister change in the wind's note. As he sought some sign of the gun-brig he became aware of the changed condition of the sea. It was no longer a dark mass delineated by streaks of spume and the roar of breaking crests tumbling to leeward. No longer did the sea rise to the force of the gale. Now it was beaten; the white breakers were shorn as the sound of the wind grew from the scream of a gale to the booming of a storm.

Beside him the mast creaked and with a sound like a gunshot the foretopsail blew out and the flogging of canvas began again, transmitted to the mainmast via the stays, a shuddering that seemed fair to bring all three of the barque's masts down. Below him Littlewood was bawling more orders and his men were laying in from the main topsail yard. Their faces, what he could see of them, were wild, fierce with desperation, excoriated by anxiety and the onslaught of salt spray which scoured the flesh and made looking to windward impossible. For an indecisive moment Drinkwater cast about him, conscious only of the vast power of the storm and the strain on the *Galliwasp*, but as Littlewood's men struggled over the edge of the top to go forward and try and secure the foretopsail, he recalled Quilhampton and tried again to make out the gun-brig in the surrounding darkness.

Littlewood was keeping his ship's head before the wind but Drinkwater was unable to see anything more than a small circular welter of seething white water, a tiny circumscribed world in which only they existed. He was aware too, that he was having difficulty breathing, that he could no longer cling to his perilous perch and retain the strength to descend the mast. Fearful of his own weakness as much as the wind's violence, he fought his way over the edge of the top, pressed into the futtock shrouds and impeded by the updraught of the wind. Like a fly in a web he struggled until he regained the comparative safety of the deck.

Littlewood had all hands mustered now, transformed by the catalyst of crisis into an inferno of energy. Unlike the complex arrangements on a man-of-war, with its chains of command extending from the quarterdeck into the nethermost regions of the ship, a merchantman's master was at once in supreme command but on an occasion such as this, driven of necessity to perform many duties himself. His mates and petty officers were also strained in the extremity of their situation, tailing on to ropes, heaving and belaying as they fought to subdue the flogging foretopsail and to brace the yards. Littlewood himself was struggling at the helm and Drinkwater crossed the deck to grab the opposite spokes and help him.

'Obliged,' shouted Littlewood. 'We've three feet of water in the well . . . Did you see . . . ease her a point, Captain . . . did you see anything of the brig?'

'Nothing.'

For a while they struggled in silence, Littlewood ducking and staring aloft, and bellowing out the occasional word to his mate who at the foot of the foremast stood holding a halliard ready to render it on its pin. From time to time, with a look over his shoulder, Littlewood eased a spoke to keep *Galliwasp* off before the wind, but no words were necessary since Drinkwater understood instinctively. There was no danger of their being pooped, for the wind prevented the high-breaking seas from rearing over the ship's stern. Their greatest worry was the strain being imposed on the gear aloft.

Drinkwater, still shaken from his own exertions, was content for a moment to let Littlewood fret over the *Galliwasp*. He stared dully at the swinging compass card, still lit by the guttering flame of the binnacle oil lamp. He felt Littlewood's tug on the wheel and responded. Then, suddenly realizing that something was wrong he looked up.

'What the devil . . . ?' Littlewood craned round anxiously.

There was a sudden, unexpected lull, the booming of the wind ceased and dropped in register, and Drinkwater shot another look at the compass card.

'We've swung her head three points in the last few –' he began, but the explanation was already upon them.

'Up helm!' roared Littlewood, thrusting the wheel over. Then the backing wind was upon them, striking them with the violence of an axe blow to the skull, stopping the ship dead, catching her aback and tearing the half furled canvas of the reefed foretopsail out of its gaskets and hurling the frayed mess at the men who sought to tame it.

The first casualty was a topman, an able seaman flung from the yard, who vanished into the sea with a scream. It seemed to Drinkwater that the shriek lasted until after the dismasting, that the renewed boom of the wind reasserted itself only after the scream had finished, and it was the falling of a man who, as a last act, tore at the stays and plucked the masts out of the *Galliwasp* in a gigantic act of protest. It was a stupid fancy, confounded by the facts that confronted them an instant later: the man lost and the barque's three masts lying in ruins around them.

There was a hiatus of shock, and then came the voices of men, some shouting in pain, others bawling for assistance, a few asserting their authority. Drinkwater fought his way through a tangle of rigging, aware that the wheel was smashed by a falling spar and that Captain Littlewood had been less fortunate than himself and was trapped by the yard that had dashed the wheel to pieces. Beneath their feet the barque began to roll as the tangle of wreckage, much of it falling over the side, dragged them beam-on to the wind. And its sudden shift now threw up a confused sea, buffeting the disabled ship and increasing the difficulties of her company.

'Captain Littlewood,' Drinkwater called, as he struggled to free the master, 'are you hurt, sir?'

'Only a trifle . . . but I cannot move . . .'

Drinkwater stood up and bellowed 'Mr Munsden!' and was relieved to hear the second mate's voice in reply. 'Can you lay your hands on a handspike or a capstan bar. Captain Littlewood is held fast here!'

They eased the weight on Littlewood after a struggle, raising the fallen yard from across his belly and dragging him out. Periodically seas crashed aboard, sluicing through the chaotic raffle of ropes, spars and torn sails like a river in spate choked by fallen trees. Elsewhere about the littered deck, other groups of men were helping to free their comrades. As Littlewood struggled to his feet they were aware that they no longer had to shout in each other's ears to make themselves heard: the storm, having done its worst, was content to subside to a mere gale again. Littlewood ordered a muster of his crew; in addition to the lost topman, two others were found dead, one was missing and three were badly injured. A dozen others had cuts, bruises and scratches of a less serious nature.

Soaked to the skin, they took stock of their situation. The backing wind was no longer so cold and they began to sweat with the effort of clearing the *Galliwasp*'s deck in an attempt to get her under command again.

When it came, the dawn found them lying helplessly a-hull, rolling constantly in the trough of the sea and making leeway. The wrecked top-hamper overside laid a wide, smooth slick to windward which prevented the waves breaking aboard. The wind continued to drop during the forenoon. With a vigorous plying of axes and knives they cut away the wreckage, salvaging what they could. Captain Littlewood proved as energetic in adversity as when things progressed well. Drinkwater, stripped to his shirt in his efforts to help, recalled Littlewood's personal stake in the ship and her cargo, content for the moment to throw himself into the urgent task of saving themselves.

It was after noon before they had brought a semblance of order to the ship, leaving her trailing downwind of her wrecked jib-boom to act as a sea-anchor and hold her head to wind and sea. The cook relit the galley range and served a steaming burgoo laced with rum and molasses that tasted delicious to the famished and exhausted men.

His mouth full, Littlewood beckoned Drinkwater aft and the two men conferred over their bowls.

'I don't like our situation, Captain Waters. There is four feet of water in the well, and as for our reckoning, well . . .' With the back of his right hand, his spoon still clutched in his fist, Littlewood rasped at his unshaven chin. A smear of burgoo remained behind.

'I have been giving that some consideration myself,' said Drinkwater, 'but with this overcast . . .' he cast a glance at the lowering grey sky, 'we have little to go on beyond our wits. Let us adjourn below and look at the chart.'

In the stern cabin Littlewood poured them both a glass of rum and unrolled a chart. The nail of the stumpy index finger he laid on their last observed position was torn and bleeding. He drew his finger tip south.

'We'll have made leeway towards the Frisians, then, with the shift of wind, east, towards the estuaries.'

Drinkwater looked from the long curve of islands that fringed the coast of north Holland and Hanover to the extensive shoals that stretched for miles offshore, littering the wide mouths of the Jahde, Weser and Elbe. How far away were those lethal sands with their harsh and forbidding names; the Vogel, the Knecht, the Hogenhorn and the Scharhorn? How far away were the fringe of breakers that would pound them mercilessly to pieces if their keel once struck the miles and miles of shoal they thundered upon?

'We have enough gear salvaged to jury rig her and run before it. With luck we might reach to the norrard.'

Littlewood's torn finger moved north, away from its resting place on the flat island of Neuwerk lying athwart the entrance to the Elbe.

'It offers us our best chance if we avoid the Horn's Reef and Danish letters-of-marque. Of course it's a risk . .' the master drowned his incomplete sentence in a mouthful of rum.

Beyond the island of Sylt lay the port of Esbjerg from which Danish privateers would swoop on the *Galliwasp* with alacrity. The Danes had not forgiven Great Britain the abduction of their fleet two years earlier, nor the bombardment of their capital, Copenhagen. A British ship falling into their hands could expect little mercy: a British naval officer none whatsoever. One caught in disguise would almost certainly be hanged or shot; Drinkwater had seen such a man, strung up by the Dutch above a battery at Kirkduin.

'D'you have a larger scale chart?' Drinkwater asked, shying away from the hideous image.

'Aye.' Littlewood turned and pulled a chart tube from a locker. From it he drew a roll of charts. Drinkwater waited, feeling the rum warm his belly. 'You are thinking of Helgoland?'

'Yes.'

They spread out the second chart and Drinkwater noted it was an English copy of a survey commissioned by the Hamburg Chamber of Commerce.

'Too risky,' Littlewood said, shaking his head. 'If we are out in our reckoning, or if we miscalculate and are swept past, then our fate is sealed.'

'We could anchor and make a signal of distress. There is often a cutter or a sloop stationed near the island.'

'There is as often as not a damned French custom-house lugger, or worse, a Dutch coastguard cutter; that damned island attracts them like a candle does moths. The fact is, Helgoland is too much of a hazard. I'd rather take my chance to the norrard and hope for the sight of a British cruiser than poke my head into that noose!'

Littlewood's voice rang with the conviction of a man who had made up his mind and would brook no interference. His eyes met those of the still uncommitted Drinkwater and he summoned a final argument to ram home his conviction.

'What would the French garrison in Hamburg say when they seized our cargo, Captain, eh? Mercy bow-coup, damn them, and all I'll get in receipt is board and lodging in a cell! You know well enough I *have* to think of my ship. We'll take our chance to the norrard.'

Littlewood let go his end of the chart and it rolled up like a coiled spring against Drinkwater's hand which held down the opposite margin. The sensation of a tiny wounding, a reminder of Littlewood's ultimate responsibility struck him. Drinkwater was not a naval officer in Littlewood's mind but an encumbrance, and Drinkwater faced a situation over which he had no real control. Matters had gone too far for him to contemplate casting aside his disguise in order to usurp Littlewood's command of the *Galliwasp*. Besides, his authority to do even that was difficult to prove and impossible to enforce. The first intimation of naval command would reek so strongly of the press in the nostrils of *Galliwasp*'s people that he would very likely be in fear of his life.

Littlewood's assessment was the truth and his solution the only practical one. Clawing their way to the north bought them sea room, time, and the chance of an encounter with a British man-of-war; running to leeward, for all that the British-occupied island lay downwind, was too much like clutching at a straw.

'Very well. I agree.' Drinkwater nodded.

'Pity about that gun-brig . . .'

Drinkwater lingered in the cabin after Littlewood returned to the deck. He could be heard exhorting his crew to further exertions as *Galliwasp* rolled and pitched sluggishly – what remained of the dead burden of her wrecked top-hamper lying over her bow – holding her head to wind. Her buffeted hull creaked in protest and Drinkwater heard the monotonous thump-thump of her pumps starting again as Littlewood sought to prevent his precious cargo being spoiled by bilge water.

'God's bones!' Drinkwater blasphemed venomously and struck his clenched fist on Littlewood's table. What in hell's name was he doing here, presiding ineffectually over the shambles of Dungarth's grand design?

The thing was a failure, a fiasco . . .

The matter was finished and Quilhampton was lost, for it was inconceivable that his little brig could have withstood the onslaught of the night's tempest. The mission – if that was what Dungarth's insane idea to force the war to a climax could be called – had foundered with the *Tracker*. Littlewood was right and there was nothing more they could do except preserve themselves and their cargo. Perhaps, if they regained the English coast, the ruse might be attempted again after the spring thaw. It was something to hope for.

But the loss of Quilhampton, Frey and their people brought an inconsolable grief and Drinkwater felt it weigh upon him, adding to the depression of his spirits. It was then that the idle and selfish thought insinuated itself: with the loss of *Tracker* had gone his sea-chest and all his personal effects.

CHAPTER 6 October 1809

# Coals to Newcastle

Drinkwater woke with a start, his heart hammering with a nameless fear. For a moment he lay still, thinking his anxiety and grief had dragged him from sleep, but the next moment he was struggling upright. Shouts came from other parts of the ship, shouts of alarm as other men were woken from the sleep of utter fatigue. *Galliwasp* struck for a third time, her hull shuddering, a living thing in her death throes.

He reached the deck as the cry was raised of a light to leeward.

'*Where* away?' roared Littlewood, struggling into a coat, his face a pale, anxious blur in the gloom.

'To loo'ard, Cap'n! There!'

Both Drinkwater and Littlewood stared into the darkness as *Galliwasp* pounded upon the reef for the fourth time and the hiss and seething of the sea welled up about her and then fell away in the unmistakable rhythm of breakers.

Then they saw the light, a steady red glow which might have been taken for a glimpse of the rising moon seen through a rent in the overcast except that it suddenly flared into yellow flames and they were close enough to see clouds of sparks leap upwards.

''Tis a lighthouse . . . Helgoland lighthouse!' Littlewood called, then bellowed, 'In the waist there! A sounding!'

Drinkwater felt Littlewood's hand grip his arm. 'Cap'n

Waters,' he said, his voice strained and urgent. 'They must have been asleep,' – referring to the watch of exhausted men who had laboured throughout the preceding day to prepare *Galliwasp*'s jury rig – 'and we've drifted . . .'

'By the mark seven, sir!'

'She's come off!' snapped Drinkwater, watching the bearing of the light and feeling the change in the motion of the *Galliwasp*.

'By the deep nine!' confirmed the cry from forward.

'They may not have been asleep,' Drinkwater said consolingly, as Littlewood, in his agitation, still clung to Drinkwater's sleeve. 'That light was badly tended.' Both men stared at the now flaming chauffer which seemed to loom above them.

'Do you anchor, upon the instant, sir!'

At Drinkwater's imperative tone Littlewood shook off his catalepsy.

'Yes, yes, of course. Stand by the shank painter and cat stopper!'

It was a matter of good fortune that they had had the foresightedness to bend a cable on to the best bower the afternoon before. Indeed they had mooted anchoring, but decided against it, believing they had sufficient sea room to remain hove-to overnight and able to get sail of the barque before the following noon.

'By the deep eleven!'

The anchor dropped from the cat-head with a splash and the cable rumbled out through the hawse-pipe. Littlewood was roused fully from his momentary lapse of initiative. Drinkwater heard him calling for the carpenter to sound the well and the hands to man the pumps. The pounding that the *Galliwasp* had taken on the reef must surely have started a plank or dislodged some of her sheathing and caulking. Littlewood must be dog-tired, Drinkwater thought, feeling useless and unable to contribute much beyond feeling for Littlewood a surrogate anxiety. He turned to the flames of the lighthouse as he felt *Galliwasp*'s anchor dig its flukes into the sea bed and the ship jerk round to her cable.

Carefully Drinkwater observed the bearing of the light steady.

Littlewood stumped breathlessly aft. 'He *was* asleep . . . the mate I mean . . . God damn his lights . . .'

'The bearing's steady . . . she's brought up to her anchor.'

'Thank God the wind's dropping.'

'Amen to that,' murmured Drinkwater.

'She's making water, sir.' The carpenter came aft and made his report at which Littlewood grunted. 'We'll have to keep the men at the pumps until daylight.' He raised his voice. 'Mr Watts!'

The mate came aft, a shuffling figure whose shame at having fallen asleep was perceptible even in the darkness. As Drinkwater overheard Littlewood passing orders to keep men at the pumps he reflected on the situation. The *Galliwasp*'s hands had laboured like Trojans, Watts among them. There were too few of them, far fewer than would have been borne by a naval vessel of comparable size. Detached, Drinkwater could almost condone their failure. Littlewood turned towards him with a massive shrug as Watts went disconsolately forward.

'I'll stand your anchor watch for you,' Drinkwater said. 'You have all been pushed too hard.' Littlewood stood beside him for a moment, looked forward, where the thudding of the pumps were beginning their monotonous beat, and then stared aft, above the taffrail, where the flaring coals of Helgoland light burned.

'Obliged to 'ee,' he said shortly, and went below.

Dawn revealed their position. To the south east the cliffs and high flat tableland of the island dominated the horizon. Their concern at the difficulties of fetching the flyspeck of rock had been confounded by a providence that had landed them on the very reefs which ran out to the north-west of Helgoland itself and which, just to seaward of them, now lay beneath a seething white flurry of breaking swells, the last vestiges of the tempest.

Drinkwater could see clearly the column of the lighthouse,

together with the roofs of some buildings and the spire of a church. To the left of Helgoland lay a narrow strait of water in which several merchant ships lay at anchor. Beyond them the strait was bounded by a low sandy isle on which a pair of beacons could be clearly seen against the pale yellow dawn. Drinkwater found the battered watchglass that nestled in a rack below the *Galliwasp*'s rail, focused and swept the cliff top. The rock rose precipitously, fissured and eroded by countless gales and the battering of the sea. Tufts of thrift and grass, patches of lichens, and the streaked droppings of seabirds speckled the grim and overhanging mass. Floating like a cloud above the cliff edge, hundreds of gulls hung on motionless wings, ridge-soaring on the updrafts of wind. Then Drinkwater saw the men, two of them, conspicuous in British scarlet. He lowered the telescope and stowed it. Striding aft he found *Galliwasp*'s ensign and took it forward. Their situation must have been obvious, even to the pair of lobsters regarding them from the cliff, but there was no harm in underlining their predicament, or in declaring their nationality.

Walking forward past the tired men labouring half-heartedly at the pump handles, he caught hold of a halliard rigged on a spar raised and fished to the stump of the foremast. Bending on the ensign he ran it up, union down in the signal of distress.

'D'you reckon on any help from the shore, Cap'n?' asked one of the party at the pumps, an American, by his accent.

'We've been seen by two soldiers on the cliff top,' Drinkwater answered confidently as he belayed the flag halliard, 'and I see no reason why those vessels at anchor shouldn't lend us a hand.'

He pointed and the men, grey faced with fatigue, looked up and saw the anchored ships for the first time.

'Say, Cap'n Waters, what is this place?'

Drinkwater grasped the reason for their anxiety. They had no idea where they were, and probably considered his act of hoisting a British ensign a piece of folly.

'It's all right, lads,' he said, 'this is Helgoland. It's British occupied; those soldiers ain't Frenchmen.'

He could see the relief in their faces as they spat on their hands and resumed the monotonous duty of keeping the *Galliwasp* afloat until help arrived.

Help arrived in the form of Mr Browne and two naval launches. The heavy boats crabbed slowly towards them, rounding the eastern point of Helgoland under oars. They were full of men and followed by several smaller boats from the merchant ships.

Mr Browne, a heavily built man with a florid face and white side-whiskers, was dressed in a plain blue coat secured with gilt buttons. On these Drinkwater noticed the anchor of the naval pattern. Mr Browne, he correctly deduced – together with his two launches – was a servant of the crown.

'Browne,' the man announced, staring about him as he clambered over the *Galliwasp*'s rail. 'King's harbour-master.'

'Litttlewood, Master of the *Galliwasp* of London, bound for the Baltic from the London River. This is Captain Waters, supercargo.'

Browne nodded perfunctorily at Drinkwater.

'You're in a pickle, to be sure,' said Browne, pushing a tarred canvas hat back from his forehead and scratching his skull.

'I've a valuable cargo, Mr Browne,' said Littlewood with a show of tired dignity, 'and I've every intention of saving it.'

Browne cast a ruminative eye on the fat shipmaster.

'We've a great deal of valuable cargo hereabouts, Mister,' he said in an equally weary tone, 'but we'll see what can be done.' He sniffed, as though the noise signified his taking charge of the situation, then turned to the ship's side, cupping two massive hands about his mouth and shouting instructions to the boats assembling round the wallowing *Galliwasp*.

'We'll tow her in, boys . . .' He turned to Littlewood, 'Is she taking much water?'

'Enough, but the pumps are just holding their own,' Littlewood replied, throwing Drinkwater a quick glance to silence him. Watts had just reported the water to be gaining on them.

'If she looks like foundering,' the harbour-master bellowed

to his boat coxswains, 'we'll beach her on the spit by the new beacon.'

Browne turned inboard again, fished in a pocket, brought out a quid of tobacco and thrust it into his mouth. 'We'll buoy-off your anchor, Cap'n, save a bit o' time and miss the worst of the ebb against us in the road. Can your men get a rope ready forrard?'

By noon, having set a scrap of sail on the jury foremast and submitted to the efforts of the boats orchestrated by Mr Browne, the *Galliwasp* lay anchored to her second bower just off the new beacon, where she would take the bottom at low water.

To the east the low sandy isle protected them from easterly winds. Extending north-west and south-east, reefs like the one they had struck twelve hours earlier protected them from the north and south.

To the west, the direction of the prevailing wind, the island of Helgoland formed a welcome bulwark. Less forbidding from this eastern aspect, the tableland inclined slightly towards them. Along the beach were situated a row of wooden buildings, some under construction. From among them a road climbed the rising land to a neat village surrounding the church spire whose cruciform finial Drinkwater had spotted from the far side of the island. On the beach, fronting the row of wooden buildings, a beacon with a conical topmark was in transit with the lighthouse beyond.

'Well, sir,' said Browne after dismissing the boats, 'you could show your appreciation in the usual way.'

Littlewood nodded as Browne rubbed a giant paw across his lips.

'Come below, Mr Browne,' said Littlewood, relief plain on his face, 'and you as well, Cap'n Waters, you've been on your pins since the alarm was raised.'

They went below and Browne's eyes gleamed when he saw the mellow glow of rum.

'Good Jamaica rumbullion, Mr Browne,' said Littlewood, handing the harbour-master a brimming glass.

'The best, sir,' said Browne expansively now that the job

was done. 'You will have to clear your cargo, Cap'n Littlewood. I will take you ashore later,' he went on, indicating there was no hurry and edging his empty glass forward across the table with the fingers of his huge hands.

'I should be obliged, Mr Browne, if you would favour me by arranging an interview with the Governor,' put in Drinkwater. Browne turned his gaze upon Littlewood's supercargo.

'The Governor's only concerned with military affairs, Cap'n . . .'

'Waters.'

'Cap'n Waters, if either of you have commercial matters to discuss, Mr Ellerman, chairman of the Committee of Trade will be able to assist.' He turned back to Littlewood. 'If you want to discharge your cargo, Cap'n Littlewood, he's the man to consult.'

'But where can we store it?'

'Them wooden shacks they're puttin' up all along the foreshore,' Browne said, draining his second tumbler of rum, 'they call warehouses. Most are empty . . . speculation,' Browne said the word with a certain disdain. 'Someone'll *rent* you sufficient space, I'm sure.'

'I'd still appreciate your arranging an interview with the Governor, Mr Browne,' Drinkwater said with quiet insistence.

Browne looked at Littlewood who nodded. 'Oblige Cap'n Waters, Mr Browne, if you please.'

'God's strewth,' growled the King's harbour-master, 'this ain't another cargo on the bleeding secret service, is it?'

'Well sir?'

The officer seated behind the desk looked up from a sheaf of papers and regarded Drinkwater over a pair of pince-nez. From the expression on his face Drinkwater expected an intolerant reception. He had been led to believe, during the stiff climb up through the village to the old Danish barracks in the company of Mr Browne, that the Governor was plagued by the merchant fraternity who seemed to regard the island as more a large warehouse than a military outpost. Some of this disdain had rubbed off on Browne, who railed against the ever-increasing number of 'commercial gennelmen' who were littering his foreshore with their hastily erected warehouses. By the time Drinkwater was shown into the Governor's presence by a young adjutant, he was more than a little irritable himself.

'You are Colonel Hamilton, the Governor?' Drinkwater asked, pointedly ignoring the fidgeting adjutant at his elbow who had just told him the Governor's name. Hamilton's face darkened.

'You sir!' he snapped. 'Who the deuce are you?'

'This is Captain Waters, sir, supercargo aboard the barque *Galliwasp* – the disabled vessel I reported to you earlier, sir,' the subaltern explained.

'I wish to see you alone, Colonel,' Drinkwater said, ignoring the two soldiers who exchanged glances.

'Do you now,' said Hamilton, leaning back in his chair so that the light from the windows glittered on the gilt buttons of his undress scarlet, 'and upon what business, pray?'

'Business of so pressing a nature that it is of the utmost privacy.'

Drinkwater turned a withering eye on the junior officer, unconsciously assuming his most forbidding quarterdeck manner.

'Captain Waters,' drawled Hamilton as he removed the pince-nez and laid them on the papers before him. 'Every confounded ship, and every confounded master, and every confounded supercargo, agent, merchant and countin' house clerk, comes here bleatin' about *private business*. I am a busy man and Mr Browne will do all he can to assist your ship and her cargo . . .' Hamilton leaned forward, picked up and repositioned the pince-nez on his nose and bent over his paperwork.

'No, Colonel. *You* will assist me . . .'

'Come sir.' Drinkwater felt the adjutant's hand on his arm but he pressed on.

'You will assist me by obliging me with a private interview at once.' As Hamilton looked up, his face as red as his coat,

Drinkwater turned to the adjutant. 'And you will wait outside.'

'Damn it, sir,' said the young man, 'have a care . . .'

'OUT!' Drinkwater roared, suddenly furiously glad to cast off the mantle of pretence. 'I demand you obey me, damn you!'

The adjutant put his hand to his hanger and Hamilton leapt to his feet. 'By God . . .'

'By God, sir, get this boy out of here. I've a matter to discuss with you in private, sir, and you will hear me out.' Hamilton hesitated, and Drinkwater pressed on. 'After which, Colonel, you may do as you please, but you are a witness that your adjutant laid a hand upon me. On a quarterdeck, that would be a grave offence.'

Hamilton's mouth shut like a trap. As Drinkwater caught and held his eyes a glimmer of comprehension showed through the outrage. Still standing he nodded a dismissal to the fuming adjutant.

'Well, sir,' Hamilton said once again, his voice strained with the effort of self-control, 'perhaps you will give me an explanation?'

'My name is not Waters, Colonel Hamilton, but Drinkwater, Captain Drinkwater, to be precise, of the Royal Navy. I am employed upon a secret service with a cargo destined elsewhere than Helgoland, and I am in need of your assistance.'

Hamilton eased himself down into his chair, made a tent of his fingers and put them to his lips.

'And what proof do you have for this claim?'

'None, Colonel, apart from my vehemence just now, but if it sets your mind at rest, the name of Dungarth may not be unknown to you. It is Lord Dungarth's orders that I am executing; or at least, I *was* until overcome by the recent tempestuous weather.'

'I see.' Hamilton beat his finger tips gently together, considering. Lord Dungarth's name was not well known except to officers in positions of trust, and Hamilton, for all the obscurity of his half-colonelcy in the 8th Battalion of Royal

Veterans, was among such men in his capacity as Governor of Helgoland.

Hamilton appeared to make up his mind. He leant forward, picked up a pen, dipped it and wrote a note. Sanding the note he sealed it with a wafer, scribbled a superscription and sat back, tapping his lips with the folded paper. For a moment longer he regarded Drinkwater, then he called out: 'Dowling!'

The adjutant flew through the door, 'Sir?'

'Take this to Nicholas.'

The junior officer's tone was crestfallen. It was clear he would rather have leapt to the rescue of his beleagured commander.

'Take a seat, Captain,' said Hamilton after Dowling had gone.

'Obliged.'

The two men sat in absolute silence for a while, then Hamilton asked, 'Are you personally acquainted with his Lordship, Captain Drinkwater?'

'I have that honour, Colonel Hamilton.'

'For a long while?'

'He was first lieutenant when I was a midshipman aboard the *Cyclops*.'

A desultory small-talk dragged on while they waited. Hamilton sought to draw personal details out of Drinkwater who gave them graciously. At last a knock on the door announced the arrival of Mr Nicholas.

'Mr Edward Nicholas, Captain Drinkwater, is in the Foreign Service.'

Drinkwater rose and the two men exchanged bows. Nicholas, a younger man than Hamilton, with quick, intelligent dark eyes, exchanged glances with the Governor, then studied Drinkwater.

'He says he's under Dungarth's orders, Ned. Got a cargo intended for a secret destination. Rather think he's your department – if he ain't a fake.'

Nicholas's eyes darted from suspect to suspector and back again. Then the slight figure in its sober grey suit sat down on the edge of Hamilton's desk and dangled one leg nonchalantly.

'What is your Christian name, Captain Drinkwater?'

'Nathaniel.'

'And what ship did you command in the summer of the year seven?'

'The frigate *Antigone*. Upon a special service . . .'

'Where? In what theatre?'

'That is none of your concern.'

'It would greatly help our present impasse if you would tell me,' Nicholas smiled. 'Come, sir, be frank. Otherwise these matters become so tedious.'

'The Baltic.'

'Good. You knew my predecessor here, Mr Mackenzie . . .'

'Colin Mackenzie?'

'The same. He was with you in the – Baltic, was he not?' There was just the merest hint of a pause before Nicholas said 'Baltic', implying the proper name was a vague reference and that both men knew more than they were saying.

'I was employed at Downing Street, Captain Drinkwater, in the drafting of the special orders prior to Lord Gambier's expedition leaving for the reduction of Copenhagen and the seizure of the Danish fleet. I recall your name being mentioned by Mr Canning in the most flattering terms.'

Drinkwater inclined his head. It was odd how pivotal that Baltic mission had been. Before it, all had been hope and aspiration; afterwards, following the approbation of Government and the meteor strike at an unsuspecting Denmark in a pre-emptive move to foil the French, fate had discarded him. It was Hamilton who interrupted Drinkwater's metaphysical gloom.

'None o' that proves he's who he says he is.' Hamilton spoke as though Drinkwater was not there. Nicholas ignored the Governor. Drinkwater guessed they did not get on.

'If you want our assistance, Captain Drinkwater, you will have to be more frank with us. Where is your cargo destined for? I assure you, both Colonel Hamilton and I are used to matters of state secrecy.'

'It is intended for Russia, and I require it to be removed from the *Galliwasp* and stored securely in requisitioned space.

I will then attempt to arrange for another vessel to relieve the *Galliwasp* if she proves too damaged to re-rig.'

'You *require*, do you, sir?' Hamilton spoke in a tone of low sarcasm.

'For what purpose is your cargo going to Russia, Captain?' Nicholas persisted.

'To break the blockade.'

'We do that from here,' put in Hamilton sourly. 'One would think it the only purpose for holding the island.'

'But you do not implicate the Tsar by such a transaction,' said Drinkwater quietly, and now his words engaged the attention of both men.

'How so?'

'The purpose of my mission, gentlemen, the reason why a post-captain of the Royal Navy is obliged to submit himself to sundry humiliations, is that this cargo is designed to draw attention to itself, to shout all the way to Paris the single fact that Alexander, faithful ally of the Emperor of the French, is trading with his friend's sworn enemies.'

'And break the accord between Paris and Petersburg,' said Nicholas, his eyes bright with comprehension. 'Brilliant!'

'And what is this cargo?' asked Hamilton.

'Military stores, Colonel. Greatcoats, boots, muskets . . .' Drinkwater began, sensing victory. Hamilton only laughed.

'Devil take you, sir, you jest. We've the *Delia*, the *Hanna*, the *Anne*, the *Ocean*, the *Egbert* and the *Free Briton* lying in the roads right now, their holds stuffed with ordnance stores, clothing, ball and cartridges. Captain Gilham of the *Ocean* has been languishing here since last May! They too were intended for a secret service! I'm afraid, Captain Drinkwater, you've brought coals to Newcastle!'

Hamilton's laughter was revenge for Drinkwater's *lèse-majesté*, an assertion of superiority that pricked Drinkwater's pride. Yet the Governor had missed the point.

'Whatever the purpose of these other ships, Colonel Hamilton, the *Galliwasp* was not intended to end up at Helgoland.'

'We will write to London for instructions, Captain Drinkwater,' Hamilton said coolly. 'Besides, even a lobster knows the Baltic will be closed to navigation in a week or two. You must perforce become a guest of the mess. I am sure that Lieutenant Dowling will be only too happy to look after you.'

'You are placing me under constraint, sir?'

'Only as a precaution, Captain,' Hamilton went on happily, 'until Mr Nicholas here has received instructions from His Majesty's Government. We are not far distant from an enemy coast, you know.'

'And Captain Littlewood and his cargo?'

'Captain Littlewood may make arrangements among the mercantile fraternity and repair his ship if he is able to. Browne will give what assistance he can, no doubt. Be a good fellow, Ned, and call Dowling in again. Good day to you, Captain.'

CHAPTER 7 October–November 1809

# Helgoland

The weeks that succeeded this unpromising interview were tedious in the extreme. Drinkwater's sole positive act was to write to Dungarth explaining his predicament and whereabouts. Of necessity, his words were terse and he carried round in his head the sentence admitting the failure of his mission: *It is with regret that I inform you that due to the tempestuous weather we have been cast up on the island of Helgoland at so late a season as to render the continuation of the voyage impracticable until the spring* . . . Diplomatic affairs, Drinkwater knew, might be entirely upset by so delayed an arrival of his cargo.

Pending word from London, Drinkwater had taken Littlewood into his confidence to the extent of allowing the *Galliwasp*'s master to give out that their cargo was intended for a secret service to Sweden. It was an open secret that the situation in that country was unstable and a shipment of military stores would raise no eyebrows, particularly as so many of the other ships in Helgoland Road seemed destined for a similar purpose.

Littlewood agreed to this proposal. He had much on his mind and Drinkwater left him to the supervision of the discharge and storing of *Galliwasp*'s cargo and the survey of his damaged ship.

For his own part, Drinkwater was allowed a small room in the former Danish barracks and the freedom of the garrison officers' mess, but he was not a welcome guest. The officers regarded him with a suspicion fostered by Hamilton and confirmed by Dowling, while Nicholas, to whom Drinkwater felt a natural attraction, maintained a polite, uncommunicative distance. Although not exactly a prisoner, Drinkwater felt he was afforded the hospitality of the Royal Veterans in order that they might the better keep an eye on him. He took to walking on the wild western escarpment of the island, losing himself among the rocks and the sparse grass in the company of the wheeling seabirds whose skirling cries seemed to echo the bleakness of his mood.

In the frustration of his situation, Drinkwater felt himself utterly bowed by the overwhelming dead weight of a hostile providence. His lonely, introspective thoughts followed a predictable and gloomy circle that bordered on the obsessive. Intensified by his isolation they threatened to unhinge him and in other circumstances could have led him to succumb to the oblivion of opium or the bottle. From his involvement in Russia to the loss of Quilhampton, the train of his tortured thoughts drove him to seek out the lonely parts of the island, to curse and fulminate and regret in equal measure, only returning to what normality was allowed him during his nightly visits to the bleak mess.

Here he found some mitigation of his misery. Lieutenant McCullock of the Transport Service, an elderly naval officer with a lifetime's service to his credit, was not unfriendly in a gruff way; nor was Mr Thomson, agent of the Victualling Board, and from these men he gleaned a little information about the island and its inhabitants.

Perhaps McCullock was cordial only because it was rumoured that the irritable grey-eyed man with the scarred cheek, the old-fashioned queue and the lop-sided shoulders was a post-captain in the Royal Navy. If it was true, it behove McCullock to mind his manners. Mr Browne seemed impervious to such a suggestion, though he was sufficiently expansive to explain that the native Helgolanders subsisted from fishing.

'They long-line for cod and 'addock from open boats in companies of a dozen or so men,' he said, 'and every one is licensed to sell liquor by hancient privilege.' Browne wiped the back of a huge hand across his mouth and grinned. 'Gives our noble Governor a parcel o' trouble.' Browne grinned and nodded in the direction of the two sentinels at the beach guardhouse.

The 8th Battalion of Royal Veterans who, with a handful of Invalid Artillery made up the island's garrison, were largely elderly or pensioned soldiers, re-enlisted for the duration of the war with France and her allies. One or two were younger men considered unfit for service with a regular line battalion in Spain.

'Weak in the arm and weak in the head,' Browne muttered, as they passed the two lounging sentries. ''Hain't worth a musket, rum nor bread,' he intoned. 'It's them young, useless buggers that give the Governor his problems.'

It was clear that Mr Browne considered his own drinking, evident from his complexion and the reek of him, to be beyond gubernatorial judgement.

'Weak 'eads can't 'old their liquor, d'ye see.'

They walked down through the village with its neat, brightly painted cottages and fantastically spired church. The helices and finial reminded Drinkwater of those in Copenhagen. Pigs and chickens ran about the cottages, each of which had its own vegetable garden set behind walls of whitewashed stone.

'Then there's the women,' Browne went on. 'Most of 'em are married, and that pastor fellow keeps an eye on 'em when their menfolk are away fishing, but we've got a spot o' bother wiv one or two.'

They watched a buxom, middle-aged woman with flaxen hair and a ruddy face peg a pair of wet breeches on a line of gaily dancing washing. She gave them a shy smile.

'*Guten tag*,' said Browne with the proprietorial hauteur of a seigneur.

'*Guten tag*, Herr Browne.'

'I observe it is the women who carry the coals to the lighthouse,' remarked Drinkwater.

'It earns 'em a few shillings,' Browne said as they reached the boat landing. Here Browne took his leave and Drinkwater, as had become his daily habit, inspected the progress Littlewood and his party were making on the refitting of the *Galliwasp*.

Emptied of her cargo, they had hauled her down and careened her, exposing the torn sheathing and a hole stove in her planking by a rock. She had escaped serious damage to her keel, though much of her false keel had been torn off in the grounding. They had replaced the damaged planks, doubled them and recaulked her strained seams until, by the end of October, Littlewood had pronounced her hull sound and they set to work on the foreshore, making new spars.

They had been fortunate in finding a quantity of timber on the island, brought by several prudent shipmasters, and they were able to make a number of purchases to facilitate the repair work.

Littlewood daily expressed his satisfaction and Drinkwater acknowledged his report with assumed gratification. In his heart he thought Littlewood would end up the loser, for they daily expected the packet boat with orders from London which would put an end to the Russian mission.

The packet *King George* left Helgoland with Hamilton's letter and Drinkwater's report in mid-October, bound for Harwich. By the end of the month, Hamilton estimated, they should have the instructions that would end Drinkwater's equivocal status, but this proved not to be the case. A breezy October turned into a grey, chill and misty November, when the wind swung east and fell light.

Such conditions, though delaying the mails from England, increased the activity of the smugglers. Fishing boats and *schuyts* of up to thirty tons burthen sailed into Helgoland Road to trade for the luxuries dealt-in by the two dozen merchant houses whose wooden stores crowded the foreshore. They came out from Brunsbuttel and Cuxhaven on the Elbe, Blexen and Geestendorf on the Weser and Hocksiel on the Jahde to smuggle the luxuries Napoleon's Continental System denied the wealthier inhabitants of his reluctant empire. Tea, coffee, spices, Oporto and Madeira wines, silk and cotton, and above all, sugar, were in demand by the new bourgeoisie created by the success of French arms. In small quantities, slipped ashore on lonely landings on the featureless coasts of Kniphausen, Bremen, Oldenburg and South Ditmarsch, these goods found their way across Europe, a reciprocal trade to the brandy, lace and claret which came across the Channel to the English coast.

Frequently the smugglers brought news: either gossip or copies of the Hamburg papers, giving the island its military justification as a 'listening post'. Occasionally they brought intelligence of a graver sort with the arrival of an agent. One such gentleman appeared on an evening in November. Lieutenant Maimburg's arrival coincided with that of His Majesty's gun-brig *Bruizer* which had returned from a patrol along the Danish coast in quest of Danish gun-boats reported to have been sighted off Syllt. The appearance of Lieutenant Smithies of the *Bruizer* and Lieutenant Maimburg of the King's German Legion, was the excuse for a riotous evening in the officers' mess.

Maimburg, whose duties were more that of a spy than a soldier, had brought with him fifteen Hanoverian lads, recruited for the Legion then serving in Spain; he had also brought news of a Turkish victory over the Russians at a place called Siliskia, and a rumour that Napoleon had ordered areas of Hanover ceded to his puppet kingdom of Westphalia, while a matching Eastphalia was to be created as a kingdom for his stepson, Eugene de Beauharnais. Such gossip had the mess buzzing with speculation, and amid the chink of bottle and glass the chatter rose. Sitting quietly, Drinkwater learned also that a week or two earlier, news of peace between France and Austria had been augmented by rumours of joint action by the Emperor of the French and the Austrian Kaiser in support of the Tsar against the Turks.

But these social occasions were infrequent. The life of the colony beat to the slow, intermittent rhythm of news from the Continent and news from England. The delay to the Harwich packet was reflected in the irritability of the garrison officers. For Drinkwater, the long wait became a purgatory.

Hamilton's continuing dislike and Nicholas's cautious indifference made his situation profoundly depressing. He could assume the character of a merchant shipmaster in the line of duty, but to be cast out into a limbo of suspicion was almost more than he could bear.

One afternoon, inspecting the decayed grate of the lighthouse, he caught sight of a sail to the westward. The Harwich packet doubled the buoy marking the Steen Rock and fetched an anchorage in the road. Too agitated to rush down to the barracks, Drinkwater maintained a stoic isolation on the western bluff, where Dowling, thundering up on Hamilton's charger, found him.

Hope leapt into Drinkwater's heart as he watched Dowling coax the beautiful dun hunter over the tussocked grass. The charger was the only horse on the island and the news must have been important for Hamilton to have allowed Dowling the use of it.

'The Governor summons your presence upon the instant, sir,' Dowling called, reining in his mount twenty yards short of Drinkwater. 'Upon the instant, d'you hear?' he added, then wheeling the horse, cantered away.

Drinkwater watched him go; there had been too much of a smirk on Dowling's chops to augur well. He made his way to the barracks as near instantly as his legs would allow and was ushered in to Hamilton's presence. Nicholas was already there.

'Sit down, Captain,' Nicholas said smoothly. Hamilton rose and stood staring out of the window on to the parade ground. It was clear that he was leaving matters to the younger man.

'I'll stand, if you've no objection,' said Drinkwater coldly.

'None whatsoever.' Nicholas picked up a letter which lay before him on Hamilton's desk. 'I'm afraid, Captain, that it appears your situation is more confused than ever. Lord Dungarth has not favoured us with a reply.'

'Not replied?' Drinkwater was taken aback. 'I don't understand . . .'

'It seems,' Nicholas went on, 'that there has been a duel in the Government. Lord Castlereagh and Mr Canning have been at pistol-point on Putney Heath.'

'Go on, sir,' said Drinkwater incredulously.

'Mr Canning has, we understand, been wounded, though not mortally. The incident has brought down the Government . . .'

'But Lord Dungarth,' Drinkwater began, only to be interrupted by Hamilton turning from the window.

'Has not written, Mr Whatever-your-name-is.'

Drinkwater met the Governor's triumphant gaze with an expression of continuing disbelief.

'I have already spoken with Captain Littlewood,' Hamilton continued, 'he reports his ship will be ready to reload in a day or two. He will return to England as soon as he is able. As for yourself, you will embark in the *King George* and are free to leave aboard her. She will depart in a couple of days. Was I not waiting for a courier from Hamburg, I should order her master to leave at once.'

The implication in Hamilton's words was clear: his disdain, surely unmerited no matter what the misunderstanding that had arisen on their first acquaintance, had developed into a passion. The shock of realization struck Drinkwater with sudden force. It dislodged him angrily from his long wallow in despair. Hamilton's overt prejudice goaded him to a reaction from which all his subsequent actions sprang.

'Sir,' he said, 'I hope fervently to meet you again in circumstances which accord me greater satisfaction.' Then, not trusting himself further, he stalked from the room.

He did not stop walking until he had regained the lonely bluff on the western extremity of Helgoland. Hamilton's perverse attitude, rooted in God-knew-what pettiness, had sent his mind into a spin. There was undoubtedly a good reason why Dungarth had not written. Whatever it was – and it most certainly had nothing to do with the duel fought between Castlereagh and Canning – it was inconceivable that it should result in Dungarth abandoning Drinkwater or his own position at the head of the Admiralty's Secret Department.

Drinkwater wished now he had been more explicit in his letter, at least intimated that Governor Hamilton did not believe he was a naval officer. If Dungarth knew he was at Helgoland, he doubtless assumed Drinkwater would make the best of a bad job. But if he did not . . .

Drinkwater recalled Dungarth's own warning that trouble was brewing between Canning and Castlereagh. The consequent ructions, he had guessed, would affect British foreign policy.

Drinkwater paused and stared at the grey sea below him. The swell broke against the rampart of the island, a filigree of white foam rolled back from the rocks, harmless-looking from this height. In the west, behind rolls of dark cumulus, the sunset was pallid. Drinkwater sniffed the air and stared about him. There were fewer birds about than earlier, most were already roosting on the cliff. He looked again at the swell and barked a short laugh.

There would be a westerly gale by morning. He would go when the packet sailed, but that would be when God decided, not Colonel Bloody Hamilton! He turned, intending to walk back by way of the lighthouse. He would achieve something following his visit to Helgoland, send a letter of censure to the Elder Brethren of the Trinity House for allowing so archaic a system as the chauffer to continue in service, when a parabolic reflector and Argand lights would provide a reliable light on the island!

With such consoling and indignant thoughts he began the return journey. He had not gone a hundred yards before he almost fell over the seaman.

The man was asleep, but woke with a start as Drinkwater stumbled and swore.

'God damn it, man, what the devil are you doing here?'

'I beg pardon, Cap'n Waters. Guess I must have fallen asleep. I came up here more or less like yourself, fixing to get some peace and quiet.'

Drinkwater recognized the American seaman he had last spoken to at the *Galliwasp*'s pumps.

'Sullivan, ain't it?'

'That's correct, sir,' Sullivan replied, brushing himself down.

'You're an American, aren't you?'

'A *Loyalist* American, Cap'n. I hail from New Brunswick now, though I was born in Georgia. My paw was with Colonel Kruger at Fort Ninety-Six.'

'Ah yes, the American War. You're a long way from home, Sullivan.'

'Aye, Cap'n, and a damned fool for it, and if I wanna get home I have to keep clear o' Lootenant Smithies. He's made threats to press some o' the boys from the *Galliwasp*. That's why I spends my liberty hours up here, away from the grog shops.'

'I see. Well, good luck to you. The sooner you get that barque refitted, the sooner you'll see New Brunswick again.'

He walked on, unaware that the encounter with Sullivan was the second event of consequence that day.

Drinkwater avoided the company of the garrison officers that night. He went, without dinner, directly to his room. There seemed little point in disobliging Hamilton. He would happily leave on the *King George*, when the packet sailed. He had begun making up an account to settle with Littlewood when a knock came at his door. It was Nicholas.

'May I speak with you, Captain Drinkwater?'

'Why the change of tack, sir?' said Drinkwater coolly. 'I thought all that was necessary had already been said.'

'Not quite, sir. May I . . . ?'

Drinkwater lit a second candle and motioned Nicholas to sit on the bed. He sat himself on the single rickety upright chair that served all other offices in the bare room. 'I shall not be sorry to leave this place,' he said, looking round him.

'Sir,' said Nicholas urgently, 'I must apologize for Colonel Hamilton's attitude as well as my own. He is a harassed man, sir, under pressure from many quarters and, if you will forgive the metaphor, you were a timely whipping-boy. The fact is, sir, that if you are who you say you are – damn it, this is difficult – but put bluntly, sir, as a post-captain you were seen as a threat . . .'

'Damn it, Mr Nicholas, I only wanted a degree of co-operation.'

'I think, sir, that you are a man of more decisiveness than the Governor. He is a trifle jealous of those whose, er, energy threatens to compromise his authority.'

'Which is why you yourself so assiduously toe his line,' said Drinkwater wryly.

'Er, quite so, sir. I have to endure a long posting here.'

Drinkwater smiled. 'Well, as for my decisiveness, Mr Nicholas, it has not been much exercised lately. In fact – well, no matter. To what do I owe your present visit?'

'A word with you privately, sir. I have given much thought to what you have told us. I have also consulted Captain Littlewood who told me that he was secretly informed in London that you were a naval officer of distinction.'

'Who told him that?' Drinkwater asked, recalling Littlewood's occasional sly 'jibes'.

'His charter-party, I understand. A Mr Solomon . . .'

'I see. Why then if you knew that, did you not intercede with Hamilton?'

'It only occurred to me to ask three days ago and since then, with the arrival of Lieutenant Maimburg, I have been much occupied with despatches. Besides . . .'

'Your relationship with Hamilton is not always easy.'

'Quite so, sir, quite so.'

'But you could have said something today.'

'I did not make the connection until dinner this evening, sir. It did not occur to me earlier and besides, there are certain matters that are exclusively my concern, as agent for the Foreign Service.'

'I see.'

'But before I can go any further, sir, before I can act on my own initiative, I have to satisfy myself that you are indeed the officer of whom I have heard.'

'And how do you propose to do that?' Drinkwater asked drily.

'You mentioned your acquaintance with Colin Mackenzie. What was it you jointly achieved in the, er, Baltic?'

For a moment Drinkwater stared silently at the young man. There were good reasons why he should remain silent, but there were equally good reasons for not doing so.

'What have you in mind, Mr Nicholas, if I prove to be who I claim? I am after all, about to be repatriated. Do you just wish to satisfy your curiosity?'

'You might yet achieve your objective, sir. You might yet convince the French that your cargo *was* bound for Russia, that the Russians *are* buying quantities of arms and that it suggests a secret accord between St Petersburg and London.'

'And how do you propose I, or should I say "we" are to accomplish this, Mr Nicholas?'

'Wait, sir. I beg you be patient. I can at present only conceive the grand design. Ever since I heard of Lord Dungarth's idea, I was struck by the subtlety of it. It understands exactly the circumstances likely to directly attract Napoleon's attention. But first, sir, answer my question: what was it you and Colin Mackenzie jointly achieved?'

It was as if a lock had been picked in Drinkwater's soul. As the candles guttered in the fervid breath of the eager Nicholas and the shadows of their figures leapt on the peeling limewashed walls of the barrack room, it seemed that his visitor was a providential messenger, sent to release him from his purgatory. Fate had decided upon a reprieve, and he felt his spirits rise with the enthusiasm of the younger man.

'Well, sir, if I hear you have breathed a word of this to anyone, I shall shoot you.' He said it without meaning it, but the flat tone of voice menaced Nicholas so that he caught his breath and nodded.

Drinkwater smiled. 'We are like conspirators, are we not, Mr Nicholas?'

'I hope not quite that, sir.'

'Lord Dungarth once said to me that he imagined himself as a puppet-master, pulling strings that made others jump. A rum fancy, but not inaccurate. Very well. Mackenzie and I were at Tilsit. There were two other men involved, one of whom is dead and neither of whom need concern us now, and what we achieved was the theft by eavesdropping of the secret compact made verbally between the Tsar and Napoleon Bonaparte. Now do you believe I am Nathaniel Drinkwater, sir?'

'I do, sir, and I am most regretful that I did not from the start. I can only say that it may be providential that I made the discovery this evening, for only today have circumstances conspired to make my new proposal possible.'

'It is pointless to engage in mutual recrimination,' Drinkwater agreed. 'Please proceed.'

'Well, Captain Drinkwater, I have already expressed my admiration for Lord Dungarth's idea. It is highly probable that he has taken other measures to augment the plan . . .'

'How do you mean?'

'Well, it would not work unless the enemy heard about it . . .'

'You are very astute, Mr Nicholas,' said Drinkwater, thinking of his success in the whore-house, 'that is indeed quite true. You think his Lordship even now might be absent from London on some such task?'

'I think it most likely, sir. If all had gone well your cargo would have been delivered by now and the veracity of his claim, wherever laid, could have been checked.'

Drinkwater's heart was thumping with excitement. It was unlikely that Nicholas was right, for Dungarth was no longer fit to risk his life in France, but the thought that he could have been absent from London for a prolonged period had simply not occurred to Drinkwater. Hamilton would not have written to Dungarth personally, and Nicholas would have written to Canning. Canning would not have had time to deal with the correspondence before his pointless duel; and Dungarth's absence, even on so innocent an excuse as taking the waters at Bath, would explain why no answer had been forthcoming.

'You may have a point, Mr Nicholas, pray go on.'

'Well, as I believe you know, there are transports lying in the road that were destined for a secret service.'

'I have met Gilham of the *Ocean*, yes . . .'

'It was intended that a rebellion was raised in Hanover in favour of King George, the legitimate sovereign.'

'But the plan misfired?'

'Yes, the troops intended for it were sent instead to Spain and we have had to content ourselves with recruiting for the King's German Legion. By the same packet that failed to bring your accreditment, I received a *Most Secret* despatch, one whose contents I am not necessarily obliged to make known to Colonel Hamilton.' Nicholas paused, as if to add emphasis to the drama.

'By which I take it you are about to strain the exact nature of the, er, obligation in my favour, eh?'

'Quite so, sir,' Nicholas said. 'The point is, that the Ordnance Board have written off the entire convoy. This was the news that arrived today. The cost is transferred to Mr Canning's Secret Service budget and Mr Canning is . . .'

'Out of office!'

'Exactly so!'

'And in the absence of Mr Canning, *you* are going to take it upon yourself to dispose of those cargoes to me in order that I may exceed my own instructions and devise a means by which the whole are delivered to Russia? No, no, Mr Nicholas, at least not until the spring. The Baltic will be frozen and by then . . .'

'The Elbe is still open.'

'The Elbe?' Drinkwater sat back in astonishment, making his chair creak. 'You are suggesting we land those cargoes in the Elbe?'

'It is only necessary that Paris believes they were *consigned* to Russia.'

'But what you are suggesting is the disposal of Crown property to the enemy!'

'Think what we would gain. The success of Lord Dungarth's mission with the enemy swallowing the bait in the belief that they had won the advantage while at the same time we should have disposed of the goods at a profit.'

'But . . .'

'The Government, Captain Drinkwater, has already written off those stores to the disposal of the Secret Service,' Nicholas repeated persuasively.

'Do we have some trusty person in Hamburg capable of acting as agent for the sale?'

'Indeed we do!' Nicholas said grinning, and Drinkwater found it impossible not to smile in response.

# PART TWO

# The Luring of the Eagle

England is a nation of shopkeepers.

NAPOLEON,
Emperor of the French

# The Lure

For a long while Drinkwater sat in silence and Nicholas watched anxiously. The longer the silence persisted, the less Nicholas thought he had convinced his listener. He began reciting a catalogue of reasons why the mission could not possibly be misjudged.

'If you have any misgivings, Captain Drinkwater, consider the facts. The funds of the Secret Service have been worse spent. We have squandered thousands on the Chouans . . . we have wasted huge amounts on fomenting the *émigrés* in Switzerland . . . the Comte d'Antraigues and Mr Wickham have gobbled up fantastic sums, all to no effect . . .'

But Drinkwater was not listening. Nicholas's words had acted like a drum beat to his tired heart. First the anger roused by Hamilton's rudeness had made him receptive to Nicholas's proposal; then the chance meeting with Sullivan, the *ci-devant* American, who had sown the seed of an idea . . .

He got up and began pacing up and down the spartan room: three paces to the wall, three paces to the bed, up and down, up and down.

'We have already enjoyed one brilliant success, sir, from this very island when Mr Mackenzie was here and superintended the mission of Father Robertson . . .'

Drinkwater stopped pacing and held up his hand. 'Stop, Mr Nicholas, you are being indiscreet. Whatever Mr Mackenzie's achievements, beware of seeking a reputation imprudently.

Your case has much to recommend it; now I desire that you listen to me.'

Drinkwater began to walk back and forth again, though at a slower pace, his head down and his forehead creased in concentration.

'There will be a gale by morning and the packet will be delayed. We must use this time to bring the Governor round. He has only to arrest and deport me for this scheme of yours to be stillborn. That I must leave to you, but I will give you some cogent reasons for pressing the point.

'To enable us to deliver a convoy would necessitate the co-operation of too many men and I doubt the fellows on those merchant ships will agree. However, we might mount an operation with two vessels. It will be known in Hamburg that these ships have been idling here for months; it would not be difficult to persuade the authorities there that their crews are disaffected, or threatened with the naval press. The Emperor Napoleon has inveighed against the application of the press against the hapless seamen of Great Britain . . .

'Apart from these two vessels, the remaining ships may be deployed as decoys in such a way as to give the impression of our sincerity, without committing them. Is there a rendezvous with the mainland that would not admit too great a risk to our people?'

'Yes, Neuwerk, an island ten leagues to the east and three from Cuxhaven.'

'Ah, yes, I recollect it from the chart. Well then, under the strictest discipline I think we might achieve something. Holding back most of the ships will perhaps serve to salve Colonel Hamilton's conscience, but he must put it about publicly that now the Ordnance Department have relinquished responsibility for the vessels, he wants them out of his charge.'

'I have no doubt but that he'd oblige you there.'

'He has no love of the mercantile lobby. Can we guarantee such an attitude will be made known ashore?'

'Gilham and company have rumbled with discontent for nigh on six or seven months, sir. The smugglers who buy from the warehouses report the movements of ships to and from the island. It cannot have escaped the notice of the authorities in Hamburg that some of them have been choking the anchorage for a long time.'

'And that they bear the distinctive marks of troop transports,' added Drinkwater, thinking of the large 'DA' painted on the bows of Gilham's *Ocean*.

'Quite so, sir, and if you make much of the disaffection of the crews when you are obliged to confront the *douaniers* . . .'

'Yes, Mr Nicholas,' Drinkwater broke in, 'but such a claim needs to be corroborated by whatever gossip precedes us. You say you have a trusted contact in Hamburg; I shall need also a German linguist. I know you to speak the language, do you know a person of such calibre that would accompany us?'

'Yes, I do. You recollect Colonel Hamilton spoke of delaying the packet until a message arrived?' Drinkwater nodded. 'And you recall me saying that it was only tonight that events conspired to make this present proposal possible?'

'I recollect.'

'There is a merchant house whose head is a man called Liepmann, a Jew, resident at Altona and master of a considerable business chiefly connected with the import of sugar. He is adept at maintaining this trade notwithstanding the present blockade and we are sympathetic to his needs. He is known to the French, having opened up a lucrative communication with the city's former Governor, M'sieur Bourrienne. He is a go-between, a broker . . .'

'And will handle the commercial aspects of this transaction of ours, eh?' Drinkwater asked, jumping to the obvious conclusion.

'Quite so. We, I mean, the Governor, is awaiting news as to how matters are to be conducted in the wake of Bourrienne's departure and under the rule of Reinhardt, the new French minister. The man who brings this, Herr Reinke, is surveyor to the Chamber of Commerce, continually mapping the shifting sandbanks of the Elbe, a man whose absence is not missed for a few days and who can be relied upon as an expert pilot and linguist. It is his arrival the Colonel anticipates.'

'I see. And Liepmann, can you communicate a matter of this complexity with him directly, or must we wait for Herr Reinke to return to Hamburg?'

Nicholas shook his head. 'I can send him a cryptogram by way of a fishing boat.'

'Very well.'

Drinkwater stopped pacing up and down and stood over Nicholas. He was resolved now, convinced that they had a chance of success.

'You will explain our intention in full to London, Mr Nicholas, is that clearly understood?' He did not want his motives misunderstood if the affair *did* miscarry, or he himself failed to return. 'Encode the message and do your best to reassure Colonel Hamilton that what we intend is a bold stroke.'

'A decisive stroke, wouldn't you say, sir?'

Drinkwater caught the twinkle of humour in the younger man's eyes.

'Indeed.' He smiled, then added, 'it would be even better managed if you could persuade him the idea was his own.'

Nicholas's eyebrows shot up. 'I could try, but I doubt that I possess sufficient tact for that.'

They laughed, just like conspirators, Drinkwater thought afterwards.

'And the communication with Herr Liepmann . . .'

'If you draft it, I will code it.' Nicholas hesitated then said, 'I think, Captain Drinkwater, that it would be to our advantage if you also knew the method of communication with Herr Liepmann. It might, after all, be useful to you in the event of any problems that might arise.'

'I see you are well cut out to be a diplomat, Mr Nicholas,' Drinkwater said wryly. 'This code is known to you and the Colonel . . .'

'And Herr Liepmann.'

'Very well. I agree. Now, Mr Nicholas, paper and ink, if you please. I will see you tomorrow when I hope to have spoken with Littlewood and, I think Gilham. In the mean time, oblige me by seeing if there is sufficient bunting on this

God-forsaken island to manufacture a dozen Yankee ensigns.'

'*Yankee* ensigns, Captain, you mean *American* ensigns?'

'That is precisely what I mean, Mr Nicholas.'

'May I ask why?'

'No, you may not. I shall tell you tomorrow evening, when I have decided whether or not this lunatic proposal of yours has the least chance of success. Now, sir, pen and ink, and then leave me alone.'

The gale came with the dawn and Drinkwater went out to revel in the rising wind that so accorded with his mood. Unshaven, his stock loosened and his eyes gritty from lack of sleep, Drinkwater felt again the electrifying thrill he had last experienced when talking to the Jew Solomon after his night of dissipation in the Wapping stew.

It seemed now a pity to waste that night of seedily shameful labour, and it was a consoling thought that the success of the resuscitated mission might avenge the loss of Quilhampton and all the brave fellows aboard the *Tracker*.

He was convinced that, given the right conditions, they could deceive the French. If neglectful providence chose to favour their endeavours they might achieve a great deal more, for the detachment of the Tsar from his alliance with Napoleon was too grand a design to baulk at for the loss of a few muskets and pairs of boots . . .

Drinkwater stretched and sniffed the damp air as it rolled a grey cloud over the heights of the island, obscuring the lighthouse tower and the church spire. It reminded him of the squadrons of His Britannic Majesty's Fleet keeping watch and ward off Ushant and La Rochelle, off L'Orient and Toulon, the Scheldt and the Texel.

Just suppose there was a rupture between St Petersburg and Paris; just suppose for a second time the Grand Army was drawn off to the east where it had narrowly missed defeat at the hands of the Russians at Eylau . . .

Just suppose the apparently senseless deaths of Quilhampton and Frey, and even of poor Tregembo, were transformed into so rich a prize as a lasting peace . . .

Then the storm-battered ships of the western squadrons and the Mediterranean fleet could be withdrawn; their people could go home to their families; he himself could go home to Elizabeth and their children.

He shivered, suddenly chilled in the damp air. Flights of such improbable fancy were inimical to the grim, omnipresent business of war. He went inside again, in search of hot shaving water and a solution to the greatest obstacle he foresaw to the enterprise.

The compliance of Captain Littlewood was essential to the success of Nicholas's idea. A second ship in support would add credibility to Drinkwater's appearance in the Elbe while the remainder could, at little risk, play their part without being committed. But without the *Galliwasp*'s cargo, nothing could be attempted, let alone achieved.

Littlewood was, therefore, the first person with whom he discussed the plan that morning. He found the shipmaster on the foreshore talking to Watts and Munsden, his two mates. Seeing Drinkwater approach, Littlewood extended his arms then dropped them disconsolately by his side. Beyond the trio, *Galliwasp* had been hauled off to a mooring buoy, one of a trot laid by Browne and his seamen to enable ships to ride out bad weather. A pair of sheerlegs rose from the barque's waist and most of her company hung about the water's edge, where a pair of boats lay drawn up on the beach.

'I'd hoped to get the main mast in her this morning,' bemoaned Littlewood, 'but this damned gale . . .'

He left the sentence unfinished.

'Well, Captain Littlewood, count your blessings,' said Drinkwater cheerfully, 'at least you have her off the shoal.'

'Just what I were sayin', Cap'n Waters,' said Watts. 'She'd not take another poundin'.'

'Perhaps, Captain Littlewood, you'd take a turn along the foreshore with me,' Drinkwater said.

They walked south in silence. To their left lay the road with its crowd of anchored ships and the sandy island beyond. To their right the steep cliffs of the island rose from the sand and rock pools of the narrowing littoral strip. Waders ran about on the tideline of bladder wrack left by the last high-water. A pair of pied oystercatchers took flight, their brilliant orange bills shrieking a piping cry of alarm as the two men disturbed them.

'I was wondering when you'd be along, Cap'n Waters,' said Littlewood as the beach narrowed beneath the beetling rock face of the cliff.

'I've passed the time of day with you most mornings, Captain Littlewood,' Drinkwater said cautiously, wondering how best to approach the subject he wished to broach.

'That's not what I mean.' Littlewood cocked a shrewd eye at Drinkwater.

'What exactly is it that you *do* mean then?'

'I'm not a fool, Captain Waters. I don't need a supercargo to deliver a cargo anywhere in the world. I know *what* you are, if not *who* you are.'

'Mr Solomon was indiscreet . . .'

'Mr Solomon was protecting his investment, Captain,' Littlewood said, according Drinkwater's rank a less than casual ring. 'I knew you'd be up in them barracks a-thinkin'. You see, I *know* my cargo's valuable, and I ain't just talking pounds, shillin's and pence.'

'Solomon told you *that*?' Drinkwater's expression betrayed his surprise.

Littlewood laughed. 'No, he ain't that indiscreet, but I knew a lot was ridin' on the sale and I wouldn't have had a shipmate like yourself, Captain, if the matter didn't stink o' Government. Besides, you don't get withdrawn from the Scheldt expedition without a deal of influence in high places.' Littlewood paused, then added, 'And I've some cargo aboard on my own account.'

Drinkwater stopped and looked at Littlewood. It occurred to him that he had been too much taken up with his own preoccupations, too morbidly bemoaning his fate to have paid sufficient attention to others whose lives were as much at hazard in the affair as his own.

'What sort of cargo, Captain Littlewood?' Drinkwater asked.

'Why sugar loaves, Captain Drinkwater, sugar loaves.'

'May I ask you then what you would now do, left to your own devices?'

'I live by profit. No Government pay supports me or my family. Doubtless I'd discharge my cargo in a Swedish port; you'd have little objection to that?'

'Only that it fails in its objective.'

'We've already failed in that. Besides, though the objective, as you call it, was set by the Government, the cargo was consigned at the expense of Solomon and Dyer. Whatever the outcome, they and your humble servant are entitled to a modest profit, Captain.'

'Very well, Captain Littlewood, suppose I was to ask you a second question: do you, or Solomon and Dyer, have an agent either here,' he paused as Littlewood's eyes narrowed, 'or in Hamburg?'

Drinkwater watched the other man's face with interest. He sucked in his cheeks and raised his eyebrows but his eyes remained fixed on Drinkwater. It was clear the idea of selling his cargo to a nearer market than Gothenburg had already occurred to him, for when he blew out his cheeks he asked, 'And if my men won't sail for Hamburg, Captain?'

'I should requisition your ship and man her with Mr Browne's ratings,' Drinkwater said, advancing a contingent argument he had discovered during the small hours of the previous night.

'Is Mr Browne now amenable to your discipline, then?' Littlewood said, alluding to the equivocal status the whole island must have known Drinkwater had been accorded.

'Mr Browne knows his duty . . .' Drinkwater bluffed, 'perhaps we managed our deception better with others than with you.'

Littlewood chuckled and looked at the horizon. 'If we pay 'em, Captain, I'll answer for ten – a dozen men.'

Drinkwater caught the significance of the first person plural and grinned as Littlewood swung round and faced him. 'How well d'you know Captain Gilham? Could we persuade him to join us?' Drinkwater asked.

Comprehension dawned large in Littlewood's eyes. 'My God, Captain, you are going way beyond a modest profit and a new gown for Mistress Littlewood.'

'I'm going for very high stakes, Captain Littlewood. With luck Mistress Littlewood will be able to take the air with four in hand.'

'Damn it, sir. If Gilham ain't game *I'll* guarantee his ship. What about the others?'

'I have plans for them, but the affair will depend upon the reliability of those that take part. Too many might lay us open to disaster; those that come must be volunteers, volunteers for a dangerous service. Only when you have those men game enough should you advertise extra payment. *Then* you can promise gold.'

'You have thought of everything, Captain, I congratulate you.'

'Thank you,' said Drinkwater ironically. 'We enter the Elbe under American colours, though ultimately there's no attempt to claim American nationality. We have been lying at Helgoland for months, our crews are unpaid and disaffected . . .'

'Where Gilham's concerned that ain't so far from the truth.'

'Then you must moot it thus among the masters. Do not reveal my part until you have sounded their opinion. When they realize they can get out of this place at little risk and with a profit, they'll fall in with my plan.'

'And you'll not risk more than the two ships, the *Galliwasp* and the *Ocean*?'

'Not if I can avoid it, though I may want the others to proceed to Neuwerk in due course. Do I recollect you mentioning to me that *Galliwasp* carried a consignment of sugar on your own account?' Drinkwater asked.

'Aye, loaf sugar.'

'I think you may find a good market for the stuff, Captain, in which case Mrs Littlewood's carriage is assured.' Littlewood chuckled and Drinkwater went on. 'I think we will have the services of a competent pilot and an agent able and willing to purchase the cargoes.'

'Would that be Herr Liepmann, Captain?' Littlewood asked.

'Damn me, yes, how the deuce . . . ?'

'He is Solomon and Dyer's agent.'

'Is he now,' Drinkwater said, one eyebrow raised quizzically. 'How very curious.'

Odd how things came together as though drawn inexorably by fate, Drinkwater thought.

'Better not make too much of our leave-taking,' he said as they approached the landing place. 'Get *Galliwasp* refitted and your cargo reloaded. We can do nothing until you are ready. Sound out the other masters and let me know in due course what their attitude is.'

'Aye, I'll see to it. As for this morning, what shall I give out as the nature of our conversation?'

Drinkwater considered the matter for a moment. 'Why, that I've overheard talk in the mess that the Ordnance Board is abandoning the convoy.'

'That should set the cat among the pigeons,' Littlewood rumbled.

'It just happens to be true, Captain Littlewood.'

He found Nicholas waiting for him when he returned to the barracks.

'Is your despatch ready, Captain?' Nicholas asked, a trifle impatiently, drawing from his breast a small octavo volume bound in brown calf. 'Dante, Captain, The Reverend Cary's translation.' Nicholas turned a few pages. 'Canto the second. You must commit these lines to memory.' Nicholas dipped the pen he had leant Drinkwater and began to scratch on a sheet of paper, quoting as he wrote:

> *Thy soul is by vile fear assail'd which oft*
> *So overcasts a man, that he recoils*
> *From noblest resolution, like a beast*
> *At some false semblance in the twilight gloom.*

Nicholas finished scrawling and looked up. 'Now, sir, 'tis perfectly simple: write the letters of the alphabet beneath each letter of the verse, omitting those already used, thus: *Thy soul is* . . . *a* to *h*, leaving the *s* of *is* blank, for you have used it in *soul*, and so on to the end. *I* and *j* are synonymous and those letters not found in the verse, *j*, *p* and *q* substitute for *x*, *y* and *z*. Cary's translation is new and not much known on the continent, though Liepmann has a copy. You have only to learn the verse.'

After Nicholas had gone, Drinkwater read the lines again as he committed them to memory. It struck him first that they uncannily described his own situation and the realization made the hairs on the nape of his neck crawl with a strange, primeval fear. And then, as he strove to remember the verse he realized that he no longer felt the oppression of spirit so acutely, that the mental activity of the last hours had roused him from his torpor.

This lift in his mood was sustained during the three days that the gale blew, three days during which he worked over and over his plan and committed Dante's lines and the information of Gilham's charts (which Littlewood had surreptitiously obtained for him) to memory. By the light of guttering candles he pored over and over them and finally burnt the blotchy copy of Cary's rendering of the Florentine poet's words in the candle flame. The plan to carry the cargoes into Hamburg had gained a powerful grip on his imagination and he eagerly awaited Nicholas's assurance that he had won Hamilton over to the plot.

He knew he could no longer dwell on the loss of his friends, only grasp the promises and seductions of tomorrow. That much, and that much alone, was allowed him. 'Hope,' he muttered to himself, '*must* spring eternal.'

Then, in the wake of the gale, as it blew itself out in glorious sunshine and a spanking breeze from the west-north-west, His Britannic Majesty's Sloop *Combatant*, carrying additional cannon for the defence of the island and confidential mail for the Governor, put an end to the dallying.

'It is providential, my dear sir, quite providential don't you know,' Nicholas said, hardly able to contain himself. 'Colonel Hamilton has received instructions from Lord Dungarth regarding yourself, Captain Drinkwater: combined with the arrival of the cannon it has quite put the backbone into him.'

'Lord Dungarth's instructions don't run contrary to our intentions then?'

'Quite the reverse . . . and here are letters for yourself.'

Nicholas pulled two letters from the breast pocket of his coat. Taking them Drinkwater tore open the first. It was from Dungarth.

*London, Nov. 26*

*My Dear Nathaniel,*

*I am sorry to hear of your Misfortune. The Venture has Miscarried in common with the Affair in the Scheldt. Your Failure is Insignificant beside this. You may also have heard of Rupture in Government. All, alas, is True. Take Counsel with Ed. Nicholas and Act as you see fit. Solomon and Dyer have Accepted Heavy Losses.*

*Yours, & Co*
*Dungarth.*

There was precious little sympathy for the Jew, Drinkwater thought as he opened the second letter. Its superscription was in a vaguely familiar hand. The letter was cautiously undated.

*London*

*Honoured Sir,*

*I am Privy to Matters closely related to your Circumstances. Your Personal Credit stands Highly here and you will Increase the Indebtedness of Your Humble Servant if you are able to Release my Agent and his Vessel to make those provisions necessary for a Small Profit to be Realized on all our Capital at Stake.*

*I have the Honour to be, Sir,*
*Isaac Solomon.*

Drinkwater could not resist a rueful smile; it was a masterpiece. As Dungarth passed the cost of the failed mission to

Solomon, the wily Jew inferred that, while the gold Drinkwater had lodged with him in good faith was of considerable value, its possession and sale guaranteed Solomon and Dyer's losses were handsomely underwritten! In short he, Nathaniel Drinkwater, would finance the expedition!

Drinkwater looked up at Nicholas. It could not have escaped either Dungarth's or Solomon's notice that Helgoland's occupation was chiefly to facilitate trade with the rest of Europe.

'I feel the strings of the puppet-master manipulating me, Mr Nicholas,' he said. 'Pray do you have any instructions regarding myself?'

'Indeed sir, his Lordship's letter to the Governor advised him to allow us to confer. But I am to take you to Colonel Hamilton forthwith.'

Drinkwater reached for his hat and both men stepped out into the passageway. 'Did you receive any further instructions about the other ships – Gilham's and the rest?' Drinkwater asked as they made their way to Hamilton's quarters.

Nicholas shook his head. 'No. I fear Government is still too disorganized as a result of Canning's disgrace . . . come, sir, here we are . . .'

Hamilton was standing with his back to them, staring out of the window. Behind him a gentle slope of grassland cropped by a handful of sheep rose to the tower of the lighthouse. Wisely, Drinkwater broke the silence.

'I am pleased to hear that matters have been happily cleared up, Colonel Hamilton. Will ye give me your hand?'

Hamilton turned and Drinkwater saw he was holding a letter. He seemed lost for words, embarrassed at the position in which he found himself.

'Come, Colonel, my hand, sir. Let us bury the hatchet . . . perhaps over a glass?' At Drinkwater's hint Hamilton unbent, took his hand and muttered something about 'spies everywhere' and 'havin' to be damned careful'.

'Perhaps, sir, you would show Captain Drinkwater the letter,' Nicholas suggested, 'while I . . .'

'Yes, yes, pour us a glass, for God's sake.' Hamilton handed over Dungarth's letter and threw himself down in his chair.

*Admiralty, London*
*26 November 1809*

*Lt. Col. Hamilton,*
*Governor,*
*Helgoland.*

*Sir,*

*I am in Receipt of your Letter of the 2d. Ultimo. The Officer You have Apprehended aboard the* Galliwasp, *barque, Jno. Littlewood, Master, is in the Employ of my Department on a Special Service. It is not Necessary to make known his Name to you, but you will know him by the following Characteristics, Viz: Engrained Powder Burns about one Eye; an Ancient Scar from a Sword Cut on the Cheek and a Severe Wounding of the Right Shoulder causing it to be much Lower than the Left.*

*You will greatly Oblige me by affording Him your utmost Hospitality and free congress with Mr Nicholas. This Officer knows my Mind and His Directions may be assumed as Congruent with my own.*

*I have the honour to be, sir, & Co*
*Dungarth.*

It was the most perfect *carte blanche* Drinkwater could have wished for, not to say the most perfect humiliation for poor Hamilton.

Drinkwater laid the letter down on Hamilton's desk and their eyes met.

'It is perhaps as well that his Lordship's letter arrived no earlier, Colonel,' Drinkwater said.

'How so . . . ?' Hamilton frowned.

'I was in damnably low spirits and had nothing of much sense to communicate. Now, Colonel, I have a proposition to make that will advance the service of our country . . .'

'A glass gentlemen,' Nicholas interposed. 'Schnapps, Captain Drinkwater.' Then he added, 'From Hamburg.'

CHAPTER 9 December 1809 – January 1810

# Santa Claus

Staring astern from the taffrail of *Galliwasp* Drinkwater watched Helgoland dip beneath the western horizon. He wondered if he would ever see it again and the thought brought in its train the multiple regrets and self-recriminations that had become a part of him in recent years. He had written to Elizabeth and the task, long postponed, had wrenched him from his deep and complex involvement with his secret mission. Nicholas would post the letter if he had not returned in two months. It told Elizabeth everything. He had left her the burden of writing to Quilhampton's fiancée and Frey's family, giving her a form of words to use.

It was no use looking back, he thought resolutely, and smacked the oak rail with the flat of his hand. He turned forward. Gilham's *Ocean* was wallowing sluggishly on their larboard beam, her bottom foul with grass despite the efforts to scrape it clean. *Galliwasp* ghosted along under topsails, keeping station on her slower sister in the light, westerly wind. Drinkwater looked up to judge the wind from the big American ensign. The stars and bars flaunted lazily above his head.

'There's Neuwerk on the starboard bow, Captain,' Littlewood pointed with his glass, then handed it to Drinkwater.

Behind the yellow scar of the Scharhorn sand which was visible at this low state of the tide, the flat surface of the island of Neuwerk was dominated by the great stone tower erected upon it.

Drinkwater studied it with interest as the young flood tide carried them into the mouth of the River Elbe. The island was to be, as it were, the sleeve from which he intended playing his ace. He handed the telescope back to Littlewood.

'Let us hope it is not long before we see it on the other bow,' Drinkwater said with assumed cheerfulness. He wished they had left Helgoland a day earlier, before the arrival of the depressing news. It cast a cloud over the enterprise, though Drinkwater, Nicholas and Hamilton had kept the intelligence to themselves.

In the period of waiting for *Galliwasp* and the other vessels to be made ready, their crews sounded and appointed and the secret messages sent to Liepmann in Hamburg, Drinkwater had been daily closeted with Hamilton and Nicholas.

On the occasion when Drinkwater had first broached the idea with Hamilton and the Governor had grasped the olive-branch thus held out to him, Nicholas had judiciously kept Hamilton's glass full of schnapps. Between them Nicholas and Drinkwater had boxed the Colonel into a corner from which his naturally cautious nature could not extricate him. In some measure a degree of bellicosity had been engendered by the arrival of *Combatant* and her cargo of cannon, and Drinkwater had insisted that the seamen of all the ships help to land and site them. This thoughtfulness on Drinkwater's part earned him Hamilton's grudging gratitude, for he himself had shown too great a prejudice against the merchant shipmasters and trading-post agents to rely on any willing co-operation from them. For his own part, Drinkwater's act was not disinterested. Requesting such assistance was a ready means of measuring his command over the odd collection of merchant seamen and naval volunteers that he would shortly lead into the enemy heartland. The fact that after months of inactivity *something* was afoot proved a powerful influence.

As a mark of their improved relationship Hamilton, Nicholas and Drinkwater got into the habit of dining together, partly to keep up Hamilton's enthusiasm and partly to discuss the progress of the preparations.

Over the dessert wine one evening Hamilton became expansive and Drinkwater learned of Helgoland's real importance as a 'listening post' on the doorstep of the French Empire.

'Hamburg has always been important,' Hamilton said. 'We nabbed Napper Tandy there after the Irish Rebellion. The place was full of United Irishmen for years.'

'They say Lord Edward Fitzgerald's wife is still resident there,' added Nicholas.

'She's supposed to be French, ain't she?' asked Drinkwater, 'though I believe her sister's married to Sir Thomas Foley. I recall *him* at Copenhagen.'

'Were you in Nelson's action, Captain Drinkwater, or Gambier's?'

'Nelson's, Colonel, just before the last peace.'

'It was after Gambier's scrap that we took this place from the Danes.'

'Yes. I was bound for the Pacific by then.'

'And after *that* Colin Mackenzie carried into effect a master-stroke,' added Nicholas.

'Ah, yes, you mentioned some such affair, a Father Robinson . . .'

'Robertson. A Jesuit who was sent from here via Hamburg to contact the Spanish forces Napoleon had isolated as a garrison on the island of Zealand – for Napoleon occupied Denmark as soon as we had seized the Danish fleet, all the while inveighing against British perfidy!'

'That would be about the time of the Spanish revolt, then?'

'Quite so. The object was to inform the Spaniards of their countrymen's uprising against the French and, if possible, repatriate them.' Nicholas refilled his glass, then went on. 'Robertson posed as a cigar and chocolate salesman and made contact with their commander, the Marquis of Romana. As a result the entire corps was withdrawn aboard the squadron of Rear-Admiral Keats then cruising in the offing.'

'Almost all, Ned, a few of the poor devils were unable

to escape. They say squadrons of riderless horses were left charging up and down the beach in perfect formation!' Hamilton amplified.

'What of Robertson?' Drinkwater asked.

'I believe he got back to England eventually. He was multilingual, don't you know, a remarkable fellow . . .' Nicholas's admiration was obvious and not for the first time Drinkwater found himself wondering how much the young man might want his own reputation enhanced by a similar *coup de main.*

'Boney was reported to be hoppin' mad, when he heard of the loss of the Spanish corps,' Hamilton said, 'Romana's troops were considered to be the best in the Spanish army.'

The story and its outcome were satisfying to men planning their own foray and added to Drinkwater's high hopes, but on the eve of their departure news of a more sinister kind reached the island, borne by Herr Reinke, whose long awaited arrival signalled the end of their preparations.

On receipt of the news Nicholas had withdrawn to write to Lord Bathurst that his nephew, lately employed on diplomatic service in Vienna, had mysteriously disappeared at Perleberg and was presumed dead.

He confided as much to Drinkwater, warning him of the dangers he ran, as a naval officer out of uniform, in going to Hamburg. 'I beg you to be careful,' he said. 'I am sure that Napoleon has taken this revenge in part for the successes Robertson and others have enjoyed at his expense. He would be especially glad to seize anyone connected with the betrayal of the Tilsit agreement.'

'I understand,' Drinkwater had said, 'there is no need to labour the point.'

'Schar buoy, Kapitan,' Herr Reinke, the pilot pointed ahead. 'You make good course a little more to ze east.'

Drinkwater nodded at Munsden, standing by the helmsman. 'Bring her round a point, Mr Munsden, if you please.'

He exchanged glances with Littlewood. To facilitate the negotiations shortly to be opened with the authorities at

Hamburg, Drinkwater was to assume the character of *Galliwasp*'s master, leaving Littlewood free to deal with matters of trade with which Drinkwater had no experience.

It was refinements of this nature which had occupied Drinkwater in recent weeks, refinements designed to make plausible the defection of several British master mariners in the cause of profit.

To these had been added another. Both *Combatant* and *Bruizer* had been ordered on cruises, so that reports that there were no men-of-war in Helgoland Road would encourage belief in the merchant masters' decision to dispose of their cargoes. In a day or two, whenever they might return, either or both *Combatant* and *Bruizer* would be sent into the mouth of the Elbe, as though seeking out the whereabouts of the missing transports.

To emphasize the anxiety of the Governor to recall his cruisers, Bengal fires would be thrown up from the lighthouse at two hourly intervals during the coming night.

Referring to the chart spread on the companionway cover, Drinkwater monitored Herr Reinke's directions. They passed between the Scharhorn and the Vogel sands and left Neuwerk Island astern, raising the Kugel beacon and the flat mainland on which the town of Cuxhaven nestled behind its sea wall. They passed the familiar fishing boats, any one of which might have been a visitor to Helgoland, and doubled the North Ground where the river narrowed. Small villages appeared, each cluster of houses nestling close to its church: Groden, with its wind-pump, Altenbruch and Otterndorf. The South Ditmarsch shore closed from the north and, with the tide now ebbing and the sun setting at the end of the short, mid-winter day, they anchored off Brunsbuttel.

'We shall have visitors soon,' said Littlewood, pointing to a boat putting off from a large, heavily sparred cutter that lay anchored inshore of them. 'She's a Dutch-manned hooker of the Imperial Customs. They're smart as mustard in these waters, those squareheads,' Littlewood said in reluctant admiration.

Drinkwater studied the cutter. The massive mainmast,

exaggerated tumblehome and huge leeboards marked her as a formidable craft amid the shallow waters of the adjacent coast. He remembered such a cutter with which he had fought at the battle of Camperdown. Whether it was the recollection, a sense of foreboding, or the cold of the December twilight, Drinkwater could not tell, but suddenly he shivered.

It was almost dark when the customs boat pulled alongside. Two officers in cocked hats and boatcloaks were followed up the ship's side by four armed seamen, one carrying a lantern.

'You are Americans, *Ja*?'

'*Nein, mynheer*, we are English!' Littlewood stepped forward. Drinkwater watched a second boat go alongside the *Ocean*. He hoped Gilham would play his part and then jettisoned the thought. It was too late to worry now, they were committed and Captain Gilham, for all his unprepossessing appearance, did not seem averse to his task. A thin man with spectacles on a long nose, his face was a mass of broken veins, suggesting he was a toper. Drinkwater had learned, however, that Captain Gilham never touched liquor, held Sunday services aboard his ship and spent much of his time recording what he termed 'the marvels of atmosphereology'. The result, Drinkwater had been told, was a meticulous log of weather observations taken every six hours, day and night for the past sixteen years.

'You are *English*?' the astonished Dutch customs officer was asking. 'Den vy do you come into ze Elbe, mit your scheeps?'

Littlewood explained. 'We have been tricked by our Government. We have been kept at Helgoland too long,' he gestured at the *Ocean*'s riding light. 'Captain Gilham has been seven months waiting for orders. We have received no pay, no provisions; my charter has expired. Now we wish to discharge our cargoes. If the British Government don't want them, perhaps we may find a market in Hamburg.'

The two Dutch officers looked at each other and the older one shrugged, saying something to the other which inferred the English speaker was the junior.

'Vat is your cargo?'

'Boots,' Littlewood said, raising one foot and waving his hand at it, 'coats, big coats, some muskets, flints, powder and shot.'

The junior *douanier*'s eyes opened wide and he translated for the benefit of his colleague. The senior muttered something, then strode to the rail and cupped his hands about his mouth, bellowing across to their friends aboard *Ocean*.

'He's asking what cargo the *Ocean* has,' Littlewood murmured.

A hail came from the other boarding party. For a few moments a shouted dialogue echoed back and forth between the two anchored ships, breaking the silence that had followed sunset and the dropping of the wind. At last the senior officer turned back to the waiting men and issued some orders. The other translated.

'You must here stay at Brunsbuttel. I vill here stay mit my men,' he gestured at the seamen with him, then accompanied his superior to the ship's side and saw him safely into the boat. As it pulled away the departing *douanier* shouted something.

'He say I am to shoot anyone who make trouble.'

'We ain't going to make trouble. Is he coming back in the morning?'

'*Ja*. He vill make zis arrival telled to Hamburg.'

'That is very good.'

'Dat is ver' good, *ja*.'

Drinkwater made a small movement of his head in *Ocean*'s direction and Littlewood took the hint.

'Captain Gilham!' he hailed, 'is everything well with you?'

'Perfectly well, sir, the temperature is falling and we'll have a touch of seasmoke on the water at dawn.'

The laughter that greeted this weather report eased the tension. Having set their own anchor watch, the crew of the *Galliwasp*, including her putative master, drifted below in search of food and sleep.

'You were right, Captain Gilham,' Drinkwater said, welcoming the master of the *Ocean* aboard the next morning. A low fog lay like smoke over the surface of the river so that the two ships seemed to float upon cloud, and in pulling across, Gilham's disembodied head and shoulders had drifted eerily, the boat beneath him invisible.

'It's not a matter of judgement, Captain Waters, but simply the appreciation of an immutable natural law.' He looked up at the cloudless sky. ''Tis a raw morning, but the sun will soon burn this off.'

'Did your guests make any objection to your paying us a visit?' Drinkwater asked, nodding towards the Dutch customs officer who stood warily watching them.

'Oh, they made a fuss, but . . .' Gilham shrugged and disdained to finish the sentence. Drinkwater smiled.

'Are your men still game?'

'Certainly. Why should they not be? They are being well paid for a little inconvenience. They were more discontented lying at anchor in that detestable anchorage.'

Drinkwater envied Gilham the cold, unemotional approach of a man whose life was guided by the simplistic principles of profit and loss.

'Every man has his price, they say,' Drinkwater said.

'And it is a very accurate saw, sir,' added Gilham, cocking an appraising eye at the mysterious 'captain' Littlewood had informed him was a personage of some importance.

'You sound as though you have done this sort of thing before, Captain.'

'I am told,' Gilham replied obliquely, 'that best Bohea is available for guests at the Tuileries and Malmaison.'

'As is cognac at the Court of St James . . . hullo, our friend stirs.'

Both men watched the uncanny sight of a large gaffed mainsail hauled aloft from an unseen deck as the Dutch customs cutter got under way. The long masthead pendant with its Imperial device trailed out in the light north-westerly wind. Littlewood joined them and in silence they observed the manoeuvre. After a few minutes they heard the splash of an anchor and the rumble of cable, then the mainsail disappeared again. The Dutch cutter was anchored closer to the two British merchant ships.

'When this seasmoke burns off,' Gilham said, 'you'll see her guns run out.'

'That ain't a matter of immutable law, Captain Gilham,' Drinkwater remarked lightly, 'but it's a damned sound judgement.'

A few minutes later, arriving as weirdly as Gilham had done, the senior Dutch customs officer clambered back over the *Galliwasp*'s rail. Seeing Gilham he frowned and addressed a few curt words to the tired junior he had left to stand guard the previous night. The younger man said something in reply, then shrugged.

The senior officer crossed the deck, his face angry. He asked Gilham a question and the younger officer translated.

'He say vy do you come this scheep?'

'To talk with my friends,' said Gilham, his expression truculent. 'How do we know you won't cheat us?'

The junior of the two Dutchmen shrugged again and relayed the message. The exchange reversed itself.

'It is *verboten* you make talk.'

It was Gilham's turn to shrug. 'I do not understand.'

Again the pantomime of translation. This time there was a longer exchange, then: 'Vy do you come here to Brunsbuttel?'

'We told you last night,' Gilham said sharply, his self-appointment as spokesman lent force by his very real frustration. 'Because I have been waiting at Helgoland for seven months to discharge my cargo.' He held up his fingers to emphasize the period. 'Now the British Government tell me it is not wanted. I have no money. I must pay my crew. I have the expenses of my ship. I have a wife. I have sons.' He punched the air with his index finger, advancing on the unfortunate Dutchman until his fingertip tapped the blue-coated breast, physically ramming at him the cogency of the simple sentences. 'Now I come to sell to the Hamburgers what the British Government does not want. Tell that to your chief, and tell him that he does not tell me what I must and must not do. I am master of the *Ocean* and by heaven, I'll not be pushed around by you, or him!'

Drinkwater watched the Dutchmen; one quailed visibly

under Gilham's onslaught, the other's face darkened as he understood the import of Gilham's speech. As his junior turned to explain, he was brushed aside. Gilham found himself under attack. The senior officer exploded into a tirade of invective in which God, swine and the English were recognizably called upon.

The senior *douanier* did not wait for this to be translated for his audience, but turned on his heel and went over the *Galliwasp*'s rail in a swirl of his cloak. His colleague began to stammer out an explanation but ceased as Gilham touched his arm.

'Never mind, my friend,' he said, impishly smiling, 'we understand.'

The customs officer stood nonplussed, then shrugging dismissively shouted something to his seamen and followed his commander over the side. A moment later another young officer climbed aboard.

'The king is dead, long live the king,' Gilham said drily.

'Well, I suppose we'll just have to wait and see what happens now,' Littlewood remarked. 'I wonder if there's fog in the outer estuary?'

By noon the visibility had improved and in the crisp, cold air, they could see the light tower at Cuxhaven and beyond it, the gaunt outline of the Kugelbacke beacon. Closer, the green river bank to the north and the white painted houses and spired kirk of Brunsbuttel spread out along the Ditmarsch shore. Closer still, the low, black hull of the Dutch cutter swum out of the dissipating mist.

'Looks as innocent as a swimhead barge, don't she,' said Littlewood as they studied her sharply raked bow.

'Not with those black muzzles pointing at us,' said Gilham.

'How d'you rate your own people if it came to a fire fight?' asked Drinkwater in a low voice.

'They don't have any practice,' replied Littlewood, 'though they'd be game enough.'

'Well, gentlemen,' said Gilham resolutely, 'if you're contemplating a private war, I'm returning to the *Ocean*. As I said to that squarehead, I've an interest in survival, never having rated glory very highly. Besides,' he added as he whistled for his boat's crew, 'it's dinner time.'

Littlewood and Drinkwater, who dined later, stood in silence for a while, curiously sweeping their glasses along the shoreline. The pastoral tranquillity of the scene was far from the blasts of war they were discussing. Cattle grazed the water-meadows and they could see the red flash of a shawl where a girl was tending poultry on the foreshore.

'Boat putting off from the Dutchman.' Munsden's report made them turn their telescopes on the cutter. Both of their recent visitors were leaving, bound for the beach where a horseman rode down to meet them.

In the sunshine they could see a green uniform topped by a plumed shako.

'French officer of *chasseurs*,' said Drinkwater, holding the figure in his Dollond pocket-glass.

'I can see some more of them, look, behind the large cottage to the left of the church . . .'

Drinkwater swung his glass to where Littlewood was indicating. He could see mounting figures pulling out of what he presumed were their horse-lines.

'I wonder why he never asked for our papers,' pondered Littlewood as the two men watched the Dutchmen leap ashore and confer with the French officer.

'I think we annoyed him too much and he was frustrated by not being able to speak to us directly. Gilham upset him and I suspect he's reporting us to his superiors. He's got us under his guns and he may be under some constraint, being a Dutchman.'

'There are some fiercely republican Dutchmen,' Littlewood said.

'Yes, I know.'

'I wonder what lingo they speak between each other?' Littlewood mused as they watched the French officer jerk his horse's head round.

'God knows,' said Drinkwater.

The French officer apparently shouted an order and four troopers, the men that had just mounted up, broke away from the horse-lines and rode after him as he set off eastwards at a canter.

'Odd that he needs an escort,' said Littlewood, lowering his glass and wiping his eye. 'Matter of waiting now,' he added.

They were compelled to wait two days before they learned of any reaction in Hamburg. Early on the morning of the first of these, however, a cloudy morning with the wind backed into the south-west, the horizon beyond the yellow scars of the exposed sandbanks to seaward was broken by the grey topsails of two ships.

In silence the observers on the decks of the *Galliwasp* and *Ocean* watched their approach with anxiety. This anxiety was real enough, for the first event of that day had been the arrival at Brunsbuttel of a jingling battery of horse artillery. The unlimbered field guns now pointed directly at them and, with the cannon of the Dutch cutter, neatly enfiladed them. Until the appearance of the distant topsails, the curious aboard *Galliwasp* and *Ocean* had occupied their enforced idleness by studying the artillerymen who, having established themselves, lounged about their pieces.

Despite the protests of their guard, Littlewood had sent Munsden aloft with the watch-glass to call down a commentary on events to seaward of them which was eagerly attended by those below.

'They are the *Combatant* and the *Bruizer*, right enough, and they're just clewin' up their main an' fores'ls.'

'Where are they?'

'Comin' up abeam of Cuxhaven . . . aye, *Combatant*'s roundin' up into the tide . . .'

'Anchoring or taking a tack inshore?' Littlewood asked anxiously, for whatever he did, *Combatant*'s commander *must* look as though he was making a determined effort to retake the truant merchant ships.

'She's opening fire!'

They could see the yellow flashes from the deck now, and the sloop's yards braced sharp up as she crabbed across the young flood tide.

'There won't be much resistance at Cuxhaven,' said Littlewood, 'if the last reports were correct.'

'No,' said Drinkwater, staring through his glass, his heart beating for those two distant ships. The thunder of that opening broadside rolled dully over the water even as *Combatant* loosed off a second and a third.

'*Bruizer*'s standin' on,' reported Munsden, unconsciously betraying the plan, the gun-brig making directly for them while the heavier sloop occupied whatever might be at Cuxhaven in the way of artillery. And then they knew. Six yellow pin points of muzzle flashes were followed by another six.

'My God, they've got two batteries of horse-artillery there! They weren't evident the other day when we passed.'

'Moved in this morning, like our friends yonder,' Littlewood said, jerking his head at the nearer shore without lowering his glass.

'*Bruizer* comes too far to the north, Kapitan,' said Herr Reinke, the pilot and surveyor. 'He must be careful.'

Drinkwater transferred his attention to the gun-brig. Unaware that any resistance would be forthcoming from Cuxhaven, a pretext for the withdrawal of the two men-of-war had to be invented. To achieve this, Smithies had been ordered to incline his course so as to take the bottom on the North Ground, the sandbank opposite Cuxhaven. The resulting confusion would offer the commander of the *Combatant* a pretext for breaking off the action. In fact there was little risk to the shallow draft gun-brig. The tide was rising and with her anchor down, she would float off in an hour or two.

But with the *Combatant* engaging artillery ashore and Smithies acting over-zealously, the ruse looked as though it might be more realistic than was intended.

'If anything miscarries, Captain,' Littlewood muttered beside him, aware of Drinkwater's apprehension for the naval ships, 'don't forget to look cheerful!'

Drinkwater grunted, his throat dry. Of course, Reinke could be wrong. At this distance it was notoriously difficult to judge angles of aspect.

'*Bruizer*'s struck sir!' Munsden called. 'And lost her foretop-mast!'

Littlewood burst into a cheer and slapped Drinkwater heartily on the back. Drinkwater staggered under the impact of the blow and coughed on his chagrin. Over the water the rolling concussions of the *Combatant*'s guns duelling with the batteries at Cuxhaven echoed the thumping of his heart.

An answering cheer came from the men ranged on the customs cutter's deck. Littlewood rounded on the Dutch officer aboard *Galliwasp*, 'Why you not weigh your anchor and go and fight?' he urged. The *douanier* shook his head.

'Cuxhaven guns make stop your scheeps.'

And so it proved. *Combatant* broke off the action and tacked across the stream as the tide slackened. *Bruizer* refloated and swung her head seaward. A boat was seen between the two ships, then, as *Combatant* went about again, she drew *Bruizer* in her wake on an unseen towline. As she tacked back towards the Cuxhaven shore she laid a few last broadsides at the enemy. Apart from holes in her sails, she appeared unscathed.

'As neat a piece of seamanship as I've seen in a long while,' said Littlewood from the corner of his mouth.

'If she had lost a mast, then things might have turned out differently,' breathed a relieved Drinkwater. He already had cause to regret the loss of one gun-brig.

'Oh, he kept out of range of those nine-pounders . . . but I'm glad to see *you* looking a little more cheerful at that spectacular British defeat.'

Littlewood grinned at Drinkwater, and this time Drinkwater smiled back.

'Russia? You are saying, Captain, that your cargo was consigned to *Russia*?'

'Yes,' said Drinkwater, staring levelly at the dark and handsome Frenchman in the sober black suit. His plain, elegant clothes reminded him of Nicholas and it was clear the two had more in common than the unaffected good taste of their dress; both were the diplomatic, and therefore the political, emissaries of their respective masters. Monsieur

Thiebault had arrived from Hamburg to carry out an examination on behalf of Monsieur Reinhard, the Emperor's minister in that city. Upon Monsieur Thiebault's appraisal of the curious submission of the two British shipmasters depended the success, or otherwise, of the grand deception. And incidentally, Drinkwater thought, driving the underlying fear from the forefront of his mind, ultimately their own survival.

'But why?'

'It is a market, M'sieur. With the continent closed to us by the decree of your Emperor, we must sell wherever we can. Had I not been driven by bad weather to Helgoland, I would not be suing for purchase by you . . .'

'Yes, yes, we have been over that,' Thiebault said testily, his command of English impeccable, 'but Russia is also under an embargo.'

Drinkwater laughed and Littlewood beside him smiled knowingly.

'We are able to trade with Russia, M'sieur, quite easily. As you see . . .' Drinkwater nodded at the three grey greatcoats and the two pairs of hobnailed boots on the table between them. 'Samples to whet their greedy appetites' Littlewood had called them when he suggested exhibiting their cargo.

'And your consignee was the Russian Government?'

'That is clear from the papers before you, sir,' said Littlewood.

'And on the papers before me it states that Captain Waters here is the master of this ship,' Thiebault said suspiciously.

'Captain Waters,' Littlewood said, brushing the matter aside, 'is new to the trade. I am acting on his behalf and as agent for the consignors.'

'And who *are* the consignors, Captain Littlewood?'

'You can see from the manifest, sir, Solomon and Dyer.'

Thiebault listened to something whispered in his ear by the senior Dutch officer. He nodded and consulted a second *douanier* on his right, a very senior French officer of the Imperial Customs Service.

'Mynheer Roos tells me this merchant house is known in

Hamburg. Is that why you have chosen to offer your cargo here, despite the embargo?'

'M'sieur, Mynheer Roos knows well that a regular trade has been opened for some time between us. The Governor of Hamburg, M'sieur Bourrienne, encouraged it as a form of relief for the citizens . . .'

'That is not quite the case,' said Thiebault hurriedly. Bourrienne had been recalled by the omnipotent Napoleon, to whom he had once been confidential secretary, on the grounds of corruption and disobedience.

'Perhaps not *quite* the case, M'sieur, but certainly the facts behind it,' Littlewood said mischievously.

'Tell me, gentlemen, as a matter of perhaps mutual interest, are Solomon and Dyer the *only* London house trading with Russia?'

'I shouldn't think so,' laughed Littlewood insouciantly, to Drinkwater's admiration. It was clear that Littlewood relished the cut and thrust of mercantile bargaining and had imbibed every detail of his assiduous coaching on Helgoland. He was proving his weight in gold, Drinkwater thought wryly.

Thiebault rubbed his chin in thought, his eyes never leaving the faces of the four men ranged in front of him.

'And you, Captain,' he referred to the report of Mynheer Roos. 'Gilham. Your cargo was under contract to the British Government?'

'As I've already explained, M'sieur, I've been buzznacking . . .'

'I do not understand that word, Captain Gilham,' Thiebault said sharply. 'Confine yourself to the question.'

'Yes, I was on a Government charter.'

'And you chose a treasonable course of action . . .'

'We were told in Helgoland that the operation was not now to be undertaken. We were told that the Government had written off our cargoes. Experience tells me that I will be extremely fortunate to recover my expenses.'

'What was this operation?' Thiebault asked.

'Oh, an attempt to raise the population of Hanover against

the French and Prussian interference. It was common knowledge.'

'Was it?' Thiebault said archly. 'And why do you suppose your Government decided, how do you say, to call it off, eh?'

Gilham chuckled and worked himself forward on his chair. 'Because, M'sieur, they are embroiled in a grand fiasco off Walcheren, that much we know both from your Hamburg newspapers and from the scuttlebutt at Helgoland.'

'*Scuttlebutt*?'

'Gossip . . . tittle-tattle . . . news by word of mouth . . .'

'Ah, yes.' Thiebault swivelled his eyes to the fourth of his interviewees. 'And you, Herr Reinke. You are a surveyor are you not? You have produced surveys for the Chamber of Commerce at Hamburg, yes? You speak excellent English, I hear.'

Reinke nodded gravely.

'It is not good to find you on an English ship.'

'I was making a survey off Neuwerk, M'sieur Thiebault, when I was captured by fishermen. They took me to Helgoland where they were rewarded. The English stole my survey and paid the fishermen for me.' Drinkwater heard the story delivered in Reinke's dead-pan accent.

'We received no report of this incident, Herr Reinke.'

'It only happened five days ago. I am gone for many days sometimes, on my work.'

'And these gentlemen obliged you by setting you free.'

'You could say his arrival made up our minds for us, M'sieur,' Littlewood said.

Thiebault looked at Littlewood. 'You mean it was providential?' he said, and something of doubt in his tone alarmed Drinkwater.

'No, I merely meant that what we had been discussing amongst ourselves was made possible by Mr Reinke's capture.'

Drinkwater's eyes met those of Thiebault and they were like two fencers, each watching for the almost imperceptible facial movement that communicated more than words, but spoke of truth and resolution.

'And how, Captain, er, Waters, do you know you can trust us? Suppose we promise you payment, then take your cargoes and throw you into gaol?'

'Because you are a man of honour and will give us a *laissez-passer*,' Drinkwater leaned forward, 'and because there are three other ships waiting at Helgoland under orders to return to England which, if they receive favourable reports from Hamburg by means which you know to exist, will also deliver up their cargoes, cargoes of ball, cartridge, clothing and small arms.'

'And how do you know we would not let this message go and lock *all* of you up?'

'Because it would put a stop to *all* British shipments . . .'

'Not for long, your countrymen are too greedy for that.'

'Of course,' smiled Drinkwater, 'they would ship their trade to Russia in expectation of a greater profit than you can offer.'

Thiebault looked at him through narrowed eyes. All the men in the *Galliwasp*'s cabin knew that illegal trade flourished in spite of the Emperor's proscription. Indeed it was connived at on every level of Imperial legislation and Hamburg was notorious for being the chief channel for this illegal traffic.

'If we agree to your proposition, gentlemen, and reach a satisfactory conclusion that is beneficial to us all,' Thiebault gestured round the table, hinting that all, though opposed in theory, shared a common interest, 'how will you explain your action to your owners?'

'There are six ships involved, M'sieur. The misfortunes of war might be invoked to explain their loss. They are of course insured . . .'

Littlewood's explanation had been devised by Drinkwater, but not its masterly embellishment. He had not considered the loss to the insurers, but clearly the thought of this additional damage to the economy of Great Britain appealed to Thiebault. Moreover, Littlewood was about to give greater proof of his fitness for the task.

'By the way, did we mention the sugar?' he asked innocently.

'Sugar?' Thiebault and his colleagues stiffened perceptibly.

'Yes, the best, we have a small amount in addition to these,' Littlewood gestured at the boots.

'Well,' said Thiebault, recovering, 'it is a most attractive offer gentlemen, assuming, of course, that we can afford it.' He conferred again with his flanking *douaniers*, then rose to his feet. 'Very well, gentlemen. I must, naturally, report this affair to Hamburg. I am sure they will be interested to know that Saint Nicholas has arrived from so unexpected a quarter . . .'

'Saint Nicholas?' quizzed Littlewood.

'Ask Herr Reinke. It is a German custom, is it not Herr Reinke? Happy Christmas, gentlemen.'

CHAPTER 10 January 1810

# Hamburg

'It is good, Kapitan,' Herr Reinke said in his flat, humourless English, 'everything is arranged.'

'There are no problems?' Drinkwater enquired, hardly able to believe what Reinke, Littlewood and Gilham accepted without apparent misgiving.

'No.' The ghost of a smile now played about Reinke's face. 'You have not been many times in this trade?' he asked, though he seemed to be merely confirming an impression rather than seeking a fact. 'You are surprised it is easy, yes?'

'Yes, I am.' Drinkwater poured two glasses of Littlewood's blackstrap, handing one to the German surveyor.

'*Prosit.* Things are a little different now. When Bourrienne was Governor it was more easy.'

Drinkwater knew of the corruption, if corruption it was, that had flourished under the city of Hamburg's disgraced Governor. Bourrienne's hand had been light on the helm, but deep in the pockets of his unwilling subjects, for he had connived at flouting the proscriptive decrees of his Imperial master on the pretext that too severe an imposition of trading embargoes would produce indigence and destitution among the inhabitants of the Hanseatic towns. Such disaffection, Bourrienne had argued, could fester and then erupt as open rebellion. It was rumoured to be happening in Prussia and other German states unhappy with their vassal status. Bourrienne's recall and subsequent disgrace was a measure of Napoleon's displeasure, and a gauge too, Drinkwater thought, of the Emperor's likely reaction to news of similar irregularities with Russia.

'In fact, Kapitan, more than one thousand English ships already discharge their cargo here, in Hamburg, every year since you take Helgoland.'

'I see. Then there is a ready supply of capital in the city?' Drinkwater persisted. Such details he had left to Nicholas, assured by him that they would encounter no obstacles and which, preoccupied as he had been by the planning and writing of orders concerning the logistic and military side of the operation, he had been content to ignore. Now, in the very heart of the great city, as he waited for the hatches to be opened and the contraband cargo discharged, he found his curiosity aroused.

'*Ja*,' said Reinke. 'Mainly Jews, like your Herr Liepmann, but also good German merchants. Herr Liepmann is knowing that the Governor must provide some stores for the Grand Army. Some things, like these boots you have, the Governor will sell to Paris. Herr Liepmann will buy from you, the Governor's agents will buy from Liepmann. Paris is happy it has boots; the Governor is happy: he has a profit because he sell at more than Herr Liepmann sell to him; and Liepmann is happy because he also has a profit when he buy from you and sell to the French. And *you* are happy because without Liepmann buy your cargo, you have nothing.'

'But how,' Drinkwater asked, feeling far from happy, 'did Herr Liepmann reach this accommodation with the Governor? And how does he preserve it when Bourrienne leaves and Reinhard arrives with new orders to enforce the embargo more strictly?'

'Ach, you don't understand *that*! Well, that is most easy.' A smile of pure worldly cynicism lit up Reinke's sober face. 'We are not barbarians. The French take Hamburg and we must live, *nein*? We must, what is word . . . ?'

'Adapt?'

'*Ja*, to adapt. Hamburg must adapt. There are ways of

doing things. Herr Thiebault, he is *un homme d'affaires*, he understands . . .'

'And has a taste for sugar?'

'*Ja!* You understand Kapitan, but also, I think, he is much interested by these boots.'

The seasmoke they had experienced at Brunsbuttel became a daily phenomenon as they lay at buoys off the city of Hamburg. The ships had worked their way slowly upstream, catching the wind and tide when they served, anchoring when they became foul and hampered progress. Reinke piloted them skilfully, for the channel wound between a vast expanse of salt marsh and shoals. The flat wilderness of reed beds where the mighty Elbe swirled and eddied over the shallows was the haunt of heron and harrier, of a myriad species of ducks and geese. Alders and willows crowded the banks and midstream aits, and cattle stood hock deep in the water-meadows near the scattered villages past which they had slipped under their false, American colours.

At Blankenese the land began to rise in a series of low hills until, beyond the village of Altona, they could see the smoke and spires of the great city that lay on the Elbe's northern bank. Here, in accordance with Thiebault's instructions, they were directed to secure to midstream mooring buoys. Their Dutch escorts departed and French soldiers, grizzled infantry of a line battalion recruiting its strength in the 'soft' posting of garrison duty, took over as their guards. The contrast they made with Hamilton's men struck Drinkwater, for these were veterans in the real sense of the word, men whose entire lives had been spent in bivouac, men used to scraping a bare subsistence from the country they found themselves in, men of almost infinite resource, easy in their demeanour like his own seamen, yet possessed of the intelligent eye, the keen weapon and that invisible yet detectable *esprit* that marked them as invincible. Their proximity increased Drinkwater's unease.

On their arrival Littlewood was escorted ashore. When he returned he reported he had met the mysterious Herr

Liepmann. He expressed himself satisfied with the transaction and said that Liepmann had undertaken to transmit a secret message through his own channels to Isaac Solomon in London. Three days into the new year lighters arrived alongside, each with a gang of workmen and more guards.

'They,' said Littlewood nodding at the blue uniforms of a platoon of *voltigeurs*, 'are proof that the French authorities themselves are taking this little lot into safe-keeping.' Here Littlewood shifted his nodding head to the first bales of greatcoats that swung up and out of *Galliwasp*'s hold.

Drinkwater was aware that he ought to have shared the obvious euphoria of Littlewood and Gilham, but he could not shake off the thought that matters had gone too well and that the plan had worked almost too faultlessly. In his mind he reviewed the interviews, Thiebault's reactions and Reinke's laboured explanations. There could be no doubt that a cargo had been shipped from London for Russia, and that the French knew about it, for if Fagan had not alerted them, Thiebault had most certainly done so and had made no attempt to disguise the fact that he had digested the information with interest.

Drinkwater ought, he knew, to have enjoyed a sense of relief far greater than that of his companions for, against the odds, he had carried out his orders. The enemy had been baited and taken the lure, and this appeared to have been confirmed by the account of the 'naval battle' off Cuxhaven in the Hamburg newspapers, for it was too preposterous a story not to have originated in Paris, a reprint of *Le Moniteur*'s account of 'two British frigates trying to force a passage into the Elbe in pursuit of neutral, American shipping. They had been engaged and driven off by horse-artillery detachments, one having been dismasted.'

It was only after Reinke had translated this mendacious account that Drinkwater realized that the 'neutral, American shipping' referred to *Galliwasp* and *Ocean*, and that the report was virtual confirmation that the French had been deceived.

There was, he realized, no absolute guarantee that the men of the *Galliwasp* and the *Ocean* would be released, though

Reinke assured him he had nothing to worry about. It was of little advantage to the French to hold merchant seamen, for they were outside the normal cartel arrangements for the exchange of prisoners and merely an expense, though their confinement did deprive the British of their services as pressed men. At a local level the pragmatic realization that their detention would deter others from bringing the desired luxuries through the blockade was a more persuasive argument in favour of letting them continue their voyaging.

'If Thiebault makes trouble,' Reinke promised, 'we will make trouble also.'

It was clearly in the interests of the Chamber of Commerce to ensure the freedom of the Britons in their midst, an action facilitated for all the parties concerned by the fiction that they were American, though it was difficult to imagine what form this 'trouble' might take.

As he leaned on *Galliwasp*'s rail and watched the beefy German lightermen swinging out the ground tier of bales with their heavy grey greatcoats hidden under the dull burlap, Drinkwater told himself he was becoming old and jittery, apprehensive that as a disguised sea-officer in enemy territory, he ran the risk of being shot as a spy.

Reinke left them that forenoon, removed now that the services of neither a pilot nor an interpreter were required. The authorities, having permitted the discharge of the cargo to commence, were content to keep the crews of the two ships in mid-stream quarantine. The work progressed slowly. Only one lighter per ship was allowed them, clear proof, Littlewood asserted, that the stores were being carefully housed under lock and key in some well-guarded warehouse.

Drinkwater waited impatiently, pacing *Galliwasp*'s poop. Pancakes of ice began floating sluggishly past them as the weather turned bitterly cold, the copper cupola of St Michelskirche standing green against the dark grey of a sky pregnant with snow. The first fall occurred on the second day of their discharging and Drinkwater woke next morning to a changed scene, the roofs of the city white and the hum of the quays and bustle of the river muted under the mantle of snow. At first he thought the lack of activity due to the snowfall, but then he marked a restiveness among their guards and noticed a propensity for the French soldiers to huddle and gossip quietly amongst themselves with more animation than was usual. Again, this too might have been attributable to the change in the weather, except that he was conscious of something else, a total lack of movement on the river. It was true there was more ice than there had been, but the Elbe was a great highway and a fishing ground, and he knew from long experience that men who earned their livelihood from trade and fishing do not cease at the first flurry of snow, rather they increase their activity before the severity of the weather stops them altogether.

'There's something amiss ashore,' Littlewood said, lowering the glass with which he had been scanning the adjacent quay.

'You've noticed it too,' said Drinkwater. 'It can't be another religious holiday, the churches are silent.'

'No, but there are soldiers on the quay there.' Littlewood pointed and offered Drinkwater his glass.

Drinkwater scanned the wharves. A troop of dragoons trotted past, their long carbines tucked in stirrup-holsters.

'Can't have anything to do with us,' Littlewood remarked, though his tone lacked conviction.

'Garrison reinforcements?' Drinkwater said. 'Perhaps the arrival of a French bigwig?'

'That might explain the stoppage of work, I suppose,' said Littlewood disconsolately, 'I hope it won't detain us for long, I don't like this ice.' He gestured over the side, where larger floes, flat glistening sheets, revolved slowly in the stream, occasionally jamming athwart their hawse before tearing free and continuing their passage to the North Sea.

The following night, during the early hours, Drinkwater was shaken hurriedly awake. Littlewood, still wearing nightcap and gown and holding a lantern, stood over him.

'Cap'n Waters, get up! There's a summons from the shore! Thiebault's come aboard and he wants you and Gilham.'

'What o'clock is it?' asked Drinkwater, but Littlewood was not listening.

'Something's afoot! Two lighters will be here within the hour. That should take the remains of our cargo. Thiebault wants us and the *Ocean* under weigh by daylight.'

Littlewood left as hurriedly as he had come, leaving a confused Drinkwater to dress and follow him. On deck he found the French customs officer muffled in a cloak.

'Captain Waters?' Thiebault's voice was tense and his tone urgent.

'Yes? What is the meaning of this?'

'Please prepare yourself for an absence from the ship.'

'But I understand you wish us to be under weigh by dawn . . .' Drinkwater protested. Thiebault interrupted him.

'I can give you five minutes, Captain, but no more.'

'I demand an explanation . . .'

'I have loaded pistols which will persuade you to do as I ask,' Thiebault hissed. 'I do not wish to summon the guards, but I give you five minutes to attire yourself.'

Drinkwater spun on his heel and returned to his cabin, his mind a whirl. The dull, persistent foreboding was proved right, he thought, as he forced his feet into Dungarth's hessian boots, rolled up his shaving tackle and stuffed small clothes into a leather valise. For a moment he thought of leaping from the stern window, then dismissed the idea as stupid. He would freeze within minutes, his wracked shoulder no aid to such heroics. Wrapping himself in his boatcloak and jamming the plain tricorne on his head, he returned to the *Galliwasp*'s poop. Thiebault was impatient to be gone.

'You are quite safe, Captain Waters, but I am under the painful necessity of securing your person, and that of Captain Gilham, as guarantors.'

'*Guarantors!* What the devil d'you mean?' snapped an increasingly angry Drinkwater.

'Against the compliant behaviour of the other ships whose cargoes you have promised . . . come sir, I will explain, but you *must* attend me at once, we have not a moment to lose!'

Drinkwater turned to Littlewood, an unpleasant suspicion

forming in his mind. 'Littlewood, are you a party to this knavery?'

'No sir! I shall do everything possible to expedite the arrival of the remaining ships, believe me!'

'I am compelled to, sir!' snapped Drinkwater.

'Come Captain . . .' Drinkwater felt Thiebault's hand at his elbow. He shook it off angrily, then Thiebault called out in a low but authoritative voice, '*M'aider, mes amis!*'

The grim infantrymen of their guard suddenly surrounded Drinkwater. He was hustled unceremoniously to the rail and down into the waiting boat. Collapsing, half-trodden on by the descending Thiebault, he found an indignant Gilham held at pistol point.

'What in God's name . . . ?' Drinkwater began, but he felt himself seized from behind and a hand clapped firmly over his mouth. As the boat shoved off from the side of the *Galliwasp*, Thiebault leaned over the two Britons.

'Not a word, gentlemen, I insist. In a moment I will explain.'

And with that they had, perforce, to be content. With a regular dip and splash, the boat was pulled obliquely across the river, dodging the ice floes and bumping gently at the foot of a flight of steps set in a stone quay. They were bundled up these and into a carriage. Its blinds were drawn and Thiebault entered after them. He set a lantern in the sconce, then turned and took a pistol from one of his assistants. The door slammed shut and the carriage jerked forward with Gilham and Drinkwater staring down the barrel of Thiebault's pistol. From time to time the Frenchman cautiously lifted the edge of the adjacent window blind and peered out. In the lantern light Drinkwater noticed an unseasonal perspiration on Thiebault's forehead.

Less than half an hour had passed since Littlewood had woken Drinkwater, and in the confusion he had felt only an angry perplexity. But it was anger tempered with the odd feeling that he had expected some such event, and now that it had occurred and he was compelled to sit and wait upon events, he noticed Thiebault's anxiety with interest. Beside him Gilham was less philosophical.

'Well,' he demanded, 'what about this confounded explanation you promised?'

Thiebault let the blind drop for the third or fourth time and lowered the pistol, his thumb and forefinger easing the hammer so that the gun was no longer cocked and the frizzen clicked shut over the priming pan.

'Gentlemen,' he said with what Drinkwater thought was an effort to assume his customary urbanity, 'there has been a development in our affairs that was unforeseen. I assure you there is nothing sinister in your predicament. It is merely a precaution.'

'I do beg to differ, M'sieur Thiebault,' said Gilham sarcastically, 'it is hard to view midnight abduction at pistol point as anything other than sinister.' Gilham leaned forward and Drinkwater shot out a hand to restrain him.

'I think M'sieur Thiebault has problems of his own, Gilham. I think we are taken not merely as guarantors against the arrival of the other ships, but as hostages . . .'

'*Hostages*, by God!'

'Hold hard, sir!'

Thiebault, clearly compromised and, judging by his obvious anxiety, preoccupied with plans of his own that took precedence over any consideration, real or pretended, shot Drinkwater an unguarded look of pure astonishment.

Drinkwater seized upon his obvious advantage. 'Who has arrived in Hamburg, M'sieur Thiebault, to compel you to take this extreme action, eh?'

Thiebault's mouth opened, then closed. He offered no explanation, and Drinkwater knew his question had found its mark.

'You see, Gilham,' he went on, never taking his eyes off the French official, 'I believe that we are hostages to be delivered up to this person if M'sieur Thiebault here has to clear his name from any charge of trafficking with the British. Is that not so, M'sieur?'

Thiebault let his breath out with an audible hiss.

'Well?' Gilham persisted, 'what d'you say to that?'

'Yesterday,' said Thiebault resignedly, 'the Prince of Eckmühl arrived in Hamburg.'

'And who in the name of Beelzebub might *he* be?' asked Gilham sharply.

'Marshal Davout, gentlemen,' said Thiebault, adding under his breath, '*le marechal de fer . . .*'

# Sugar

Captain Gilham had never heard of Davout, and the muttered soubriquet – evidence of Thiebault's fear of the marshal – made no impression upon him. Instead he raged against the Frenchman's perfidy, subjecting Thiebault to a tirade of abuse until Drinkwater silenced him, to Thiebault's obvious relief.

'Where are you taking us?' he asked.

'To a property of Herr Liepmann's, Captain Waters, where you will be quite safe.'

Drinkwater suppressed a smile. It was clear to him that Thiebault's action was on his own account, or at least on the account of those engaged in illegal trade. Drinkwater knew little about Marshal Davout, but what he did know was enough to make him sympathetic to Thiebault's plight. Davout's Third Army Corps had held the main body of the Prussian army at bay at Auerstädt while Napoleon thrashed the remainder at Jena, accomplishing in a single day the destruction of the Prussian army. He was reputed to be unswervingly loyal to the Emperor, incorruptible and humourless, a man of ruthless severity and no private weaknesses. It was no surprise that Thiebault had been driven to the extremity of seizing the two masters of the British ships just then lying in the Elbe. It was bitterly ironic, Drinkwater thought, that by exchanging positions with Littlewood, he had thus compromised himself.

'I did not wish to disturb the safe despatch of your ships,

gentlemen,' said Thiebault, 'that is why I left Captain Littlewood in charge as your – what do you say? Comprador?'

'Supercargo,' offered Drinkwater.

'Ah, yes . . .'

The carriage jerked to a halt and rocked on its springs for a moment before the door was opened. Thiebault hoisted himself from his seat. 'No trouble, gentlemen, I beg you.'

They descended into a dark, cobbled alley, barely wider than the coach. On either hand tall buildings rose and the air was filled with strange, exotic smells. Drinkwater knew at once that they were among warehouses.

In the Stygian gloom a blackness opened beside them with a creak and they were ushered into a cavernous space filled with a sweet, sickly smell. Then followed the crash of the closing door, the click and tumble of catch and lock, and the knock of a heavy cross-timber being put in place. A moment later the snick of flint on steel, and a flicker of light.

'Follow me, gentlemen,' Thiebault commanded, holding up the lantern.

As they made for a ladder between stacks of bales and cases, Drinkwater looked in vain for evidence of the boots or greatcoats that had come from either the *Galliwasp* or the *Ocean*. At length they ascended several flights of wooden stairs and found themselves in a small room, boarded with tongue-and-groove deals in the manner of a magazine.

'There is water here, gentlemen, and food will be brought to you twice daily. I will return soon. I do not think that you will be compelled to remain here above a week or ten days.' Thiebault gestured at the straw-filled palliasses that presumably furnished accommodation for a watchman. 'I regret, however, to tell you that escape is impossible. Herr Liepmann maintains a pair of hounds to guard against intruders. They were removed during our arrival. When I leave, they will be returned.' Thiebault paused. 'Also, I should advise you that there are many troops in the city.'

Thiebault made to leave them, but Drinkwater said, 'One thing I do not understand, M'sieur Thiebault.'

'What is that, Captain?'

'If you are so anxious to discharge the cargoes of the *Ocean* and the *Galliwasp* and want them to drop downstream by dawn for fear of discovery by Marshal Davout, why are you so anxious that the other ships come in?'

'That is no concern of yours!'

'What the deuce d'you make of all that?' rasped Gilham as the door closed behind Thiebault. 'I hope to heaven Littlewood's been paid.'

Drinkwater flung himself down on the nearer palliasse.

'I must say you seem damnably cool about this predicament, Waters. Ain't you worried about your cargo, man?'

'To be frank, sir, no.' Drinkwater propped himself up on one elbow. 'I don't think that Herr Liepmann will leave us here unattended, Gilham, so pray simmer down and let us do some thinking.'

'Or some praying,' said Gilham seriously.

'As you wish.'

Whatever the arrangements that Thiebault had made with Liepmann, it was inconceivable that the Jew should ignore the two British shipmasters held in his warehouse. Further ramifications of the affair occurred to Drinkwater as he lay in the cold and nursed the ache in his shoulder.

Thiebault was clearly heavily implicated in the illegal traffic passing through Hamburg. As a senior officer of the Imperial Customs Service he would be in an incomparable position to feather his own nest. But he would need to distance himself from his contacts, the merchants with whom he dealt, men like Liepmann who must never be left in any doubt that if Thiebault himself was ever threatened with Imperial retribution, he would strike them down first before they were able to lay evidence against him.

The presence, therefore, of his hostages in Liepmann's property, fully implicated the Jewish merchant. If Davout gave the slightest hint that he suspected Thiebault of collusion, Thiebault only had to order his own officers to apprehend Liepmann, together with two British shipmasters, to ingratiate himself with the marshal and prove his own zeal, efficiency and trustworthiness.

'If we can but make contact with Herr Liepmann,' Drinkwater reassured Gilham, 'I do not think we have much to worry about.'

'I hope you are right.'

Shortly after dark they heard the snarling bark of dogs below. The sound faded to whimpering and was followed by the noise of feet upon the stairs. A moment or two later a young man entered the watchman's hutch bearing a basket of food. Laying out cold sausages, bread and a bottle of wine on a napkin, he smiled and withdrew. As the two Britons bent to help themselves to the food they were aware of a tall man in the doorway. Drinkwater rose to his feet.

'Herr Liepmann?'

The man bowed gravely. Like Isaac Solomon he wore the long hair of Orthodox Jewry. '*Ja*, mein English ist not goot. You are Kapitan Waters, *ja*?'

'At your service, sir.'

'Goot. I know somet'ing of you from Herr Solomon . . .'

Drinkwater turned slightly so that his back was towards Gilham, and making a negative gesture with his right index finger held close to his breast, he then pointed it at his chest, indicating Gilham's ignorance.

'Ach . . .' Liepmann's head inclined in an imperceptible nod of understanding.

'Herr Thiebault is a very clever man, Herr Liepmann,' Drinkwater said slowly. 'I understand he must hold us hostage against your good behaviour.' Drinkwater accompanied this speech with a deal of gesturing and was rewarded by more nodding from Liepmann.

'*Ja, ja.*'

'Why does he want to bring in more English ships, the ships now at Helgoland? We know he is frightened of Marshal Davout . . .'

Liepmann looked from one to the other. His tongue flickered over his lips and a faint smile followed.

'Ze scheeps at Helgoland have guns, no?'

Drinkwater nodded.

'Marshal Davout he like guns. Herr Thiebault vill get guns. Make money and pleez Marshal Davout. You understand?'

Drinkwater nodded. 'Yes.'

'Damned if *I* do.'

'It is ver' dangerous for you here. You must not stay . . .'

Liepmann had his own game to play, Drinkwater thought, but it was essential that *Galliwasp* and *Ocean* escaped from the river before Drinkwater or Gilham made an attempt at getting out of Hamburg.

'We must wait, Herr Liepmann, until we hear from Helgoland that our ships are safe.'

'*Ja, ja*,' the Jew nodded. 'It will be ver' dangerous for you stay here. Zis is best place. When time come we take you out of Hamburg *mit* ze sugar.'

'Can you send a message to Helgoland,' Drinkwater asked, 'if I write it?' Liepmann nodded. 'Herr Nicholas has told me . . .'

'*Ja*,' Herr Nicholas tells me also.' Liepmann threw a glance in Gilham's direction and pointed at a ledger lying on a shelf. Inkpot and pen stood close by.

'In English, Kapitan . . .'

Drinkwater exchanged glances with Liepmann.

'It is safe?'

'*Ja*.'

Drinkwater took up the pen and wrote carefully in capitals:

G AND W TAKEN OUT OF THEIR SHIPS BY FORCE BUT PRESENTLY SAFE ENJOYING HOSPITALITY OF OUR MUTUAL FRIEND. ARRANGEMENTS SET AWRY BY ARRIVAL OF MARSHAL DAVOUT. SHIPS DISCHARGED OUTWARD BOUND.

He paused a moment, wondering how to sign himself, and then added: BALTIC.

Straightening up he handed the torn-out page to Liepmann. The Jew took the pen, dipped it in the inkpot and on another piece of paper began to write a jumble of letters, having memorized the crazy alphabet from Canto II of Dante. When he had finished the transliteration he opened the lantern and held Drinkwater's draft in the candle flame. The incinerated ash floated lazily about the table.

'There is one more thing, Herr Liepmann. You should understand that it was never intended that more ships would come, only that they would pretend to come. Do you understand?'

'They not come?' Liepmann regarded Drinkwater with surprise.

'No. They were to have gone only to Neuwerk . . . to look as if they were coming into the Elbe.'

'You do not wish to sell ze guns, *nein*?'

'No, only the greatcoats and boots.'

'Ach . . . and ze sugar, *ja*?'

'Yes,' Drinkwater said, matching the Jew's smile, 'and the sugar.'

Liepmann had turned to go when Gilham, his mouth full of the food which he had been busy eating during this exchange, asked, 'Herr Liepmann, did you pay Littlewood?'

Liepmann turned to Gilham, a look of mild surprise on his face. '*Ja*. I pay him goot . . . also for your scheep, ze *Ocean*, two thousand thalers . . .'

In the wake of Liepmann's departure Gilham grunted his satisfaction. With a wry look at his compatriot, Drinkwater helped himself to what was left of the sausages and bread.

He felt better with food inside him, aware that the winter's day, short though it had been, had passed slowly and been full of the uncertainties that kept a man from feeling hungry until actually confronted with food.

With a little luck they would be all right. A day or two lying low and then, when *Galliwasp* and *Ocean* were clear, Liepmann would smuggle them out of the city. Drinkwater was content to leave the details to the Jewish merchant. Davout would be settling in, receiving reports from the French officials and administrators, all of whom would be wary, and it would take even so dynamic a soldier as the marshal was reputed to be, a few days to decide upon what course of action to settle. There was no doubt that he had been sent to shut the gaping door that Hamburg had become in his master's Continental System.

'You seem to know a deal of what's going on,' Gilham said, suddenly jerking Drinkwater from his complacency and reminding him that if his real identity or position were known, then capture meant certain death.

He shrugged. 'It is not so very difficult to deduce,' he said with affected nonchalance, undecided as to whether to take Gilham into his confidence. 'D'you trust Littlewood?' he asked, deliberately changing the subject.

'I don't have much choice, do I?'

It was bitterly cold in the watchman's room and Drinkwater slept fitfully, waking frequently, the knotted muscles of his wounded shoulder aching painfully. Beside him Gilham snored under a blanket with a full belly and the sailor's facility for sleeping anywhere.

Drinkwater envied Gilham. He himself was desperately tired, tired of the burden Dungarth had laid upon him and tired of the interminable war. He had done his best and was no longer a young man. Now his shoulder pained him abominably.

He thought of his wife, Elizabeth, and their children, Charlotte Amelia and Richard. He had not seen them for so very long that they seemed to inhabit another age when he was another person. He found it difficult to remember exactly what they looked like, and found all he could call to mind were the immobile images of the little portraits that used to hang in his cabin when he was in command of a frigate and not cowering under borrowed blankets in a Hamburg garret.

Where were those imperfect portraits now? Lost with his other personal effects when the *Tracker* foundered and poor Quilhampton died, together with Frey and Derrick.

He tore his exhausted mind from horrible visions of his friends drowning, deliberately trying to recall the items of clothing, the books, charts and equipment he must have lost along with his sea-chest and the pictures of his family.

There was his sword and sextant, his journals and the little drawing case Elizabeth had given him, pretending it came from the children . . .

Mentally he rummaged down through the layers of clothing in the chest. The polar bear skin, presented by the officers of His Britannic Majesty's sloop-of-war *Melusine* and there, at the very bottom, cut from its wooden stretcher, the paint cracked and flaking, another portrait, found when he captured the *Antigone* in the Red Sea, ten, eleven years earlier.

Odd how he could recall *that* portrait in all its detail: the beautiful French woman, her shoulders bare, her breasts suggestively rendered beneath a filmy wrap of gauze, her hair *à la mode*, piled up on her head and entwined with a string of pearls. Hortense Santhonax, now widowed, though an unmarried woman when he had first seen her . . .

He closed his aching eyes against the moonlight that flooded in through the lozenge shaped window set high in the apex of the gable-end. It was all so long ago, part of another life . . .

Somewhere below him Liepmann's dogs stirred. Johannes, the young man who brought them their food and served as the Jew's watchman, was probably doing his rounds.

The whining suddenly rose to a bark of alarm. Once, twice, the hounds yapped before shots rang out. The barking ended in a mewling whine.

For a moment Drinkwater lay still, unable or unwilling to comprehend what was happening, then a muffled shout was followed by a curt, monosyllabic command.

Drinkwater threw off his blankets and reached for his boots.

'Gilham! Wake up!'

He kicked the recumbent figure into consciousness.

'What's the matter?' Gilham asked sleepily.

'The bloody French are here!'

Drinkwater pulled on his coat and kicked his blankets into the shadows. Feet pounded on the wooden ladders, the floor of their hideout shook. Gilham was on his feet, picking up the empty wine bottle from the table.

'Get in the shadows, man, and keep quiet!' Drinkwater hissed, though his own heart was pounding loud enough to be heard.

The door to the watchman's room was flung open. Three dragoons, clumsy in their high jackboots, burst into the room. For a moment they froze, staring about them, the moonlight gleaming on the bronze of their high, crested helmets and the steel of their bayonetted carbines. Then a fourth, a sergeant holding up a lantern, shoved past them. Drinkwater was aware of more men on the landing outside and the terrified whimper of a young prisoner. They had already seized Johannes.

The sergeant's lantern light swept the room, falling on the absurd gilt tassels on Drinkwater's hessian boots. A second later it played full in his face.

'*Qu'est ce que vous foutez là?*'

The lantern's light found Gilham, then the basket and utensils used to bring their supper, the pen and ink, the extinguished lamp and the torn pages of the ledger. A few black wisps of ash stirred in the air.

The dragoons stepped forward and Gilham shattered the wine bottle and raised its broken neck with a defiant cry. The noise terminated in a grunt as he doubled up in pain. The nearest dragoon's toecap struck him in the groin and vomit splashed on to the floor.

The dragoons secured their prisoners in a silence broken only by the rasp of Gilham's tortured breath. The sharp reek of spew filled the stuffy air. With cords about their wrists both Drinkwater and Gilham were pushed forward to join Johannes on the wooden catwalk that served as a landing from the topmost ladder.

They stumbled downwards, the sergeant and his lantern ahead of them, the shadows of themselves and their escort leaping fantastically on the stacks of baled and cased goods piled on all sides. At ground level the sergeant paused, ordering his patrol into rough formation. The circle of lamplight illuminated his boots and the long tails of his green coat with the brass eagles securing the yellow facing of the turn-backs. It fell also on the corpse of one of Liepmann's watchdogs, the pink tongue lolling from its gaping jaw. The sergeant kicked it aside.

'*Ouvrez!*' he ordered, and a blast of cold air struck them as the door was swung open. The sergeant lifted the lantern and walked down the line of his men, peering at the three prisoners pinioned between the double files. He said something in a low voice which made his men snigger, then he swung round and Drinkwater saw the sabre in his right hand. Holding up the lantern in his left, he let the beam play on the stack of bulging sacks beside them.

'Hippolyte,' he commanded, '*allez . . . votre casque, mon ami.*'

The dragoon who had thrown open the warehouse door trotted obediently up and doffed his helmet. He held it upside down as the sergeant lifted his sword arm.

'*Qu'est que ce?*' he asked mockingly, slashing at a sack. Sugar loaves tumbled into Hippolyte's helmet and the dragoons roared with laughter.

'*Voila!*' cried the sergeant with a flourish. '*Nom de Dieu! Sucre!*'

And the patrol lurched forward into the dark cobbled alleyway in high spirits, locking the warehouse door behind them.

CHAPTER 12 January 1810

# The Iron Marshal

They were not long in the custody of the sergeant and his troopers. At the end of the alley they found a mounted officer whose helmet, scabbard and horse furniture gleamed in the flaring light of a torch held by an orderly on foot. The leaping flame, lighting his face from below, gave it a demonic cast as he stared down at the prisoners, listening to the sergeant's report. The officer's bay mount shifted uneasily beside the flickering brand, tossing its head and throwing off flecks of foam from curling lips. The officer soothed its arched neck with a gloved hand.

With the stately clip-clop of the charger bringing up the rear they marched off, crossing a moonlit, cobbled square, to halt in the high shadow of the Rathaus. Despite the midnight hour, messengers came and went, clattering up to the waiting orderlies who grabbed flung reins as the aides dashed into the lit archway, the flanking sentries snapping to attention and receiving the most perfunctory of salutes from the young officers.

Drinkwater, Gilham and Johannes were marched off to a side door, entering a stone flagged passage that opened out into an arched chamber guarded by two shakoed sentinels and containing a staff officer who sat writing at a desk. The escort of dragoons was dismissed, infantry took over and the dragoon officer made a *sotto voce* report to the staff captain. The latter barely looked up, though his pen scribbled busily across the uppermost of a small pile of papers. These formalities over, the three prisoners were taken through an iron-bound door and locked into a small chamber which had clearly been used as a storeroom.

Gilham and Drinkwater exchanged glances but their silence did nothing to reassure the young German. Johannes was agitated to the point of visible distress and would have broken down completely had not their incarceration ended suddenly. A tall corporal of fusiliers, his shako plume raking the lintel of the door as he ducked into the makeshift cell, called them out.

'*Allez!*'

They trooped out and followed the corporal; two soldiers with bayonets fixed to their muskets fell in behind them. At the staff officer's desk they were motioned to pass, and climbed a flight of stone steps to halt outside impressive double doors guarded by two further sentries.

'The holy of holies,' muttered Gilham and in the silence that followed Drinkwater could hear the chatter of Johannes's teeth. When the doors opened it startled the three of them.

Monsieur Thiebault advanced towards them. His face was pale and he wrung his hands with a nervous compulsiveness.

'Gentlemen . . .' he said, attempting a reassuring smile, stepping aside and ushering them forward, 'His Excellency will see you now . . .' He nodded at the guards.

Drinkwater and Gilham started forward with Johannes in their wake, but Thiebault, Drinkwater noticed, made a sharp gesture with his hand and turning his head Drinkwater saw the boy's arm seized by one of the soldiers. He caught Thiebault's eye and the customs officer raised his shoulders with a fatalistic shrug.

Drinkwater's heart was pounding. If he let slip the slightest hint of his real identity, he would be shot as a spy. Though Gilham did not know of his status as a sea officer, he might make some indiscreet reference . . .

'Leave the talking to me, Gilham,' he snapped in a low voice as they were ushered into a high chamber, lit by a dozen candelabrae. A fire blazed in a grate and above the mantelpiece hung the mounted heads of a pair of tusked boars. Between them were emblazoned the castellated arms of the Hanseatic City of Hamburg. More hunting trophies were displayed on the dark panelling of the burghers' council chamber that was now occupied by the commander-in-chief of the Army of Germany.

Louis Nicholas Davout, Prince of Eckmühl, Duke of Auerstädt and Marshal of France, sat at a desk in the centre of the room, his balding head bent over a pile of papers, his polished boots reflecting the fire and his gold-laced blue coat tight over powerful shoulders. Beside him, in a similar though less splendid uniform, a plumed bicorne tucked neatly under his elbow, an aide-de-camp stood in a respectful attitude.

The marshal said something in a low voice, the aide bent attentively, replied as the marshal dashed off a signature, took the document with a click of his heels and left the room. The jingle of the aide's spurs ceased as the double doors closed behind him and Drinkwater, Gilham and Thiebault were left in a silence broken only by the crackle of the fire.

Slowly the marshal lifted his head and stared at them. The firelight reflected off his pince-nez hid his eyes, but Drinkwater was conscious of a firm mouth and round, regular features. When Davout removed the spectacles his expression was intimidating. The light danced on the coils of oak leaves embroidered upon his breast as he sighed and leaned back in his chair.

'M'sieur Thiebault . . .' he murmured, looking at the two Britons before him. Thiebault launched into a speech punctuated by ingratiating '*Monseigneurs*'.

Whatever the content of Thiebault's discourse, Drinkwater was conscious of the unwavering gaze of Davout, the man the French themselves called 'the iron marshal', the archangel of the Emperor Napoleon. He tried at first to meet Davout's eyes, then, finding the scrutiny too unnerving and with the thought that such a wordless challenge was dangerous, Drinkwater tried to make out the gist of Thiebault's explanation while his eyes roved about the chamber with the affected gaucherie of a man aroused by curiosity. He hoped his apprehension was not obvious.

He heard, or thought he heard, Thiebault mention the word '*Russie*' but could not bring himself to look at the marshal. Then Thiebault said it again and Drinkwater, conscious that Davout was still staring at him, dropped his own gaze. At the marshal's feet, amid a small heap of dispatch boxes, a leather wallet and a travelling valise, lay a frayed roll of canvas. It had been kept tight-rolled but now untied, it had sprung open enough for Drinkwater to see its inner surface.

The shock of recognition brought a wave of nausea so strong that for a moment he thought he might faint. Instead he moved, shifting his weight forward before recovering himself with a cough. He was better placed to see now the familiar portrait.

Looking down beside Davout's shining black boot heels Drinkwater saw the crown of the woman's head, the coils of auburn hair wound with pearls and the arch of a single eyebrow set against the eau-de-nil background that the artist had painted. He saw too the star shaped flaking where the unstretched canvas had shed the slight impasto of the flaming hair and the white gesso ground showed through. The position and shape of that bare patch confirmed what Drinkwater had already guessed, that the rolled canvas beneath the desk of Marshal Davout was the portrait of Hortense Santhonax that once hung in the cabin of the *Antigone* and which had, until very lately, rested at the bottom of his sea-chest.

He felt the flesh on the back of his neck crawl and brought his incredulously staring eyes up to meet those of the marshal.

'M'sieur Thiebault speaks that you had cargo for Russia, *oui*?'

Recovering himself, Drinkwater nodded. 'Yes, Excellency, military stores . . .'

'*Et sucre, n'est-ce pas?* And sugar . . . ?' Davout's accent was thick, his English uncertain. 'Why come to Hamburg, not Russia?'

'My ship was damaged in a storm, sir. We,' Drinkwater gestured vaguely at Gilham who had the presence of mind to nod, suggesting their circumstances had been identical, 'put into Helgoland. Then the winter, the ice in the Baltic . . .' he made a helpless gesture of resignation, 'we could not go on to Russia. At Helgoland the Government told us they had abandoned us and we decided to sell our cargo here, in Hamburg.'

Drinkwater paused. Without taking his eyes off the two Britons, Davout queried something with Thiebault who appeared, by his nodding, to be confirming what Drinkwater had said. Drinkwater decided to press his advantage, mindful of the rolled and damaged portrait at Davout's feet.

'We had an escort of the British navy, but we became separated . . .'

'What name this ship . . . this escort?' Davout's poor English, learned during a brief period as a prisoner of the Royal Navy when a young man, could not disguise the keenness of his question.

'*Tracker*,' said Drinkwater, noticing the exchange of glances between Davout and Thiebault and the half-smile that crossed the marshal's face.

'You have news of her?' Drinkwater asked quickly. Davout's eyes were cold and he made no answer, while Thiebault was clearly unnerved by Drinkwater's effrontery in asking such a question.

'You sold your cargo, *Capitaine*?'

'Yes . . .'

'The sugar?'

'Yes.' Drinkwater looked at Thiebault. Perspiration was pouring from the customs officer's forehead and it was clear that Thiebault's future, as much as that of Drinkwater and Gilham, rested upon this interview. Such anxiety argued that Davout's hostility must be at least in part aimed at Thiebault. This consideration persuaded Drinkwater to press his question again.

'Do you have news of *Tracker*, Excellency?'

Behind Davout Thiebault, his face twisted with supplication, made a gesture of suppression. Davout ignored the question.

'*Peut-être* . . . perhaps you not go to Russia . . . perhaps you only make these papers.' Davout struck the desk and Drinkwater saw the *Galliwasp*'s confiscated documents with the crown stamp of the London Customs House upon them, among those on his desk. The pince-nez were lifted to the bridge of the marshal's nose, then lowered as Davout got to his feet and came round the table to confront Drinkwater.

'You come to Hamburg as a spy?'

'*Monseigneur, l'explication* . . .' began Thiebault despairingly.

'*Assez!*' snapped Davout, turning away from Drinkwater with a contemptuous wave of his hand. He returned to his desk and picked up the pince-nez he had left there. Casting a baleful look at Thiebault he spoke a few words.

'Was the *Tracker* coming to Hamburg?' Thiebault translated.

'The *Tracker*?' Drinkwater said with unfeigned surprise, 'No, of course not.' He turned towards Davout, an alarming thought forming in his mind. 'No, Excellency, the *Tracker* was under orders for Russia . . .'

Drinkwater was unable to gauge whether or not the marshal believed him, for a knock at the door was followed by the reappearance of the aide-de-camp. It was clear that he was expected and that the matter was of greater importance than the interrogation of two British shipmasters caught breaking the Emperor's Continental System. Davout returned to his desk and curtly dismissed Thiebault and the prisoners. He did no more than nod at the young French officer, who left the doorway immediately.

Thiebault accompanied them to the foot of the steps where a weary glance from the staff officer still shuffling paper was followed by a bellow for their guard.

'What in God's name was all that about?' asked Gilham unable to remain silent.

'Oblige me a moment longer,' muttered Drinkwater motioning him towards Thiebault who was addressing the staff officer. Thiebault turned towards them, his expression one of relief. His tone was suddenly preternaturally light, the manner an attempt to recover his former insouciance. He had clearly suffered an ordeal.

'Well, gentlemen, I think His Excellency is satisfied with the, er, arrangements . . .'

'You mean the boots?' said Gilham sarcastically.

'Indeed, Captain . . .'

'What the devil was all that about the *Tracker*, M'sieur?' Drinkwater asked, frowning.

'Are our ships clear of the river?' Gilham added.

'Gentlemen, gentlemen, please; His Excellency has ordered that you be taken to Altona, to the military hospital there, just for a few days. It is a mere formality, I assure you.' Thiebault lowered his voice, 'His Excellency is due to inspect the defences of Lübeck shortly. I will send you word . . . now, if you will excuse me . . .'

Thiebault turned to go as two fusiliers approached. At the same moment the door at the far end of the room opened, admitting a blast of cold air which set the flames of the candles on the staff officer's desk guttering. A French officer escorted a cloaked figure towards them. The officer was resplendent in the campaign dress of a lieutenant in the horse chasseurs of the Imperial Guard. His scarlet pelisse was not draped, *à la hussard*, from his left shoulder, but worn over the dolman, the gold frogging buttoned to his neck against the cold. His overalls were mud spattered, evidence of a long, hard ride, and his face, below the fur rim of his busby, was fiercely mustachioed. He drew the cloaked person after him, reached down to the sabretache that trailed over the flagstones with his scabbard and drew out a sealed document.

'*Lieutenant Dieudonné à votre service*,' he said, holding out the letter. '*Pour le Maréchal* . . .' He nodded at the cloaked figure, his green and red plume throwing a fantastic shadow on the wall.

The momentary distraction had provided Thiebault with an opportunity to escape, and though Gilham protested, more questions on his lips, Drinkwater was rooted to the spot, overcome by a moment of premonition that prepared him for the shock as the cloaked figure threw off its hood.

As she shook her head the auburn hair fell about her shoulders, and although he could not see the woman's full face, there was no doubt about that profile, at almost the same angle as she had assumed for the artist Jacques Louis David. He knew the face so well, for David's portrait – painted for her dead husband and later captured by Drinkwater – now inexplicably lay rolled under the desk of the Prince of Eckmühl.

In his distraction Drinkwater resisted the tug of his guard so that the soldier became angry, stepped behind him and thrust his ported musket into the small of his prisoner's back with a sharp exclamation. Drinkwater stumbled forward, losing his balance and attracting the attention of Lieutenant Dieudonné and the woman. Gilham caught Drinkwater's arm; recovering himself, Drinkwater looked back. Beyond the menacing guard the woman was staring after him, her face in the full light of the leaping candles on the staff officer's desk.

There was no doubt about her identity: she was Hortense Santhonax and she knew Nathaniel Drinkwater to be an officer in the Royal Navy of Great Britain.

# The Firing Party

Outside stood the carriage that had brought Madame Santhonax, its door still open. A dozen chasseurs sat on their horses round it, exchanging remarks. Drinkwater moved forward in a daze. He was tired, cold and hungry, and the night's events had become unreal. For months – since the terrible events in the jungle of Borneo – he had been deprived of all energy, overcome by a mental and physical lethargy impossible to throw off. There had been brief moments when he felt he was recovering, when Dungarth had inspired him to take on the mission to Russia, when Solomon had entertained him that morning after his night of filth and subterfuge, and when young Nicholas had revived the failed project at Helgoland.

But these had been brief and faltering revivals and, he could see now, merely fatal circumstances conspiring to bring him to this strange encounter. He was deep in blood, the killer of Edouard Santhonax, the executioner of Morris and murderer of poor Tregembo. Now he was to be called to account, to die in his turn, shot as a spy on the denunciation of a French woman within the Rathaus. He was convinced she had recognized him, for their eyes had met and she could have read nothing but fear in his expression. Nausea rose in his gorge, he missed his footing again and again Gilham caught him.

'Are you all right?'

'Aye,' gasped Drinkwater, feeling a cold sweat chill his brow in the icy air.

'I think they want us in the carriage,' Gilham said, his hand under Drinkwater's elbow.

Not *her* carriage, surely, he thought, that was too ironic a twist of fate. In any case, at any moment . . .

'*Arrête!*'

This was it. The denunciation had been made, the staff officer was running out after them and he was about to be arrested, unmasked as a spy and on the summary orders of Marshal Davout, shot like a dog.

But Drinkwater was wrong.

The staff officer called something to the chasseurs, one of whom was a non-commissioned officer. They were bundled into the carriage and Drinkwater caught the elusive scent of the widow Santhonax. He sank shivering into the deep buttoned leather of the seat and closed his eyes as the carriage jerked forward.

'Are you well, Waters?' Gilham asked again.

'Well enough. Just a little tired and hungry . . .' No denunciation had come; perhaps she had not recognized him. Why should she? It had been a long time; they had changed, though age seemed to have enhanced rather than diminished her beauty. Nor did she possess a portrait of him to remind her of his features . . .

Drinkwater's relief was short-lived. The carriage swung round a corner and jerked to an abrupt halt. The door was flung open and they were ordered out.

'*Regardez-là, messieurs*,' the non-commissioned officer said, leaning from his creaking saddle.

They stood at the entrance of a courtyard. It was lit by flaring torches set in sconces and seemed to be full of soldiers, infantrymen under the command of an elderly, white haired captain who was tucking a written order inside his shako before putting it on.

'What the devil . . . ?' Gilham began, but Drinkwater cut him short, his heart thumping painfully in his chest. Far from feeling faint, the greatest fear of all had seized him and he felt a strong impulse to run.

'It's a firing party!' he hissed in Gilham's ear. A word of

command and the milling rabble of soldiers lined up in two files. A moment later a man was led out from an adjacent doorway. It was Johannes.

'God's bones!' Drinkwater swore. He wanted to move, to do something, but his legs would not respond and he watched helplessly as a bag was pulled down over Johannes's wildly staring eyes. He saw the young man's legs buckle, heard the muffled screams as he was dragged to the wall. With the ease of practice Johannes's trussed hands were tied to a ring bolt in the masonry and the boy fell forward in a faint. The double file of fusiliers raised their loaded muskets on the captain's command and a volley rang out, echoing round and round the courtyard as the body of Johannes slumped downwards. Pulling a torch from a sconce the white haired captain walked forward and leaned over the boy's shattered body. Casually he emptied a pistol into the left ear. A surgeon came forward; Drinkwater and Gilham were ushered back to the carriage. As they climbed in and the door was shut, Gilham echoed Drinkwater's own thoughts.

'Poor fellow. For a moment I thought that was for us.'

They sat in silence for a while, the death of Johannes and their part in it weighing heavily upon them.

'That was because of the sugar, wasn't it?' remarked Gilham, seeking some quieting justification for his conscience.

'Yes, I believe so,' muttered Drinkwater.

'It allowed that bugger Thiebault to clear his own yardarm,' Gilham went on. 'Which was what he was doing with all that jabbering to Monseigneur What's-his-name, eh?'

'Yes, I imagine so . . .'

'Sacrificed that poor young devil to save his own skin.'

'I do not think,' said Drinkwater, slowly recovering himself, 'that whilst Marshal Davout would turn a blind eye to the military stores, he could countenance the sugar. It was too blatant a breach of the Emperor's proscription of British imports.' He paused. Gilham's face was no more than a pale blur in the darkness that had come with moonset and an overcast sky promising more snow. 'I am surprised a man of

Davout's stamp did not have us shot out of hand too. I think Thiebault must have pleaded for us . . .'

'You think we are out of danger, then?'

'I think you are, Captain, but as for myself, I am not so sure.'

'Why ever not?'

'It is probably best that you do not ask that question. I will answer it only by saying that your association with me places you in the greatest danger.'

'What on earth are you talking about?'

'I sincerely wish I could tell you, Gilham, but prudence dictates that I hold my tongue at least for a little longer. What you are ignorant of cannot be held against you. The example of Johannes might have been intended to warn the people of Hamburg against obtaining sugar, but we were made to witness it as a warning to ourselves. No doubt His Excellency the Marshal considers his act magnanimous . . .'

'But I . . . oh, very well,' Gilham said before lapsing into a perplexed silence.

Opposite him, Drinkwater strove to order the chaos of his thoughts. There was no doubt about the accuracy of Gilham's assessment of Thiebault's conduct. He had indeed 'cleared his own yardarm' and sacrificed Johannes to satisfy the Marshal's notion of loyalty to the Emperor's edicts. Davout's clemency to both himself and the British shipmasters had been purchased along with the Northampton boots. The profit and loss of that account was a matter between Littlewood, Liepmann, Thiebault and the minister of war in Paris, but possibly Davout had retained his reputation for incorruptibility. What ought to have brought Drinkwater a measure of satisfaction was the clear indication that so unimpeachable and elevated a servant of the Empire as Davout was convinced that the original destination of the boots had been Russia. It made the desperate charade Drinkwater had endured in Mrs Hockley's brothel an unnecessary farce.

But he derived no consolation from these considerations, for far more disturbing were the appearances of the portrait and its subject. It was an inescapable fact that the former had come from his very own sea-chest, taken aboard His Britannic Majesty's gun-brig *Tracker* for safe-keeping. Its survival argued a case for the survival of the brig, for had the brig foundered, the chest – stowed in her hold – would have sunk with her. The only possible explanation was that *Tracker* had been captured, probably disabled in the tempest and driven ashore as *Galliwasp* had been, but on less hospitable shores.

Perhaps then, Quilhampton and Frey, Derrick and the others were still alive! He felt a surge of hope, of revitalization, kindle in his heart. If only it were true, how much of the burden would it lift from his shoulders! Surely, in a world that could disinter the portrait of Hortense Santhonax, so small a miracle was possible?

And what of her; had she recognized him? And if so, had she denounced him to Davout?

He tried to recall the strange encounter in the Rathaus. She had undoubtedly seen him, as he had seen her. He had known her not merely because he had kept her hidden likeness for years, but because he had met her, rescued her from revolutionaries and carried her safe to England, an *emigrée* refugee.

She had been exquisitely beautiful then, a proud young aristocrat, Hortense de Montholon, whose association with the equally proud republican, Edouard Santhonax, had led to their eventual marriage and the turning of her coat. She had gone back to France at the end of the Terror and been landed on the beach at Criel by Lord Dungarth and an unknown master's mate called Nathaniel Drinkwater. He thought her more beautiful in her maturity, grown stately as Republic had given way to Empire and the *parvenu* crown had need of a new aristocracy.

And now their paths had crossed again; the widow Santhonax was in Hamburg, and their eyes had met!

But she had been a prisoner!

The realization hit him like a pistol ball, so that he exclaimed out loud.

'Damn it, Waters, are you unwell?'

'I have just recalled something. Tell me Gilham, did you

notice the cavalry officer who came in as we were leaving?'

'The hussar fellow with the lady? Yes, of course I did, striking pair.'

'What did you make of 'em?'

'What d'you mean?'

'How did you interpret their relationship?'

'Their relationship?' Gilham asked in astonishment.

'Was there *anything* that struck you about it?'

'Well, she was brought in under constraint, like us . . .'

'Precisely!' said Drinkwater, relieved the impression had not been the work of his highly charged imagination. 'She was a detainee.'

'Is that what you wanted me to say?'

'It was what I hoped you would think. She was brought under escort, and an escort of Guard chasseurs is no ordinary escort, in this very carriage . . .'

'But what in heaven's name has this woman to do with us? Look, Waters, there's something damned fishy going on.' Gilham's tone of voice had changed, become guarded, suspicious. 'Why did you insist on doing all the talking back there? You were accustomed to taking a back seat, letting Littlewood jabber. I think you owe me an explanation.'

Drinkwater sighed, staring at the pale oval of Gilham's face as he leaned forward in the gloom.

'Very well,' he said resignedly. It was perhaps better to level with Gilham. There might be no time for explanations later, and Gilham seemed a cool enough fellow in his way.

'My name is not Waters, Captain Gilham. I will not worry you with such details; suffice it to know that I am a post-captain in the navy . . .'

'Dear God!' Gilham fell back in his seat.

'You need not worry. Your treasonable act of selling military stores to the enemy was only achieved with the assistance of both His Majesty's navy and His diplomatic service.'

'I have been duped.'

'I suspect we have all been duped a little, in one way or another. Hardly anyone in this affair is precisely what he seems, but to keep to the point . . .'

There was considerable relief in confessing things to Gilham. He felt better for the confession, felt that speaking aloud conferred a kind of existence upon his theories, delivered them from the dark womb of his turbulent mind to the harsh reality of this bitterly cold winter's night.

'It was intended to ship *Galliwasp*'s cargo to Russia; you may have realized from Davout's reaction that it would have been contrary to French interests, casting suspicion on the Tsar's reliability as their ally.'

'And having failed to do that, a shipment into Hamburg in so public a manner achieved the same objective.'

'Exactly, except that the French profited from the boots.'

'But at a cost,' added Gilham, and Drinkwater could almost hear the smile in his voice.

'Aye, at a cost. You may recall Littlewood speaking of the loss of our escort.'

'The brig *Tracker* that you mentioned tonight? I wondered why that came up.'

'We thought she had foundered, but I now know her to have fallen into enemy hands.'

'How the deuce d'you know that?'

'Because beneath Davout's desk was a rolled canvas portrait. That portrait was my property, held aboard the brig with the rest of my personal effects.'

'Your wife?'

'No.' Drinkwater shifted uneasily, glad of the darkness, aware that the relief of confession came at a price. 'It was captured aboard a French frigate, the *Antigone*, years ago, when it was cut-out by the people of the brig *Hellebore*. I brought her home and subsequently commanded her. I kept the portrait as a curiosity; you see I knew the lady in my youth . . . I was much struck by her . . .'

'And she was the woman brought in tonight by M'sieur Moustache, eh?'

'Yes.'

'So she knows you are the spy that Davout suspected.'

'I think that is the gist of it,' Drinkwater said slowly. 'She has no reason to think well of me, though I once did her a small service.'

'She will denounce you then, if she was under detention, perhaps to gain her own freedom.' Gilham's tone was confidently matter-of-fact, as though the thing was a *fait accompli*.

'Did the marshal strike you as a man to be swayed that easily?'

'He was certainly not a man who would compromise his position for a woman's blandishments, no, but if he had already made some connection between a captured portrait, a portrait in the possession of the enemy . . .'

'D'you think that the finding of an old, damaged portrait would have aroused any suspicion unless the lady was well known to the discoverer, and under some suspicion already? If I told you that she was the mistress of a highly placed but disgraced French official all of whose intimates might have fallen under suspicion, would you not think the matter took a different turn and might be seen in another light?'

'It would depend on how eminent this fellow was.'

'The Emperor's former minister for Foreign Affairs?'

'*Talleyrand?*'

'Just so.'

'Whew! Then it is a coincidence she's in Hamburg?'

'No, I don't think so. The lady is here on her own or Talleyrand's account, perhaps to contact London through Helgoland. The coincidence is that *we* are in Hamburg . . .'

'D'you think she will hold her tongue? About your identity?' Gilham asked anxiously.

'I think she will keep her own counsel until it suits her, which does not mean I may rely upon her silence. I imagine she might be tempted to seek a private squaring of accounts *after* she has contacted Helgoland.'

'So we must wait upon our friend Thiebault?'

'Altona is on the Elbe, Gilham, and we are both seamen.'

Gilham chuckled in the darkness and shortly afterwards the carriage drew up at the military hospital at Altona.

*

Drinkwater had thought the night could spring no more surprises on him, but he was wrong. The military hospital at Altona was a complex of long, low wooden buildings surrounding a snow covered parade ground. It was almost dawn when they arrived and a few figures were about, dark visaged men in tattered fatigues.

'Who the devil are they?' asked Gilham of nobody as they stood shivering while the chasseurs handed them over to more of the ibiquitous blue-coated infantry Napoleon had planted across the face of Europe.

A soberly dressed man hurrying past with a small bag stopped beside them.

'English, yes?'

'Yes, we are English,' announced Gilham. 'You are not French?'

'I am Spanish, *Señor*. My name is Castenada, Doctor Enrico Castenada, before in the service of the Marquis de la Romana.'

Comprehension dawned on Drinkwater. 'You were left behind when the Marquis's army was withdrawn from the Danish coast by the Royal Navy.'

'*Si, señor*, that is correct.' He switched to French and said something to the guards. They shrugged and closed the gates behind the departing chasseurs.

'Come, I will take you to the English quarters,' Castenada said beckoning them to follow.

'There are other Englishmen here?'

'*Si, señor*, I practise my English with them.'

They crossed the parade ground as a bugler started to blow reveille. More men appeared, most in worn, darned clothing, some wearing bandages, a few on crutches. There was something familiar about them . . .

'Sir? Is it you? Captain Drinkwater, sir?'

The speaker's carious teeth grinned from an unshaven jaw, his breath stank of poor diet and personal neglect. He swung round and called out, 'Hey, lads, it's the Cap'n!'

'You're from *Tracker*, ain't you?' Drinkwater asked grinning. 'How's Mr Quilhampton?'

The man turned and shook his head. ''E ain't so good, sir, but 'e put up an 'ell of a fight, bless yer!'

'What about Mr Frey?'

'I'm all right, sir!' said Frey running up and seizing Drinkwater's outstretched hand. His eyes were full of tears and the two men clasped each other with relief.

'Why, I'm damned glad to see you, sir, damned glad!'

# Altona

'How many of you are there?' asked Drinkwater eagerly, his mood transformed by the meeting with Frey. 'No, wait.' He turned to the grinning seaman who had first recognized him. 'I'd be obliged if you'd warn the men not to use my name.' He lowered his voice. 'I'm here incognito, d'you see.'

The man laid a finger beside his nose, winked and grinned lop-sidedly, exposing his foul teeth. 'Aye aye, sir, I understands, we'll hold our tongues, don't you worry.'

'Very well then, be off and see to it!'

'Aye, aye, sir.'

Drinkwater turned his attention back to Frey. 'So, how many of you are there?'

Frey looked away. 'Eleven.'

'*Eleven?* God's bones, is that all?'

'That excludes the badly wounded, sir; there are seven of them, plus the Captain, Lieutenant Quilhampton. They took him to Hamburg last night.'

'Last night?' Drinkwater frowned. Had Quilhampton been somewhere within the Rathaus at the same time as he and Gilham? Had Davout summoned him for questioning in connection with the discovery of that damned portrait?

'He's badly wounded, sir,' Frey said, breaking his train of thought.

'How badly?'

'He took a sword thrust, sir, in his left arm, above the

stump. It was gangrenous when we arrived here and Doctor Castenada had to perform a second amputation. Mr Quilhampton was in a high fever when they took him last night.'

'God damn!' Drinkwater blasphemed impotently. For a moment his thoughts were with his friend, lying delirious in the hands of the French, then he mastered himself. 'Is there somewhere less exposed that we can talk? This is Captain Gilham, by the way, the master of the *Ocean*, transport. Mr Gilham, a protégé of mine, Mr Frey.'

The two men shook hands perfunctorily.

'They are very lax here, sir. There is talk about a new Governor having arrived . . .'

'We know,' Drinkwater cut Frey short, 'but somewhere to talk, for the love of God, it's too cold here . . .'

Frey led them into a barrack hut that appeared to be a sort of officers' mess. It was full of Spaniards, the remnants of Romana's Army Corps, left behind when Rear-Admiral Keats evacuated the bulk of the Spanish forces from Denmark.

Frey indicated a table and two benches reserved for the *Tracker*'s pitifully small number of surviving officers.

'You had better make your verbal report, Mr Frey.'

Frey nodded, rubbing his hands over his pinched face. Drinkwater noted the grime of his cuffs and neck linen. His hollow cheeks had not been shaved for several days and his eyes were red rimmed and sunken.

'You recall the night of the tempest, sir?'

'Yes, very well.'

'We lost our foretopmast within the first hour. It was badly sprung and the stays slipped at the cap. As we strove to clear the wreckage we were continually swept by the sea and lost several men in the confusion, both aloft and from the deck. We burnt bengal fires for assistance, but were not certain of your whereabouts by then . . .'

'We saw them and put about, but were unable to find you. Soon afterwards we were in like condition and drove ashore on Helgoland, but pray go on.'

'We were less fortunate, sir. By daylight we had three feet

of water below and in so small a vessel it damned near had us foundering. We had precious little freeboard and were wallowing abominably. Mr Q., sir, was a tower of strength. Though we had lost a deal of our company, including both the bosun and carpenter, we got sail on her and strove to make northing . . .'

'But the wind backed and drove you east.'

'Aye sir, you were in like case no doubt?'

'Aye.'

'We fetched upon a bank, drove over it and anchored in its lee. When the gale abated we began to set things to rights. We had men at the pumps three hours out of every four and one fell dead from the labour. But Mr Q. drove us near as hard as he drove himself; we found the leak, clapped a fothered sail over it and began to gain on the water in the hold. We planned to empty half our water casks and wing 'em out in the hold for buoyancy, but the Danes came out in their confounded gunboats. They lay off and simply shot us to pieces with long twenty four pounders. We didn't stand a chance until they boarded us. Then we gave them cold steel, for there was scarce a grain of dry powder in the ship and that had been spent in the carronades. I think there were about forty of us when the action began . . .'

'And James was wounded when the Danes boarded?' Drinkwater prompted.

Frey nodded. 'Aye, sir. He did his damndest . . .'

'Mr Frey,' Drinkwater said after a moment, drawing Frey from the introspection he had lapsed into on recounting the fate of the *Tracker*. 'I would not have you think I ask this question from meanness of spirit, but what became of my personal effects?'

'We took some care of those, sir. Mr Q. had your chest sown into canvas and the whole tarred over. They weren't in the hold, d'you see, Mr Q. had 'em stowed in his cabin. When the Danes took the *Tracker*, they looted her of anything moveable. I'm afraid, sir,' Frey admitted, lowering his eyes, 'your chest was seized along with the ship's orders, sir.' He paused and looked Drinkwater full in the face. 'That was my fault, sir. I had forgotten about them in the heat of the action, sir, after Mr Q. was wounded . . .'

Drinkwater looked at the crestfallen Frey. After Quilhampton had fallen the command of *Tracker* would have devolved to him, and in the bitter moment of surrender Frey had forgotten to destroy the brig's secret orders.

'So the enemy know we were bound for Russia?'

'Yes sir, and the private signals for the . . .'

'Yes, yes, I realize that!' said Drinkwater sharply, aware of the irony.

'I'm mortified, sir, there's no excuse . . .'

'I'm sorry, I spoke hastily, I implied no reproach, it's just that . . . well, never mind. You will have to admit these things in your written report, but I do not think you need concern yourself over much.'

'Sir?' Frey looked puzzled.

'No court martial will condemn an officer who has been through what you went through, Mr Frey and, by your account, gallantly defended his ship. You must submit to the court's judgement, of course.'

'I have already written my report, sir,' Frey said gloomily.

'Well, no matter of that now,' Drinkwater said. He was impatient to reassure Frey and though both he and Quilhampton – if he survived – would have to appear before a court martial, such considerations were in the future and Drinkwater was more urgently pressed by the present.

'Just one thing more, Mr Frey, before we decide what is to be done.' He noticed Frey's expression change, responding to the positive note in Drinkwater's voice. 'What happened after you submitted to the Danes? By what authority were you brought to Altona?'

'Oh, the French appear to control the Danes, sir. As soon as we got ashore, after the *Tracker* was looted and burned – for she was hulled and aground by the time we struck – we were turned over to the French garrison at a place called Tönning. The Danes, though willing to fight us at sea – for revenge on our attack on Copenhagen three years ago I reckon – seem to lack independence ashore. There are French troops quartered upon them. It was the French that finally took the ship's orders . . . and your effects, sir,' Frey added as an apologetic afterthought. But what of you, sir?'

Drinkwater looked at Frey. He had been wondering about the precise circumstances in which the portrait had come to light and compromised Hortense. He would never know, of course, and there were far more immediate things to consider.

'Me? Oh, I will tell you one day, Mr Frey, when we are in better spirits and have put these present misfortunes behind us. Come, sir, tell me something about this place. You spoke – ah, Gilham, you have found something with which to break your fast.' Drinkwater looked up at the merchant shipmaster.

'This is for you: burgoo, though a thin stuff compared with our usual British fare, but 'twill warm you.'

'I'm obliged to you.'

'I will get some for your young friend if you'll hatch some way out of this damnable place.'

'You'll take your turn with us, not wait for Thiebault?'

'I don't trust that lizard, damn him, not now he's under the thumb of Marshal What's-his-name.'

Drinkwater could not resist a grin. 'Very well, now Mr Frey . . .'

'Well, 'tis a hospital really, as you doubtless guessed. We were brought here because so many of us were wounded.'

'Were you one of them?'

'Only a trifle, sir, a scratch, that's all. Several men have died since we arrived, but we have been tolerably well treated, allowed to bury our dead, and the commissioned officers permitted, on parole, to walk on the river bank.'

'Ah, that's good. Have you given your parole?'

'I wouldn't, sir.'

'Why not?'

'Mr Quilhampton forbade it, sir. He said 'twas enough to lose his ship, but he would not surrender his honour.'

'A Quixotic notion, but I apprehend he had ideas of escape, eh?'

'He did not know how ill he was.'

'I see,' Drinkwater paused, 'and are visits permitted to Altona itself?'

'Oh yes, we sent a man in to purchase foodstuffs . . . before we ran out of money.'

'D'you think it possible to send a message to Altona? Do any of the villagers enter the hospital at all?'

Frey's brow creased in a frown. 'Well there is a boy that comes up with fresh bread and the Commandant has some intercourse with the place for his table . . . Doctor Castenada would be the man to ask, sir. He is a remarkable fellow.'

'Is he to be trusted?'

'Aye, sir, as far as I can judge. He professes a dislike of the French.'

Drinkwater grunted and rubbed a hand across his stubbled chin. 'I used,' he said, 'to have some sneaking regard for 'em – unpatriotic, don't you know – but it seems to me that the Rights of Man was a not entirely dishonourable banner to fight under. Then last night Gilham and I saw a boy shot for hoardin' sugar . . .'

'We hang smugglers, sir,' Frey said.

'That's rather why I had a sneakin' regard for the Frogs,' grinned Drinkwater. 'Now tell me, if I asked you to plan the seizure of a boat large enough to take two dozen men down stream, what would you say?'

Frey's face was transformed by sudden enthusiasm. 'I've thought about it, sir! There is little time, for the ice is already forming along the reed beds, but there's a ballast bed just below the village and they bring barges down from Hamburg and fill 'em there. They've sails and sweeps, a dozen of us could easily . . .'

'How the devil d'you know all this if you refused your parole?'

'I didn't say I hadn't had a walk along the river bank, sir!'

'I think, Captain Gilham,' Drinkwater said, 'that we may have discovered an exit from our impasse.'

'I hope to heaven you're right, my dear fellow, for if your

friend chooses to denounce you, well . . . I don't think we have much time.'

Drinkwater needed no reminding that time was pressing. For all he knew Davout might have despatched a galloper that very morning with a message to Altona to have a certain 'Captain Waters' placed under close arrest.

Even if Hortense had not recognized him – and he was certain in his heart that his face had stirred some memory – it was likely that when confronted with the portrait and the story of its being found aboard a British man-of-war, the connection was inevitable.

Seeking a quiet corner, Frey took him to consult Castenada. The worthy surgeon provided ink and paper, nodding when Frey explained the new prisoner wished to communicate with someone in Altona.

For his own part, Drinkwater carefully wrote out the lines of Dante and encoded his message to Liepmann. It told briefly of their seizure in the warehouse, the interview with Davout and the suspected duplicity of Thiebault. Drinkwater also informed him of the fate of Johannes. Finally he made his request: *I ask that you find the whereabouts of Lieutenant Quilhampton, commander of the British ship seized at Tonning.*

'Do you know of a Herr Liepmann, Doctor Castenada?' Drinkwater asked, 'I believe he lives in Altona.'

'*Si* . . . yes, yes. He is well known. You want that I, er, convey that message?' Castenada pointed at the final draft Drinkwater had copied out.

'Yes, is it possible, without risk?'

'Yes . . . I will take it myself,' Castenada held out his hand and took the paper and stared at it. 'This is not English?'

'No . . .' said Drinkwater cautiously, unsure of the Spaniard's trustworthiness.

'It is like the pharmacopoeia, eh?' Castenada smiled and folded the paper. 'Fortunately, Herr Liepmann is supplying me sometimes, my, er,' he frowned and scratched his head, failing to find the right word and ending his unfinished sentence with a shrug.

'Ah, medicines!' offered Frey.

'Yes, yes, of course, medicines.' Castenada smiled with satisfaction.

'How soon can you go into Altona?' Drinkwater asked.

'Today, I go today. In hospital like this I always want more of the, er, medicines, no?'

Drinkwater nodded. 'Very well . . .'

He and Frey walked back across the parade ground where the snow was falling again. 'If he brings me a reply I shall know I can trust him, but it is better that I am not seen talking to him, for his sake as much as mine. Do you watch him, Mr Frey, and when he returns question him. This man Liepmann knows me and will reply in code. If Castenada plays his part, you may offer to get him and the twelve fittest Spaniards out of this place in your barge. Promise them that they will be repatriated to Spain at the expense of the British Government, d'you understand?'

'Perfectly, sir.'

'Now, have you given any thought as to how to get out of this place?'

'The main gate is locked at sunset, early at this time of year, after which a general curfew is imposed upon us all. It is never broken – there has been no need to break it . . .'

'Did you not think of escape before now?' Drinkwater broke in.

'I have thought of little else, sir, as I told you,' said Frey in an aggrieved tone and looking askance at Drinkwater, 'but I did not contemplate it without Mr Quilhampton, sir.'

'Of course, my dear fellow, forgive me, I have a lot on my mind. Pray go on, do.'

'The party to leave will break out on a given signal. When the guards shut the gates they invariably congregate in the guardhouse for a hot drink – chocolate if they can get it – after which they take up their night duties. They are very slack, most of them, being invalids themselves recuperating from wounds or sickness. Castenada tells me several have a disgusting and intractable disease, others are malingerers. If we secured them, I estimate we have an hour before the alarm is raised, time enough to get to the river and seize a barge.'

'And the keys of the gates are kept in the guardroom?'

'The corporal of the guard has them.'

'What of the officers? Don't they make rounds?'

'The Commandant has a German mistress in Hamburg, Captain Chatrian is fond of the bottle and Lieutenant Blanchard is not known for his zeal. They make their rounds before turning in, but we have at least an hour. Immediately after curfew has been sounded the officers go to dinner.'

'The virtues of military routine, eh?' said Drinkwater drily. 'I think you can rely on some revision of this regime if Marshal Davout hears of it.'

'I don't think anyone was perturbed, sir, as long as it was only the Spanish that were held here.'

'Well, Davout may be a new arrival in Hamburg, but he ain't ignorant of the fact that a British brig was taken; my personal effects were in his possession.'

'*What?*' Frey was incredulous, but Drinkwater hurried on without amplifying the statement. 'I want you to leave tonight, Mr Frey.'

'*Tonight*, sir?'

'Yes, tonight, that is what I said. You have objections?'

'Only insofar as Mr Q. is concerned, sir.'

'I shall attend to James, Mr Frey. I am not coming with you. You will take Captain Gilham as pilot and make for Helgoland. Keep your eyes open for a Dutch cutter of the Imperial Customs Service, otherwise drop downstream by night if possible. On arrival at Helgoland you will deliver a message to the Foreign Service agent, Mr Nicholas, and report to the senior British naval officer. Is that clear?'

'Yes, sir . . . but what about you, sir?'

'*Exactly* what happens to me rather depends on the news Castenada brings from Herr Liepmann. One thing is certain, however, I have no intention of staying here a moment longer than you. I have had my fill of hanging around waiting upon events. I shall break out with you and require only that when you secure the guards you seize a pistol, some ball, flints and powder. A sword would be useful . . .'

Drinkwater wished he had the sword cane with which he had terrified the frightful whore in Ma Hockley's flop-house. 'A French sword bayonet will do.' He smiled at Frey. 'Very well, Mr Frey, any questions?'

'No sir.'

'Until tonight then. I leave you to make all arrangements, muster your men, and so forth. Let us say our farewells now and as inconspicuously as possible. Good luck my dear young fellow.'

Drinkwater nodded abruptly at Frey, then turned on his heel. It was going to be a damnably long day and at any moment, he thought, glancing at the sentries lounging at the gate, Lieutenant Dieudonné, or the overworked staff officer, or, God forbid, Hortense Santhonax herself, might appear at the entrance, demanding his further presence in Hamburg.

Castenada proved as good as his word; nor did Liepmann abandon him. His message was both coded and cryptic; translated it read: *This thing already known. I am your servant.*

Drinkwater frowned over the last sentence, recalling Liepmann's competence as an English speaker. Was it a mere awkward formality, or did he imply a more sincere and pragmatic attachment? Castenada, in whose quarters Drinkwater had deciphered the message, caught his eye.

'I speak with Herr Liepmann, Captain. Your friend Mr Frey he tells me he is to leave this place tonight; he asks me to find some of my men to go with him. I ask him how he is to escape and, after him not telling me, I, er, persuade him that my men will not make a foolish try. He tells me by barge. I know all the barges belong to Herr Liepmann . . .'

'Yes . . . go on.'

'I tell Herr Liepmann . . .'

'You *what*?' Drinkwater snapped.

'Of course, Herr Liepmann say you must take. He will not report the barge missing.' Castenada smiled. 'You understand? Herr Liepmann is your friend.'

For a moment Drinkwater felt an ungracious, xenophobic

suspicion, but the value of Castenada's helpful intervention could not be denied. Besides, he had no time to waste.

'I am indebted to you, Doctor Castenada, perhaps in happier times I will be permitted the honour of repaying you.' Drinkwater felt the stiff formality of the stilted phrases sounded insincere, but Castenada bowed with equal courtesy.

'There is one other thing, sir,' Castenada said. 'Herr Liepmann suggested a possibility of helping you, *señor*, if you made your way to his house.'

Drinkwater tried to recall if he had said anything in front of Castenada to indicate whether or not he himself intended to escape with the others – and decided he had not. Perhaps Liepmann guessed from the question in the note that Drinkwater would remain behind; perhaps it was a simple offer, an expansion of that coded phrase, *I am your servant*. Drinkwater had no way of knowing, but Liepmann was one of the confraternity of Isaac Solomon, and, oddly, he inspired in Drinkwater the same confidence. He nodded at Castenada. 'Thank you.'

Castenada told him the whereabouts of Liepmann's house. 'You will find the house, it is not difficult.'

'I am most grateful.' Drinkwater paused, then added, 'Doctor Castenada, I am aware that things may be made very difficult for you after we have escaped.'

Castenada shrugged. 'After the Marquis de la Romana escaped it was difficult, but I live. A doctor can always live, especially in war.'

'Is there anything I can do for you, after I return to England. Do you have a wife to whom I can pass a message? If you do not already know, there is a British army in Spain now . . .'

'I know, Captain, and it marches into Spain and out again, and just now it is marching out again. Like Spanish armies, Captain, eh? You have a piece of song they tell to me when I am speaking English for the first time: The Grand Old Duke of York, yes? He had ten thousand men, he march them up to the top of the hill, eh, Captain? And he march them down again.'

Castenada began to laugh and Drinkwater found it impossible not to laugh with him.

'Well Gilham, are you ready?'

'As much as I ever will be. I think you're mad to stay, but good luck.'

They shook hands and took a look round the bare room with its crude wooden beds. 'I have to admit that I am not keen to sleep here,' Drinkwater said, adding, 'you will be able to take your atmosphereological observations again soon.'

A gleam showed in Gilham's eye and he drew a small notebook from his pocket.

'I have not stopped, Captain.' He smiled, then asked, 'By-the-by, what *is* your name?'

Drinkwater grinned. 'Ask Frey when you get to Helgoland. He'll tell you.'

'It's Drinkwater, isn't it? That fellow called you Drinkwater.'

'Maybe. Now let us see if the others are ready?'

They peered across the parade ground. A thick fall of snow obscured the far side and they could see nothing. Curfew had already been sounded and the 'patients' had all been locked in their wooden billets. They did not have long to wait. The stolen pick, a trophy of latrine digging, split hasp and staple from the pine planks of the building.

'You're the last,' hissed Frey.

'Privilege of rank,' murmured Drinkwater, feeling the old, almost forgotten thrill of action. Outside he and Gilham joined the crouching column of silent men sheltering in the lee of the hospital wards.

'I'd be obliged if you'd bring up the rear, sir. That's where the Spanish are.' Frey whispered in his ear then motioned his men on. Even in the snow and darkness Drinkwater recognized faces. Men he had flogged, men he had sailed with round Cape Horn and into the Pacific, men who had fought the Russian line-of-battle ship *Suvorov* to a standstill. Some of them saw him and grinned. With a pang of conscience he realized his clerk Derrick was not among them. He had not asked after Derrick and the omission bothered him. Then Gilham was tapping him on the shoulder and the faces passing him were no longer familiar. Drinkwater and Gilham fell in at the rear of the column.

Like a snake they moved round the perimeter of the parade ground. By the gate they could see a yellow loom in the snow where the guardroom door stood open. It was suddenly cut out and a man's silhouette appeared. With wonderful unity, the crouching, loping column froze, every man watching the guard pitch a cigar to the ground. A faint hiss came to their straining ears and the guard turned back amid the sound of laughter. The yellow light shone out illuminating the snow again.

From the rear Drinkwater could see Frey massing his men about the door. They appeared like dark sacks until, at a signal, they moved forward amid a few shouts.

Suddenly the gates were open and Drinkwater caught a glimpse of the guardroom and half a dozen trussed and gagged men. He began to run.

Beyond the gate the road swung to the right and Drinkwater almost collided with Frey.

'Good luck, sir. Two cables down this road there is a junction. It is the road between Hamburg, Altona and Blankenese. We turn right for the river, you must go left for Hamburg.'

'I know, Castenada told me. Good luck.'

'I could only find you a sword bayonet.' Frey thrust the weapon at him. The steel was bitterly cold to the touch. When he looked up he was alone. In the snow he could hear no sound of the retreating men, nor of the struggling guards. The loom of the hospital wall threw a dark shadow and he experienced a pang of intense fear and loneliness. A moment later he was walking swiftly south to the junction with the main road.

He had no trouble locating Herr Liepmann's house. It was set back off the road behind a brick wall, but the iron gates were open and the light in the porch beyond the formal garden gave the impression that it had been illuminated for his benefit.

It was, he thought as he felt the scrunch of gravel below the snow, a welcoming sight.

There were signs of wheel tracks in the snow, a recent arrival or departure, he judged, for they had not yet been covered. Perhaps the generous lighting was for the carriage, not for him. The thought made him pause. Should he simply walk up to the front door?

At his tentative knock it was opened, and guiltily he flung aside the sword bayonet.

'*Kapitan, Wilcomm* . . . please . . . you come . . .'

Liepmann held out his hand and drew Drinkwater inside. The warmth and opulence of Liepmann's house seemed like the fairyland pictures of his children's books. He had not realized how cold he had been, nor, now that the heat made him perspire and his flesh crawl, how filthy he was.

'I have clothes and *wasser*, come . . .'

It was ironic, he thought, that he should again clean himself in the house of a Jew, but he did not object. Liepmann led him to a side chamber where a servant waited upon him, standing impassively while, casting dignity aside in the sheer delight of washing off the past, Drinkwater donned a clean shirt and underdrawers. Silk breeches and stockings were produced, together with an embroidered waistcoat. Finally, the man servant held out a low-collared grey coat of a now unfashionable cut which reminded him of the old undress uniform coat of the British naval officer. As he threw his newly beribboned queue over the collar and caught sight of himself in the mirror, he caught the eye of the servant.

The man made a small, subservient gesture of approval, stood aside and opened the door. Ushering Drinkwater back into the hall, he scuttled round him and reaching the door of a withdrawing room leading from it, threw it open.

Drinkwater was disoriented by the luxury of his surroundings and entered the room seeking Liepmann to thank him for the splendour of his reception. But Liepmann was not in the room. As the door was opened a woman rose from a chair set before a blazing fire. She turned.

He was confronted by Hortense Santhonax.

PART THREE

# The Snaring of the Eagle

'Napoleon went to Moscow in pursuit of the ghost of Tilsit'

*Napoleon*,
J. Bainville

CHAPTER 15 January 1810

# Beauté du Diable

In the shock of encounter Drinkwater's mind was filled with suspicion. He felt again the overwhelming dead weight of a hostile providence with sickening desperation. Suddenly Castenada's obligingness and Liepmann's absence seemed harbingers of this entrapment. He regretted the sword bayonet cast aside in the box hedge and felt foolish in borrowed finery before this breathtakingly handsome woman.

She wore travelling clothes, a dark blue riding habit and scuffed boots, about her throat a grey silk cravat was secured with a jewelled pin that reflected the green of her eyes. Hat and cloak lay beside her chair and she held nothing more threatening than a glass of Rhenish hock.

'We have met before,' she said, tilting her head slightly to one side so that a heavy lock of auburn hair fell loose from the coils on her head. She spoke perfect English in a low and thrilling timbre.

'Indeed, Madame,' Drinkwater said guardedly, acutely aware that this woman possessed in abundance those qualities of grace and beauty for which men threw away their lives. He footed a bow, wondering at her motives.

'Will you take a glass of wine, sir?' Her cool courtliness was seductive and she turned aside, sure her offer would not be rejected.

The hock was refreshing. 'I am obliged, Madame,' he said,

maintaining a fragile formality despite his inward turmoil.

'You rescued me from the *sans-culottes* on the beach at Carteret, do you remember?' she went on, watching him over the rim of her glass, 'and you were with Lord Dungarth the night I was left ashore on the beach at Criel . . .'*

He did not respond. She had turned her coat by then, having met Edouard Santhonax and thrown her lot in with the Republicans. He let her lead the conversation to wherever it was going, wondering if she knew he had given her husband his death thrust.

'But that was a long time ago, when we were young and *impetueux*, was it not?'

She stepped closer to him so that he could smell the scent of her. She was undeniably lovely with a voluptuously mature beauty made more potent by the confidence of experience. He felt the male hunger stir him, mixed with something else: for years that damned portrait had symbolized for him the essence of a ruthless enemy, battening on the unsatisfied passions of his young manhood. Its power lay in both its imagery and association with her, a synthesis of wickedness, of desire denied, of lust . . .

'It was no coincidence that you were with Marshal Davout, was it? No coincidence that my portrait had come into his possession?'

There was an edge in her voice now, keen enough to abort his concupiscent longing.

'You are deceived as to that, Madame,' he replied. 'It is true the portrait was once my property, but Marshal Davout acquired it from a British brig wrecked on the Jutland coast. I was not aboard the brig, Madame, you have my word on it.'

'Your word? And what reliance may I put on that? You are a British naval officer, you are in the territory of the French Empire and,' she looked him archly up and down, '*that* is not a uniform, M'sieur Drinkwater.'

Oddly, he felt no apprehension at the unveiled threat, rather that cool resignation, that surrender to circumstances he had

* See *A King's Cutter*

experienced in action after the fearful period of waiting was over. He knew they were nearing the crux of this strange encounter and the knowledge exhilarated him. He smiled. 'You remember my name.'

'As I remember Lord Dungarth's.' She turned away to refill her glass.

'You have met him, have you not,' probed Drinkwater, 'since the business on the beach at Criel?' He did not wait for a reply, but asked, watching her keenly, 'Did you have him blown up?'

She swung round angrily. 'No!'

'I must perforce believe you,' he said, unmoved by the violence of her denial, 'and you must believe me when I tell you it was indeed coincidence that we met in Marshal Davout's antechamber. As to your portrait, I acquired it many years ago when I captured the French National Frigate *Antigone* in the Red Sea. She was commanded by your husband, Edouard Santhonax. It was among my belongings aboard the *Tracker* when she was herself taken a fortnight or so past.'

'Why did you keep it for so long, M'sieur?' She seemed calmer, as though his explanation satisfied her, and extended her hand for his empty glass. He gave it her, but did not immediately relinquish his own hold.

'I was struck by your beauty, Madame. You had already made an impression upon me.'

She could not doubt his sincerity, but his serious tone betrayed no sudden flare of passion.

'A lasting impression?' she asked mockingly, her eyes sparkling and a smile playing about the corners of her lovely mouth.

'So it would seem, Madame, though your husband had a more palpable effect . . .' He let the glass go.

'Your wounds?' she asked as she replenished the hock. She turned and held out the refilled glass. A coquettish gleam lingered in her eyes. 'Did you know I am a widow now?'

'Yes, Hortense,' he replied, his voice suddenly harsh, 'it was I who killed your husband.'

The words escaped him, driven by a subconscious desire to

hurt her, to hide nothing from so bewitching a woman with whom this extraordinary intimacy existed.

Her face turned deathly pale, her eyes searched his face and her outstretched hand trembled. 'It is not possible,' she murmured in French. He took the glass and with his left hand steadied her, but she drew back, frowning. '*Mais non . . . l'Empereur . . .*'

She seemed to be considering something, seeking the answer to some personal riddle. 'I was told he was lost in Poland . . . then the disgrace . . .'

'There was no disgrace, Madame. He was a man of uncommon zeal. He was killed at sea aboard the Dutch frigate *Zaandam*.'*

'A *Dutch* frigate? I do not understand . . .'

'Madame,' he said with sudden intensity, 'I had obtained some information of considerable importance to London. I believe it was acquired at your husband's expense. He was attempting to stop me reaching England . . .'

She was no longer listening. It was as though he had struck her. Two spots of high colour appeared on her cheeks and her eyes blazed. '*Diable!*'

If Drinkwater felt he had wrested the initiative from her he realized now he had made a misjudgement. She seemed suddenly to contract, not out of fear or weakness, but with the latent energy of a coiled spring.

'So, *that* is why . . . !'

And then he saw that the hatred he had kindled was introspective, for when she spoke to him again her voice was flat, explicatory, rationalizing things to herself, but in English for his benefit.

'Then you also killed Hortense Santhonax, M'sieur Drinkwater, for my husband is numbered among criminals, a man disgraced in the service of the Emperor.'

'I can assure you,' he said quietly, 'your husband did his duty to the utmost. It was his death or mine; your widowhood or my own wife's.'

She sighed and shook off her abstraction. 'Since Edouard's

* See *Baltic Mission*

disgrace I have received no pension, nor a *sou* of his due pay. I was abandoned by the Emperor, left destitute.'

'I believe the manner in which I harmed your husband was of very great importance to your Emperor,' Drinkwater said. He could not tell her the enormity of the secret he had brought home, that it was nothing less than the seduction of Tsar Alexander from his alliance with Great Britain and the intention of the two autocrats to partition Europe. Nor could he tell her it was that very alliance that his present mission sought to undermine. 'He was not alone in paying a price. I have not seen my wife since the event.'

She regained her composure and raised her glass. 'Do we drink to the misfortunes of war then?'

'It seems that we must, though I suspect your motives in doing so.'

'You thought I would denounce you to Davout and you do not trust me now?'

'I am not certain of anything, though in Hamburg you seemed to be under some constraint.'

'*Le bon Dieudonné?*' she smiled beguilingly. 'He is a man, M'sieur Drinkwater, and like *most* men,' she went on, 'predictable. Perhaps now you understand why so loyal a servant of Napoleon Bonaparte as the Prince of Eckmühl wished to question me when my portrait was found on a British ship.'

'Then your presence in Hamburg . . .'

'Was a coincidence as much as yours.' She seemed oddly relaxed. Could she so easily forgive the author of her downfall, or was she about to manipulate him as she intimated she had Dieudonné? Her next remark gave him no cause to think otherwise.

'Shall we sit down?'

Drinkwater's reply betrayed his unease. 'Where is our host?'

'Herr Liepmann?' she shrugged. 'I asked him to leave us alone for a few moments.' She had seated herself so that she was half turned towards him in the chair beside the fire. 'Pray sit. You have all the advantage standing, and that is unfair.'

'You forgive your enemies easily.'

She laughed. 'No. *You* are not my enemy, M'sieur Drinkwater, you are an agent of providence. Do you believe in providence?'

'Implicitly.' He sat himself opposite her. 'So why, when providence so neatly delivered me into your power, did you not denounce me in order to rehabilitate yourself with Davout and the Emperor? And why have you come here to Liepmann's house at Altona seeking this interview with me?'

'M'sieur Drinkwater, why have *you* come here? Or to Hamburg, eh? To sell boots to the French?' She laughed, a low chuckle that vibrated in her long throat. 'La, sir, it is common gossip in Hamburg, probably in Paris by now, that two British ships, cheated of a Russian market, sought their contemptible profit elsewhere.' She paused to sip her wine, then added, 'But that would not concern a naval officer, would it?'

'Quite so,' Drinkwater said, suppressing the satisfaction that the news gave him and ignoring the sarcasm in her voice.

'I will not press you for an explanation of your presence here,' she said after a pause, studying him. 'But you should know I did not make the attempt on Lord Dungarth's life. You must lay that at the feet of Fouché, or perhaps even the Emperor himself, who knows? But I have made his acquaintance, in France twice, and once in England.' She sighed. 'Edouard was my life; without him I would be an embittered *emigrée* living on charity in an English town. But he is dead and I must live; I have friends . . .' She caught his eye and then looked quickly away. She was discomfitted and he recalled Dungarth alleging an intimacy with Talleyrand. 'They are powerful friends and I am here in Hamburg on their behalf . . .'

'Go on,' he prompted, for she seemed suddenly indecisive.

'Will you do a service for me?' she asked, looking him full in the face.

'If it does not compromise my honour.'

'Will you take a message to London, to Lord Dungarth?'

Drinkwater sat back in his chair. 'Is that the coincidence that brought you to Hamburg?'

'More, it is the coincidence that brought me here to Altona. Lord Dungarth informed me that the Jew Liepmann, a merchant of Hamburg, was in touch with the British agent on Helgoland.'

Drinkwater wanted to laugh. The tension in his belly seemed to unwind, tugging at his reactive responses.

'You are not laughing at me?'

'No, Madame,' said Drinkwater with an effort, leaning forward and holding out his glass. 'Is there a little more wine with which to toast this alliance of ours. 'Tis a pity too much lies between us to be friends.'

'You have a wife, M'sieur.' She had become serious again as she poured, paying him back in his own, barbed coin. He felt again the strong animal attraction of her. For a foolish moment he persuaded himself that it was, perhaps, not unrequited.

'*Touché*, Madame,' he murmured, dismissing the fancy as conceit. 'Yes, I will take your message, but after another matter has been attended to.'

'What is that?'

'The release of a British sea officer; he is badly wounded and has a lady awaiting news of him.'

'I know, Herr Liepmann has told me.'

'He was indiscreet . . .'

'No, no, he knew I could help. He knows both you and I are dangerous; I think he would be pleased to see us both satisfied and gone.' She paused, adding, 'This is *trés domestique, n'est-ce pas*, M'sieur?'

Drinkwater looked at her across the fire, returning her conspiratorial smile.

'Very.'

'I think we should call the Jew now.'

She rose and he stood while she rang the bell-pull. Letting the braided cord fall she turned to him and took a step closer. Looking him full in the face she raised her hand and touched his cheek with the tips of her fingers.

'Providence, M'sieur Drinkwater, providence. Perhaps it has not yet finished with us.'

And reaching into the breast of her riding habit she drew out a sealed packet and handed it to him.

CHAPTER 16 January–February 1810

# The Burial Party

Long after she had gone and Liepmann had shown him to a small bedroom beneath the attic, Drinkwater sat by the open window, the quilt from the bed about his shoulders. It was impossible to sleep, for his wounded shoulder ached and his head spun with an endless train of thought.

The mood of intimacy had been broken after Liepmann's arrival. He came with news of the church bells ringing a tocsin to alert the countryside to the breakout from the hospital. They stood in silence to listen as the Jewish merchant drew aside the heavy brocade curtains and opened the tall French windows a little. Muffled by the falling snow, they could faintly hear men shouting and dogs barking.

'They go to the Elbe,' Liepmann said, closing the windows. He turned to Hortense and asked, 'You have told the Captain about the British officer, Madame?'

'Not yet.' She turned to Drinkwater. 'I knew of the ship wreck,' she said, 'and that my portrait was taken there. It was when I knew you were not a prisoner that I thought – that I decided to seek you out. As for the wounded officer from the wrecked ship, he was too ill to be questioned. *M'sieur le marechal* will have to be content with my own explanation. They said the Englishman was dying.'

Anxiety for Quilhampton must have been plain upon Drinkwater's tired face, for Liepmann added, 'Doctor Castenada is to travel to Hamburg tomorrow to return him to Altona.' The news brought Drinkwater little relief and Liepmann had his own worries. He drew a watch from his waistcoat pocket. 'Madame, it is late . . .'

Hortense bent and retrieved her hat and cloak. Liepmann helped her.

'Do not concern yourself, Herr Liepmann,' she said in her perfect English, darting a glance at Drinkwater. 'A woman seeking an assignation may pass freely anywhere. *À bientôt* Captain Drinkwater.'

'Madame.' He bowed as she swept out, leaving him prey to misgivings as to her motives. He heard the faint crunch of her conveyance on the snow covered gravel and then Liepmann came back into the room.

'She drives herself?' he asked.

'*Ja*, she is dangerous, that one – but I think . . .' he paused, 'she gave you papers for London?' Drinkwater nodded. 'Good. I can tell you that your two ships passed Brunsbuttel this morning.'

'Excellent,' said Drinkwater. 'Herr Liepmann, the British officer of whom we spoke earlier, he is a friend. I must get him out.'

The long-suffering Liepmann nodded slowly. 'We must talk . . .'

He was dog-tired when they at last retired. He had eaten nothing since the thin burgoo Gilham had obtained for him that morning. The hock had left him with a headache but he could not compose his mind for sleep and sat at the open window listening to the distant sounds of the search parties fade.

The night yielded no secrets. The dying away of the shouting proved nothing. Drinkwater thought of Frey and his men drifting slowly downstream amid the ice-floes, desperately hoping they had evaded their pursuers on the river bank. He thought, too, of James Quilhampton lying delirious a few leagues away, and of Elizabeth alone in her distant bed. But again and again his thoughts returned to Hortense with a fierce mixture of desire and suspicion.

Outside the snow had stopped. A few stars appeared, and

then the moon. By its light he turned over and over the sealed packet she had given him. Was it for London? Or was it a piece of incriminating evidence deliberately planted on him? And was the 'assignation' to which she claimed she was going, a meeting to denounce him, a British naval officer out of uniform in the house of a well-known Jewish merchant? Marshal Davout would delight in seizing a British spy caught red-handed in Hamburg whilst at the same time destroying the centre of the apparatus by which his master's Continental System was being cheated. In self-preservation Thiebault would corroborate the suspect Madame Santhonax's story and they could expect cavalry in Altona by dawn!

What had Hortense to lose? By so simple a denunciation she could secure the Emperor's gratitude; Santhonax's back-pay and her pension would be assured. He had not only confessed to having murdered her husband, but also provided her with a reasonable explanation which, made into a deposition before an advocate or a notary in Paris, would restore her husband's reputation at a stroke.

How could she not adopt such a course of action?

And yet . . .

And yet he would still have rather spent that sleepless night in her bed than anywhere else on earth.

Drinkwater woke to the alarming jingle of harnesses. He had fallen asleep across the bed fully clothed, as he might have done at sea. He had left the window open and was chilled to the bone. On leaping up and staring from the window, his worst fears were realized. A troop of brass helmeted dragoons, their grey cloaks thrown back to reveal their green coats, stood about the drive holding their tossing horses' heads. Immediately below, where the tracks of Hortense's chaise could still be seen, Herr Liepmann stood talking to a beplumed officer. A maid emerged bearing a tray of steaming *steins* and was made much of by the cavalrymen.

At almost the same instant, or so it seemed, the manservant who had attended him the previous evening entered Drinkwater's room after a perfunctory knock. Balanced on one hand he too bore a tray, with the other, its index finger at his lips, he commanded Drinkwater to silence.

The aroma of coffee, bread and sausages filled the cold air and Drinkwater relaxed. The appearance of breakfast and the raised finger did not, he judged, signal betrayal. To divert himself from being caught at the window, and compelled by hunger, he settled to the welcome food.

From time to time he rose, cautiously peering down to the driveway and was finally rewarded by the sight of the troopers mounting up. A few moments later Liepmann entered the room.

'I have news.' He held up a note. 'M'sieur Thiebault writes to tell me that trade is to stop . . . for a little while, you understand.' Liepmann smiled wryly.

'Thiebault sent the message by that officer of dragoons?'

'Lieutenant Boumeester is a Dutchman; they were Dutch dragoons. Their loyalty is, er, not good.' Liepmann shrugged. 'It is not only fat burghers who like to sugar their coffee, Captain. I have other news: Boumeester tells me more soldiers come to guard the hospital. Marshal Davout is angry.'

'So we do not have much time.'

'I go to Hamburg today. My carriage and Doctor Castenada's will –' Liepmann held out his hands, palms flat towards him and brought his finger tips together, seeking the English verb.

'They will meet?' offered Drinkwater.

'*Ja*, and I will speak. You must stay here. If I am not come back, do not worry. Go to the place we talk about last night.'

Drinkwater nodded, yawning. 'Your servants can be trusted?'

'They are paid by me, Captain. I will tell them what you need. *Auf weidersehen.*'

They shook hands. When Liepmann had left Drinkwater lay back on the bed. A moment later he was fast asleep.

It was almost dark when he awoke. The manservant was gently shaking him and indicating a tray of food, some rough, workman's clothes and a pile of furs. Drinkwater threw his legs out of the bed and rubbed his eyes. The manservant drew back a corner of the furs. A large horse pistol, a bag of balls and a flask of powder lay exposed. The weapon reminded Drinkwater with a shock of what the night held in store. He felt his heart thump as the lethargy of sleep was driven away.

'Herr Liepmann,' he asked, 'is he returned from Hamburg?'

'Eh?' The servant frowned and shrugged.

Drinkwater tried again. 'Herr Liepmann, is-he-come-from-Hamburg?'

'*Ach! Nein, nein.*' The servant shook his head, smiled and backed out.

After eating, Drinkwater changed his clothes. Over woollen undergarments he drew a coarse pair of trousers and a fisherman's smock. Two of the furs he rolled tightly and secured across one shoulder, the rest he bundled up with his cloak. Liepmann had provided a pair of sabots, but instead he drew on Dungarth's worn, green hessian boots, for they were comfortable and he had formed an attachment to them as a talisman. Pausing a moment, he shoved Liepmann's borrowed silk stockings in a pocket. Loading the pistol he stuck it in his belt. Then he picked up the sealed packet given him by Hortense. Perhaps after all he had misjudged her. Drawing a pillow-slip from the bed he improvised a bag and lanyard, pulled the latter over his head and tucked the bag inside his smock. Finally he pulled his queue from its ribbon and shook his tousled hair so that it fell about his unshaven cheeks.

By the time he had finished it was quite dark. He heard the curfew sounded at the hospital and made his way downstairs. The manservant was waiting for him and beckoned him to follow. The heat of the kitchen made Drinkwater sweat. Lantern light was reflected from rows of copper pans and a large joint of meat lay half butchered on a large scrubbed table. But apart from Drinkwater and the servant, the stone flagged room was empty, cleared of cooks and scullions by the trusted manservant who now handed Drinkwater a heavy leather satchel. A glance within revealed cheese, bread, wine, schnapps and sausage. A door from the kitchen led directly from the house and the servant lifted the latch for him.

Nodding gratefully, Drinkwater slipped out into the night; it was snowing again.

Lieutenant James Quilhampton drifted in and out of consciousness. The sound of hoof beats and the swaying of his narrow stretcher seemed to have accompanied half his lifetime. Periodically, familiar faces swam before him: his mother, Captain Drinkwater, young Frey, and Derrick the Quaker clerk he had inherited from Drinkwater. There were others too: Catriona MacEwan, elusive as always, and laughing at him as she ran perpetually away. He kept trying to follow her, but every time he tripped and fell, amid the terrible crashing of breakers and hideous thunder of cannon that made the abyss into which he descended shake in some mysterious way which he did not understand. Here *they* were waiting for him. The dark man with the saw and the knife whose kindly voice spoke in a foreign language and who thrust the knife into his arm so that he felt the white fire of amputation as he had done years ago during the bombardment of Kosseir.

When the man with the knife had finished another foreigner would appear. A man with spectacles and ice-cold eyes whose bald skull seemed too large for his shoulders and who took only a single look at him before uttering a curse. The bald man was God, of course, consigning him to the pit of hell, because Catriona was laughing at him and he fell again further and further, to where the dark man with the knife reappeared, pushing his hands into Quilhampton's very flesh. He knew the dark man was the devil and that he had been judged a great sinner.

Sometimes he heard himself shouting, for words echoed in his head and once another demon peered at him, a pale face with coiled hair that framed a face lit by the light from a lantern.

He felt better when the demon had withdrawn, cooler, as if he had been reprieved from the most extreme regions of hell, though the swaying rhythm of his body went on and on.

He must have slept, for when he was next aware of anything he was quite still, lying on his back in total darkness. There was a great throbbing in his left shoulder, as though all the pain of his punishment were being applied there. He found it difficult to breathe and, with growing consciousness, felt no longer the supine, indifferent acceptance of the feverish but the horror of the trapped. He tried to move: his right arm was pinned to his side. He raised his head: his forehead met obstruction. The sweat of fear, not hypothermia, broke from his body. The crisis of his amputation had passed but they had taken him for dead.

He was in his coffin.

Drinkwater found the boat quite easily, where the road from Altona to Blankenese dipped down to the very bank of the Elbe and a shingle strand marked the ballast bed. It must have been here that Frey had first seen Liepmann's barge, for large stakes had been driven into the ground as mooring posts. The fisherman's punt was drawn up in the centre of the little beach, a light craft such as a wild-fowler or an eel-fisherman might have used. Inside was a quant and a pair of oars, and he found it fitted with nocks intended for the latter cut in the low coaming.

Ice had formed at the water's edge but he could make out the darker unfrozen water beyond the shallow bay. Carefully he stowed the satchel and the spare furs, his boots crunching on the shingle. Once he stood stock-still when a dog barked, but it was only a mongrel in the village close by. When he was satisfied with the boat he moved up the beach, wrapped himself in the cloak and settled down to wait. A low bank some five feet high gave him a little protection from the snow and he squatted down, drawing his knees up to his chin.

He had slept too well during the day to doze, and the time passed slowly. He took his mind off the cold and the pain in his shoulder by trying to calculate long multiplication sums in his head, forcing himself to go over the working until he was confident of the answer. Faintly, borne on the lightest of breezes, he heard the chimes of a distant clock and realized it was that of the Michaelskirche in Hamburg. For him to hear it so far downstream meant that the snow was easing. When he heard ten strike, as if by magic, the sky cleared. He got up and moved cautiously about to restore his circulation; it was getting colder.

Then he heard the stumbling feet and rasping breath of men carrying something. Drinkwater crouched until he could see them, four men bearing a coffin and a fifth bringing up the rear. His heart thumping, Drinkwater rose and showed himself.

Who the four men were he had no idea beyond knowing that Liepmann would pay them well for their work and their silence, but the fifth was Castenada, bag in hand. He came forward as the mysterious bearers lowered the coffin on to the shingle beside the punt.

'Captain . . . ?'

'All is quiet, Doctor.'

Both men bent anxiously over the coffin and Castenada began to lever up the lid. Drinkwater waited. He wanted to ask after Quilhampton's condition and, at the same time, to warn his friend to keep silent.

With a grunt, Castenada pulled the lid aside. In the starlight the pale blur of Quilhampton's face was suddenly revealed, his mouth agape as he fought for air.

Castenada swiftly produced a bottle of smelling salts from the bag he had brought with him. He handed it to Drinkwater.

'Under his nose!' he ordered and Drinkwater did as he was bid while the surgeon chafed his patient's cheeks. Quilhampton groaned and Castenada transferred his attention to Quilhampton's shoulder, feeling the heat of the wound through the dressing and the sleeve of his coat.

'It is God's will, Captain,' he said, 'he is past the crisis, but he will have suffered from the shock.' Castenada put a hand on Quilhampton's forehead and clicked his tongue. Quilhampton groaned again.

'James . . . James, it is me, Drinkwater. D'you understand? You are among friends now, James. D'you understand?'

'Sir? Is that you?' Quilhampton raised his right hand and Drinkwater seized it, squeezing it harder than he had intended in the intensity of the moment.

'Yes, James, it's me. We're going for a boat ride. Be a good fellow and lie quiet.'

'Aye, aye, sir,' Quilhampton whispered, his fever-bright eyes searching the blur that he could not really believe was Drinkwater's face.

Drinkwater stood up. 'Come.' he said, motioning with his hand, 'into the boat.'

They lifted him as gently as they could, laying him on the furs Drinkwater had prepared and covering him with more furs and the blankets Castenada had packed in the coffin.

The four Germans helped Drinkwater drag the punt out over the ice, until it gave way and the boat floated.

'*Danke*,' he gasped, his breath coming out in clouds that were already freezing on the stubble about his mouth. He lifted one foot to steady the punt and half turned towards Castenada.

'Thank you, Doctor,' he hissed at the grey shape standing at the edge of the ice.

'Wait!' Castenada bent and picked up his bag and handed something to the four men. Then he was plunging awkwardly through the broken ice and, teetering uncertainly alongside Drinkwater, grabbed his arm for support.

'I come with you. He will not live without a doctor, not in this cold!'

Drinkwater looked doubtfully at the narrow punt, then patted Castenada.

'Very well! Get in!'

Drinkwater tried to steady the narrow punt as Castenada climbed clumsily aboard, but it rocked dangerously. When the surgeon had settled down Drinkwater followed, seating himself amidships on the single thwart and shipping the oars. He looked briefly ashore. The four men had already gone, taking the coffin with them. They would fill it with earth and it would be buried in the morning.

Leaning forward he could see in the stern Quilhampton's face. 'Shall we go home, Mr Q.?'

'If you please, sir,' came the uncertain, whispered reply.

Drinkwater turned his head and murmured over his shoulder, 'Are you ready, Doctor?'

'*Adelante, señor!*'

Drinkwater dipped his oars and pulled out into the stream, feeling the mighty tug of the great river. He could just make out the skyline broken by the roofs of Blankenese and the spire of its little kirk. Tugging at the oars he watched their bearing draw astern as the Elbe bore them towards the sea.

CHAPTER 17 February 1810

# Ice

At the first brightening of the sky Drinkwater sought shelter for the hours of daylight. Helped by the river's ebb they had dropped well downstream to where the Elbe widened, spreading itself among the shallows of shingle beds and islets towards its southern bank. Drinkwater pulled them up to a small reef of gravel which extended above the flood level far enough to support a sparse growth of low alder and willow bushes. Along the northern margin of this ait the stream ran deep enough to keep it ice-free, since a shallow bend in the main channel scoured its shore.

With his hands protected by the purloined stockings, Drinkwater was warm enough from the steady exertion of pulling and Quilhampton gallantly professed he felt warm enough, wrapped as he was in furs and blankets. Castenada was rigid with cold, so that, having run the punt aground, it was only with difficulty Drinkwater managed to assist first Quilhampton and then the Spanish surgeon into the shelter of the alder grove.

It was clear that the cramps of immobility as much as the cold were affecting Castenada, and watching him, Drinkwater concluded he suffered also from a heavy conscience; in his impetuous desire to assist Quilhampton he had abandoned his other charges.

Drinkwater busied himself gathering all the dry driftwood he could find, supplementing it with dead alder and willow branches. Paring a heap of kindling with the kitchen knife given him for cutting the sausage, and catching a spark from the horse pistol, he contrived to get a fire burning.

'This wood is dry enough not to make much smoke,' he observed, fanning the crackling flames as they flickered up through the sticks.

Quilhampton stared about them. 'The air is marvellously dry,' he said, and Drinkwater looked up from his task. The light easterly wind they had experienced during the night had died away. The sun was rising as a red ball and the Elbe reflected the perfect blue of a cloudless sky. The distant river banks seemed deserted as Drinkwater painstakingly surveyed them. He had no idea how far downstream they had dropped, but by the width of the river he guessed they had made good progress.

'If the weather stays this fair,' Quilhampton said as Castenada kneeled beside him to change his dressing, 'there will be little wind to worry us.'

'True,' said Drinkwater, and both sea officers looked at the low freeboard of the punt and thought of the long, exposed stretch off-shore, beyond Cuxhaven.

'Perhaps we can lay our hands on another boat,' said Drinkwater with feigned cheerfulness, though both knew the risks such a course of action entailed.

'I expect we could do something to make her more weatherly,' Quilhampton said, the perspiration breaking on his face as Castenada tried to draw the ligatures from his stump after sniffing the wound.

'Do you use the lead acetate dressing, Doctor?' Drinkwater asked, hardly able to bear the pain on Quilhampton's drawn features.

Castenada looked up. 'Ah, you know the French method, eh, Captain? The method of Larrey, yes?'

Drinkwater shrugged. 'It was shown me by a French surgeon on the *Bucentaure* during the action off Cape Trafalgar.'

Castenada frowned and rewound the bandage over Quilhampton's hot stump. 'The *Bucentaure* . . . I thought . . .' he motioned Drinkwater to help him draw on Quilhampton's coat again.

'She was French? Yes, she was. I was a prisoner.'

'Ahhh.' Castenada sat back on his haunches and stared unhappily at Drinkwater.

'Doctor, I understand something of what you are feeling. When we are a prisoner we dream of freedom: when we are free we mourn for those left behind. Is that not the case?'

'*Sí, sí* . . . yes.'

'You should not judge yourself too harshly. Left to my tender ministrations, Mr Q. here would probably be dead by now.' Drinkwater leaned forward and patted Castenada's shoulder. 'You are an agent of providence,' he said, aware that he had borrowed the phrase from Hortense Santhonax.

Towards sunset on that short winter's day, the cooling air laid a low mist over the Elbe and Drinkwater determined on an early start. He had spent part of the day asleep, but having first eaten from the scanty stock of supplies provided by Liepmann, he had observed the build-up of ice about them, certain it would encroach further during the following night. Having taken the precaution of placing the largest stones he could find on the islet in the fire, he raked them out and with Castenada's help, succeeded in rolling them in a blanket and placing them in the punt between Quilhampton's legs.

'Insurance against freezing my assets, eh, sir?' joked Quilhampton as the boat bobbed with its forefoot still aground on the shingle beach.

After each gulping a slug of schnapps, Drinkwater and Castenada shoved off and clambered in, settling themselves for the long night ahead.

'Very well gentlemen,' Drinkwater said, leaning forward with his oar blades just above the water, 'are we ready to proceed towards England?'

'I am ready to go to España,' chuckled Castenada from the bow and Drinkwater exchanged glances of amusement with Quilhampton.

Drinkwater set himself an easy pace, knowing it was not difficult to row for many hours with a favourable current, but the cold attacked his legs at once, for they were not subject to the constant movement of his upper body. Quilhampton kicked his blankets aside below the extended furs and shared the warmth of the stones.

'I'm obliged to you, James.'

They could hear Castenada's teeth chattering and invited the surgeon to sample more schnapps until all that could be heard from the bow of the punt was a light snore.

'I'm sorry about your arm, James,' he said, tugging an oar clear of a pancake of ice that spun, ghostly, on the dark water.

'Having already lost half, the remainder don't come as so much of a shock,' Quilhampton jested feebly. They fell silent and Drinkwater knew Quilhampton was thinking of Catriona.

'How did you lose it?' he asked, seeking to divert his friend's tortured mind. 'I know it was in defence of the *Tracker*, but specifically?'

'Foolishness,' Quilhampton said, a grim chuckle in his voice. 'Like most precipitate acts, it was one of pure folly. I had engaged a big tow-headed Danish officer, hand-to-hand. The fellow had the reach of an octopus and I had to get inside his guard, and damned quickly. He came at me like the devil and thinking I had a subtle advantage, I put up my timber hand and parried his low thrust, at the same time twisting my trunk to extend my own sword. The fellow was quicker than I thought: he disengaged, cut under my false hand and ran his blade to the hilt, clean through my elbow.'

'What happened to him?' Drinkwater asked, curiously.

'He took Frey's sword at the end,' Quilhampton said miserably, relapsing into silence. After a while he too slept.

Drinkwater pulled steadily at the oars, looking over his shoulder from time to time. By now his night vision was acute and he could make out the odd feature on the nearer bank. At last he sensed the ebb ease, then the slack water and the first opposing thrust of the flood. He pulled closer to the shore, seeking the counter-current, determined not to seek a resting place until dawn.

The rhythmic exertion of his body lulled him and he allowed his mind to wander. He felt a surge of confidence in himself.

Now that the outcome depended solely upon his own efforts he felt a greater ease than he had enjoyed at the mercy of Thiebault and Liepmann, and even Captain Littlewood.

As for Hortense, he was certain now that she had not betrayed him. The papers that he felt stiff against his breast were genuine enough, and he recollected other facts to buttress her claims. He remembered Lord Dungarth telling him he had been in France twice, the same number of times Hortense had said she had met his lordship there. Moreover, Hortense had added that she had also seen Dungarth in England, a fact that might indicate she spoke the truth, for her English was flawless and she had lived there as an *emigrée* during the nineties.

It seemed that Dungarth had been right, all those years ago, in setting her free on the beach at Criel. If he had thought that having turned her coat once, she might do the same thing again, he had been proved correct.

Despite the desperation of their position, there were other considerations that gave him a ridiculous pleasure as he listened to the snores emanating from both ends of the punt. The squalid and shameful subterfuge he had embarked upon in Ma Hockley's whore-house in order to sow the seed in the informing ear of Mr Fagan, and the consequences of the Russian convoy and its near disastrous end on the island of Helgoland had at least achieved more than he had expected. The tale of British trade with Russia had been successfully carried to Custom House officers and a Prince-Marshal of the French Empire. That Hortense had joked about it was evidence enough that it would likely reach the ears of the Emperor Napoleon. He had, he thought, as he stared up at the star-spangled arch of the sky, every reason to be modestly pleased with himself . . .

The ice-floe was heavy and spun the punt round so that Drinkwater almost lost his starboard oar.

As he grabbed for it his arm was soaked to the elbow and the freezing water chilled him enough to make him gasp. A moment later the wildly rocking punt grounded and his passengers woke.

'God damn,' Drinkwater swore and easing a booted leg over the coaming, he tested the depth of the water. It took him twenty full, laborious minutes to work the punt back into navigable water, twenty minutes during which he discovered that Lord Dungarth's cast-off hessian boots, though of a fashionable style, let water damnably.

'I wonder,' he said in an attempt to restore the morale of his party after the incident, 'whether our Northampton manufactures are entirely waterproof?'

They holed up for the second day on a larger, lower islet than the first. It did not yield the same amount of dry wood and they spent a miserable day. Their only high spot was in getting Quilhampton on to his feet and making him dance about a little, supported between Drinkwater and Castenada.

'Who looks a damn fool now?' Drinkwater asked as, puffing and blowing, they eased the invalid back on to his furs. As the sun westered they plundered the diminishing stock of food in Liepmann's satchel.

As the time for departure approached, Drinkwater tried to search the river ahead, but he had no vantage point and, apart from discovering the main stream appeared to swing a little to the north-west, he gleaned little information.

They set out an hour before sunset. The ice in mid-river was more noticeable, and Drinkwater had frequent trouble with floes impeding the oars as he waited for the ebb tide. The punt bumped and spun violently at times, so that stifled grunts of pain came from Quilhampton. Castenada became increasingly silent as the desperation of their plight dawned upon his landsman's perception.

In the small hours they ran aground for the sixth or seventh time. Drinkwater got out and paddled, splashing round the punt, aware that as much ice as water lay underfoot.

It seemed colder than ever, the river running over a vast area of shallows which had frozen solid where pools had formed between the gravel ridges. Walking in a circle about the boat to the limit of the painter, Drinkwater discovered a section of shingle that rose two or three feet above the water. Returning to the punt he ordered Castenada on to his feet and between them they manhandled first Quilhampton and then the punt out of immediate danger.

Casting about they discovered the ubiquitous supply of driftwood which proved sufficient to light a fire, though the effort expended with flint and steel tested Drinkwater's patience to the utmost.

'We must shield the fire glow from observation,' he said, indicating Castenada's cloak, 'I have no idea where we are, though the villages about Cuxhaven cannot be too far away now.'

In blankets, cloaks and furs they lay as close to the fire as they could. Shivering and miserable the three of them fell into a light sleep so that, after their exertions, dawn found them still unconscious.

The nightmare assailed Drinkwater shortly before dawn. It was an old dream, filled with the noise of clanking chains that might have been the sound of a ship's chain pump, or the fetters of the damned in hell. There was a woman's face in the dream, pallid and horrible, and she chanted dreadful words that he heard as clearly as if they were being whispered in his ear:

*Thy soul is by vile fear assail'd which oft*
*So overcasts a man, that he recoils*
*From noblest resolution, like a beast*
*At some false semblance in the twilight gloom.*

He could not make out whether or not it was the face of Hortense or Elizabeth, or some harpy come to warn him, but he woke to her scream and knew the dream for an old foreboding.

He was bathed in perspiration and felt a constriction in his throat presaging the onset of a quinsy.

The long scream dissolved into the unimagined reality of a distant trumpet note.

Drinkwater was on his feet in an instant, hobbling with cramp. He looked about them.

'God's bones!'

During the night they had become separated from the main stream of the river and he had pulled them unwittingly into an extensive area of shallows bordering the southern shore. The sand and gravel banks here gave way to marsh and reed bed, a landscape frozen solid, as was the water about them. Here were no comforting deep runs of moving water, instead the petrified glitter of acres of thick ice, of brittle, frosted reeds and ice-hardened, snow-covered samphire.

Beyond the marsh, not a mile away on rising ground that commanded a view of the river, stood a village, its church spire clearly visible. Drinkwater scanned the lie of the land further west. Roughly equidistant with the village a broad sweep of the Elbe ran inshore, separated from their present resting place by the ice.

Crouching low, his leg muscles tortured with the pain of cramp, he returned to the encampment.

'Wake up,' he hissed, shaking Castenada and Quilhampton. 'There are troops in a village not a mile away. Wake up!'

Drinkwater slung the satchel over Quilhampton's good shoulder and helped him to his feet. Then he and Castenada gathered up their coverings and the three of them hurried towards the punt. Stowing their belongings Drinkwater bent to the task.

'James, I want you to walk very slowly, testing the ice, ahead of us. Doctor, lift that damned bow . . . the boat, man, the boat . . .'

They broke the punt out of its bed of ice and began to slide it over the ice, negotiating the frozen reeds and finding the going easier as they moved away from the bank. They were within half a mile of open water when Quilhampton, tottering uncertainly, looked back. Drinkwater saw his jaw fall as he stared over their struggling shoulders. He turned his head, almost losing his footing on the ice.

'God's bones!'

'*Dios!*' Castenada crossed himself, an unconscious, instinctive gesture.

The cavalryman sat on his mount just below the village and watched them. Their suddenly increased exertion confirmed his suspicions. He wheeled his horse and cantered up the snow-covered incline, jerking the animal's head round again as he broke the skyline. Turning in his saddle, one hand on the rump of his horse, he appeared to be shouting to someone behind him, then he was facing them, and kicking his horse forward.

As he spurred towards them they saw the sunlight glint on the curved blade of his sabre.

CHAPTER 18 February 1810

# The Scharhorn

'James! Can you help?'

Quilhampton, pale from the effort of walking, nodded and took the painter in his right hand. Drinkwater motioned Castenada to the stern and fiddled with the toggled beckets that retained the quant pole alongside the coaming of the punt. Hefting it at its centre he pulled it clear and swung clumsily round, wheeling it as Castenada and Quilhampton ducked.

'Get moving!' he ordered, turning to face the horseman. In the wake of his struggling companions he backed along the scored ice with the painful slowness of retreat. The cavalryman was urging his nervous horse on to the ice. Somewhere behind him the shrill rapid notes of the alert cut through the bitter morning air. Letting one end of the long quant drop on to the ice, Drinkwater drew the pistol from his waistband, throwing his cloak back over his shoulders to leave his arms free.

The cavalryman had succeeded in getting his horse on to the ice and it skittered nervously, throwing up its reined-in head so that flecks of bloody foam flew from its mouth. Drinkwater waited, the advancing man clearly visible, the scarlet pelisse hooked to the neck, the overalls and the tall-plumed busby marking him as an officer of the horse chasseurs of the Imperial Guard. Drinkwater knew in his gut that it was Lieutenant Dieudonné.

At fifty paces Drinkwater lifted his pistol. The misfire

clicked impotently in the clear air and he thrust the weapon back in his belt.

'Pox!'

He gripped the quant and lifted it across his body like a quarterstaff. The uneven weight of the thing made him unsteady on the ice and he slithered, recovering his balance with difficulty. He looked back. Quilhampton and Castenada seemed a long way away from him, but so did the water. With a dry mouth he confronted Dieudonné.

'Ah! Capitaine Boire l'eau, eh?' The man was grinning beneath the fierce moustaches as he kicked his reluctant mount forwards. The horse was angled in his approach, apprehensively rolling its eyes. Dieudonné's left hand held both reins tight and the poor beast's neck was arched by the restraint. Drinkwater saw Dieudonné was trying to pull the animal's head round in order to clear his sword arm for the line of attack.

Cautiously Drinkwater slid his feet forward. He knew he had one chance, and one only, for his weapon was too cumbersome to retrieve after a first thrust.

Dieudonné succeeded in getting the horse's head swung long before Drinkwater's improvised lance was within striking distance, but his cautious advance had closed the distance a little more than the Frenchman had reckoned on.

The charger, mouth foaming and teeth bared as it fretted on the bit, loomed over him. Drinkwater foreshortened his weapon and allowing himself to be carried by the inertia of its swing, flung himself forward, thrusting the lance not at Dieudonné, but at the animal's legs. At the same time Dieudonné leaned forward, cutting down over the crupper, the sabre whistling past Drinkwater's head as he slipped and fell headlong. The charger reared with a screeching neigh, lifting its front hooves clear of the ice.

For a moment it pawed the air in a furious attempt to keep its balance but its weight, bearing now on its hind legs, was too much for the ice. The sudden and ominous crack provided Drinkwater with the stimulus he needed to galvanize his aching muscles. As he rolled clear of the horse it reared still further. Caught off balance Dieudonné slipped sideways, lost his left stirrup and lurched towards Drinkwater. He attempted to recover his sword, which dangled from its martingale, but Drinkwater seized his wrist and pulled back with all his weight. With a crash, the ice gave way beneath the horse and it was plunging up and down, neighing frantically and tossing its head as the cold water struck its loins. The turmoil broke the ice further. Dieudonné floundered half in the water, desperately trying to keep in the saddle and recover the sword that had slipped from his wrist. Drinkwater retreated on to firm ice, then saw the chasseur's sabre lying between them, on the edge of the hole the plunging horse was enlarging every second in its terror. Drinkwater edged forward; with the toe of a hessian boot he caught the sabre and drew it from Dieudonné's reach.

'Sir! Sir!'

As he bent to pick up the gilt-mounted sabre, Quilhampton's voice impinged on his consciousness. He looked round. Castenada and Quilhampton had the punt poised on the ice-edge. Quilhampton was waving frantically for him to follow. Beyond Dieudonné's desperately struggling mount more men, on foot and carrying carbines or muskets, were advancing across the frozen salt marsh.

He looked again at Dieudonné. The man was up to his breast in water. The terrible shock of the cold was plain on his face.

'*M'aider! M'aider, M'sieur, j'implore . . . !*'

Drinkwater thrust the long quant pole across the hole. '*Votre amis attendez-vous*,' he managed in his best French and turned away.

The ice grew dangerously thin at the water's edge, but Quilhampton and Castenada, by luck or foresight, had found a ridge of gravel and launched the punt from its farther limit.

'Get in!' Drinkwater gasped as he slipped and slithered towards them.

Quilhampton lay in the stern as he reached them. 'Give the Doctor your pistol!' he called and Drinkwater did as he was bid, tumbling into the punt and collapsing breathlessly on the single, centre thwart. He felt the punt lurch and roll as Castenada clambered in, the big horse pistol in one hand, the powder flask in the other. A musket ball buzzed past them, then another, and they heard the sharp cracks bite the still air.

'You have to row, sir,' Quilhampton was saying, rousing him. 'Neither I nor the Doctor can do it, sir! You *have* to row!'

Still gasping, Drinkwater realized that he had stupidly considered himself safe once he reached the boat, so great had been his concentration in dismounting Dieudonné.

He shipped the oars and spun the boat round. What he saw when he was facing the shore spurred him to sudden, back-breaking effort. Twenty or thirty dismounted hussars, some kneeling, some standing, were aiming their carbines at the retreating boat and he could see the innocent puffs of smoke as they fired, and then the skilful manipulation of cartridge and ramrod. Little spurts of water jumped up all round the boat and a section of the coaming disintegrated in a shower of splinters, one of which struck Castenada in the face. He let out a yelp and the punt was struck again while several balls leapfrogged across the river's surface like stones thrown by boys playing ducks and drakes.

Mercifully the tide was ebbing and swept them swiftly out of range. As he pulled away, Drinkwater could see a group of men go to the assistance of Lieutenant Dieudonné and the last he saw was his charger being hauled from the broken ice.

'Are we making water, James?' Drinkwater asked anxiously.

'No, I don't think so. We've one hole near the waterline, but we can plug that.'

'With what?'

'We'll try a piece of sausage, sir.'

And looking at his friend leaning outboard, his one good hand thrusting a long slice of Liepmann's *wurst* into a shot hole, he began to laugh with relief.

They ate the rest of the sausage by way of breakfast and Castenada dressed his own wound. He also expressed his anxiety about Quilhampton and the delay in drawing the ligatures from blood vessels, pointing to the high colour forming on the young man's cheeks.

'I'm all right, sir,' Quilhampton protested, 'never felt better.'

'You are light-headed, James, Doctor Castenada is right. You have lost a lot of blood and these present trials must be placing a strain upon you.'

'Fiddlesticks, sir, er, beggin' your pardon,' he added, and Drinkwater nodded silent agreement with Castenada. They did not have any time to lose.

The skirmish with Lieutenant Dieudonné had thoroughly alarmed Drinkwater, for Dieudonné had made a jest of his real name and it was impossible not to ascribe that knowledge to any source other than Hortense.

To divert his mind from the agony he felt in his arms and especially his shoulder, he tried to reason out her actions. Had she really betrayed him?

If she had done so immediately on her return to Hamburg, Dieudonné would have caught him napping in the bed at Liepmann's where, had she acted with malice aforethought, she could have had him bound and trussed as a spy.

Or had she given him time to get away and *then* denounced him, as though suddenly recollecting the identity of the man she had seen when brought before Davout? If so she played a bold game of double bluff.

To deceive the Marshal she could have pretended to fret and puzzle over the origin of that battered portrait. Having at last recognized the stranger in the Marshal's antechamber, what would be more natural than to seek an interview with him? She could then share her recollection and suggest the Englishman Drinkwater had come to Hamburg for almost any nefarious purpose she liked to fabricate!

Such an action would clear her own name and might restore her to the Emperor's favour and her husband's withheld pension.

Dieudonné catching up with them on the river bank was sheer bad luck, for Hortense had no way of knowing how long it took to drop a boat down the Elbe, while the fact that it was Dieudonné – an officer of an élite unit employed on missions of delicacy and daring – who was poking about the marshes east of Cuxhaven, argued strongly for the accuracy of Drinkwater's guesswork.

'Town ahead.' Quilhampton struggled into a sitting position, pointing. His words jerked Drinkwater back to the present. A single glance over his shoulder told him the place was Brunsbuttel, and the tortuously slow way in which features on the bank were passing them told its own tale: they would pass the town in broad daylight against a flood tide.

For a moment Drinkwater rested on his oars.

'Flood tide's away,' remarked Quilhampton.

'Aye.' Drinkwater thought for a moment, then said, 'That officer, I know who he is, James – no time to explain, but he wasn't just on the lookout for escaped prisoners like Frey and his men. He was looking for us. For me to be precise.' He began to tug on his oars again, inclining the bow of the punt inshore.

'I daresay the alarm's been raised on both banks, but word may not have reached Brunsbuttel yet that they are after three men in a duck punt. D'you see?'

'Because that scrap was on the south side of the river?'

'*Si, si*, that is right,' exclaimed Castenada from the bow.

'So we will pull boldly past Brunsbuttel and you, James, will lie down while you, Doctor, will wave if you see someone ashore taking an interest.'

'*Wave*, Captain, I do not understand . . .'

'Like this,' snapped Quilhampton, waving his only hand with frantic exasperation.

'Ah, yes, I understand, *wave*,' and he tried it out so that, despite themselves, Drinkwater grinned and Quilhampton rolled his eyes to heaven.

There was less ice now, the salt inflow from the sea inhibiting its formation, although there were pancakes of the stuff to negotiate close to the shore.

Drinkwater pulled them boldly past the town. In the corner of a snow-covered field a group of cows stood expectantly while a girl tossed fodder for them. A pair of fishing boats lay out in the river half a cable's length apart, a gill net streamed between them. Their occupants looked up and watched the punt pull slowly past them. One of them shouted something and Castenada waved enthusiastically. The man shouted again and Castenada shouted back, revealing unguessed-at talents as a German speaker, for the fishermen laughed.

'What did you say?' Drinkwater asked anxiously.

'They ask where we go and I tell them to Helgoland for some food!'

'The truth is no deception, eh?' Drinkwater grunted, tugging at the oar looms. 'I did not know you spoke German.'

'In Altona it is of help to speak German and I speak already some English. When these men come from the English ship, I make my English better. I speak French too . . .'

They were almost past Brunsbuttel when Drinkwater caught sight of the sentry. The bell-topped shako of a French line regiment was familiar to him by now. Perhaps he stared too long at the fellow, or perhaps the soldier had been attentive during his pre-duty briefing, but Drinkwater saw him straighten up and stare with interest at the boat.

'Hey! *Arrête! Halte!*' The sentry's voice carried clearly over the water, but Drinkwater pulled on as the man unslung his musket and aimed it at them. He seemed to have second thoughts, his head lifting, then lowering again as he sighted along the barrel. Just then an officer ran up and the man raised his gun barrel to point at the escaping punt. When he at last fired they were out of range and the ball plopped harmlessly into their wake.

'*Dios!*' said Castenada crossing himself.

'James,' asked Drinkwater when he was certain they were clear, 'about south-west of us, somewhere on the larboard bow, can you see the Kugel beacon at Cuxhaven?'

'I see it!' said Castenada, pointing ahead.

Quilhampton raised himself and nodded. He seemed flushed again. 'Yes, yes, it's there all right.' He slumped back amid the furs.

'Very well,' Drinkwater went on, suppressing his anxiety over Quilhampton's deteriorating condition. 'That is where they will intercept us. Dieudonné – that officer – is bound to raise the alarm there. There ain't a black-hulled Dutch cutter in sight, is there? She's a big Revenue Cruiser . . .'

He stopped rowing and looked round himself, for Quilhampton appeared to be asleep. Castenada was staring at the horizon. 'I do not see any ships, Captain . . .'

Drinkwater touched his arm and pointed anxiously at Quilhampton in the stern.

The doctor frowned and shook his head. 'He is not good.' Castenada made a move as though to rise and pass Drinkwater, but Drinkwater shook his head.

'No, no, Doctor, you will have us over . . . listen, I think I may have an idea . . .'

He rowed on, occasionally glancing over his shoulder. After a while Castenada asked, 'Where is this idea, Captain?'

'Ahead of us, Doctor, a secondary channel I recall from the chart, to the north of the Vogel Sand. We do not have to pass close to Cuxhaven and it is not many hours until dark now.'

'You would like more food?'

'Yes, and the last of that wine unless you want it for him,' he nodded at Quilhampton.

'No, it is better for you now. We are near the ocean, yes?'

'Yes.'

'And Helgoland is not far?'

'Far enough,' said Drinkwater grimly.

The end of the short winter's day came prematurely with an overcast that edged down from the north. Once the sun was obscured the leaden cheerlessness circumscribed their visible horizon. More snow began to fall. Their only consolation was that they were safe from pursuit, but this had its corollary in that they could see nothing.

The ebb came away at last and Drinkwater and his companions devoured the last of the food. All they had left was a mouthful of schnapps each, which they determined to preserve. The question of where their next meal was coming from no one mentioned.

Drinkwater was reasonably certain that they had entered

the secondary channel north of the New Ground which led past the Vogel Sand, but beyond that he had no idea where they were in the darkness.

They had been nearly ten hours in the punt without being able to stretch their cramped limbs and this, combined with the cold, the aches of old wounds and general fearfulness reduced their spirits to rock bottom.

To make matters worse Quilhampton was sliding in and out of consciousness and relapsing into fever. Castenada was silent, a man of undoubted courage, thought Drinkwater, but nonetheless profoundly regretting his impetuous action in joining them.

For his own part Drinkwater was suffering from a severe quinsy, the chronic pain in his distorted shoulder and the debilitating effects of having plied the oars for three days. He had no real idea where they were and, worn out with worry and exertion, he dozed off.

He woke with Castenada shaking him. The punt was aground, the pale loom of a sand hummock seemed almost totally to surround them.

'It must be low water,' he muttered, dragging himself with difficulty from the seductive desire to sleep. He had a faint notion that to sleep was to be warm . . .

'Is this Helgoland?' Castenada asked, and the ridiculous question finally dragged an unwilling Drinkwater back to his responsibilities.

'No . . . no, it ain't Helgoland, though I'm damned if I know where it is.'

With a tremendous effort he drew back the furs over his legs and forced himself to crouch. The silk stockings he wore as gloves were barely adequate to keep the cold from paralysing his hands, but somehow he levered himself so that he could swing his feet over the side.

The hessian boots leaked immediately and the freezing sand gave beneath him. He knew that at the tideline, where the water still drained from the recently uncovered sand, it was not dense enough to support any weight. Higher up though, where the sand had dried, it would bear and he floundered as quickly as he could through the dragging quicksand, taking the painter with him. He found firmer footing and dragged the punt as high as he was able, until Castenada joined him and, with Quilhampton's weight in the stern, they got it higher still.

The bare sandbank yielded no fuel but the movement restored their circulation. The pain of returning feeling was intense, beyond imagination, so that they both crouched apart on the sand, sobbing uncontrollably until it eased and they were able to act together again.

'*Dios*,' muttered Castenada speaking for both of them. 'Never, not the pain of the stone, nor sear of the brand can compare with that!'

When they had recovered, Drinkwater said, 'We must leave Quilhampton his furs, Doctor, but you and I must give up two of ours.'

'I do not understand.'

'We have fifteen leagues yet to go, across the open sea. The boat is not suitable: she is too low. If there is any wind the water will come in . . .'

'Ah, yes, I understand. You need furs to cover . . .' Castenada made draping gestures over the well of the boat with his hands.

'Yes, like an Eskimo's *kayak*, then we have a good chance. You will have shelter underneath.'

They found a long eel-line stowed in the forepart of the boat and with this and the skilleting knife they fashioned covers and passed lashing beneath the hull. Despite the risk of incoming breakers, Drinkwater decided to brave the rising tide. He knew that the tides were neap and hoped the bank they had landed on might not cover at all. If it looked like doing so they might have to make a portage to its eastern side and launch from there. Besides, he thought to himself, accepting the cogent argument of the only certainty, he was lost and he needed daylight to get his bearings.

He was certain afterwards that had they spent that night in the Elbe, fire or no, they would have perished. Their bodily reserves were almost exhausted and the cold of a land frost would undoubtedly have killed them. As it was the surrounding sea mitigated the temperature and this helped sustain them until they faced another bleak dawn.

The tide was already rising and they had to drag the punt higher and higher several times. The eel-line did not part and they decided prudence dictated they launch on the side of the bank away from the incoming breakers. They were low enough, but both men were anxious to avoid getting wetter than was absolutely necessary.

At the first light Castenada peeled off Quilhampton's dressing and sniffed the stump. Drinkwater waited for his diagnosis. He knew the slightest whiff of putrefaction signalled Quilhampton's inevitable death. His heart beating, Drinkwater bent over the exposed wound, shielding it from the cold as Castenada tugged the ligatures. Quilhampton stirred, opened his eyes and grunted as Castenada, with an appreciative hiss, drew the ligatures cleanly.

'I think his fever is not so much from this,' said the surgeon, replacing the lead acetate dressing, 'as from this . . .' He nodded about them. Quilhampton was asleep again. 'He is strong but,' Castenada clicked his tongue and shook his head, 'one more night . . . I don't know.'

The wind came up with the sun, a northerly breeze that kicked up vicious little waves and produced the low grumble of surf on the shoal.

Drinkwater knew the advancing tide would shortly cover their retreat and told Castenada they would have to make a move. Crossing himself the Spaniard nodded. They pushed the punt into the water and, wet to the knees, struggled aboard. Immediately the difference in their circumstances was obvious. They were no longer borne on the smooth, dark bosom of the Elbe; now they faced the open sea. It was more difficult to row and they realized very soon that they would make little progress under oars.

Drinkwater caught a glimpse of a distant beacon. He was certain that it was not the Kugelbacke at Cuxhaven, but could not remember how many beacons there were in the outer estuary, and though he recalled some on Neuwerk he could see no sign of the island. The beacon lay to the southward of them, and it seemed that during the early part of the night, just before they had grounded again, the ebb had carried them through one of the gullies that cut into the Vogel Sand, so that they had travelled south instead of west.

All that grey forenoon Drinkwater kept the frail craft hove-to with the northerly wind on the starboard bow and the flood tide setting them back into the Elbe.

They were too low in the water to see anything beyond the wave caps lifting on a horizon less than two miles away. Once they saw a buoy and Drinkwater tried desperately to reach it so that they could secure to it and await the ebb but the strength of the tide was against him and he was compelled to give up and it was soon lost to view. Then, some time towards noon, the sky began to clear again and the wind backed into the north-west and freshened, cutting up a rough sea that threatened, with the turn of the tide in their favour, to get far worse.

Two hours later Drinkwater lost an oar. Stupidly he watched it drift away, unable to do anything about it. Castenada said nothing. He was prostrated with sea-sickness, vomiting helplessly over the fur cover so that the wind bore the sharp stench to even Drinkwater's stupefied senses.

The punt lay a-hull, rolling its way to windward and at the same time being blown south. Darkness found them aground again, no more than a few miles from their starting-off point, having made good a course of west-south-west.

Castenada and Drinkwater floundered carelessly ashore. Their only thought was for Quilhampton and it occurred to Drinkwater in a brief moment of lucidity that they were wasting their time: Quilhampton was going to die because they were incapable of saving him.

They sat shivering on the punt listening to the delirious ramblings of their charge whilst they shared the last of the schnapps.

'In the bull-fight,' Castenada said, 'they watch to see if the bull makes a good death.'

Drinkwater nodded sagely and said, 'Scharhorn . . . this is the Scharhorn sand . . .'

He was pleased with himself for remembering the chart, and grinned into the darkness.

'That is not a good name,' said Castenada.

Drinkwater never had any recollection of the succeeding hours until waking to the grim thunder of breakers. The noise reverberated through the very sand upon which he lay and it was perhaps this appeal to his seaman's instinct that roused him from a slumber intended by nature to be his last. But this may not have been the only cause of his awakening, for a large, predatory herring gull had already drawn blood from his cheek and his sudden movement sent the bird screeching into disgruntled flight.

He sat up. It took him several minutes to fathom out his whereabouts and how he came to be lying exposed on the Scharhorn Sand. He cast about him and spotted Castenada, some distance off, and Quilhampton lying as though dead in the punt. Just beyond his friend, the white mist of spume rising over incoming breakers finally goaded him to action. The sudden fear of drowning overcame the pain of movement. He got to his feet and began to hobble towards Castenada. He tried shouting, but his quinsy and the schnapps he had drunk before his collapse made his throat dry. He began to feel the first tortures of severe thirst.

And then he saw it: not half a furlong distant, rising from the sand on a framework of massive timbers, the Scharhorn beacon.

CHAPTER 19 February–April 1810

# Refuge, Rescue and Retribution

Acting Lieutenant Frey stood beside Lieutenant O'Neal on the heeling deck of the twelve-gun cutter *Alert*. From time to time he went forward, levelled a battered telescope and scanned the horizon. It was broken at two points: by the Vogel sand to the north and the Scharhorn to the south. Beyond the Scharhorn lay the low island of Neuwerk with its stone tower and beacons. The crew of the alarm vessel marking the entrance of the River Elbe – technically the enemy – waved cheerfully as the heavily sparred cutter with its huge gaff mainsail carried the wind and tide on her daily reconnaissance into the estuary. The deck-watch on the *Alert* waved back.

Frey walked aft again and shook his head.

'Nothing?' asked O'Neal in his Ulster accent.

'Nothing,' said Frey disconsolately.

'We'll take the tide up as far as Cuxhaven,' O'Neal said encouragingly.

The incoming tide had covered the Scharhorn Sand by the time Drinkwater had got Castenada and Quilhampton up on to the massive beacon. The heavy baulks of timber tapered to a platform halfway up, access being provided by a ladder so that during the summer months carpenters from Cuxhaven could repair the ravages of the winter gales. Above the platform the structure rose further, culminating in a vertical beam of oak about which, in the form of a vast cage, the distinctive topmark was constructed.

The effort of gaining the safety of the beacon cost them all dear. The three of them lay about the platform as though dead, and it was more than an hour before coherent thoughts began to stir Drinkwater's fuddled brain from the lethargy of relief at having found a refuge. He began to contemplate the bleak acceptance of eventual defeat. He knew death was now inevitable and thirst more than cold and exposure was to be its agent. They were still reasonably well provided for against the cold, having salvaged all the furs and blankets from the punt. Damp though they were, the furs provided a windbreak and some means of conserving their body heat. They were already thirsty and the task of dragging Quilhampton and their own unwilling bodies up the beacon made it worse.

It was not long before Drinkwater could think of nothing other than slaking his burning throat. His tongue began to feel thick and leathery, and his head ached. The more the desire for water increased, the more fidgety he found he became, fretting irritably, moving about and eventually standing up, clinging shakily to an upright and staring wildly round about them. He could see to the east the low island of Neuwerk with its tower and beacons, and beyond it the masts and yards of two or three anchored ships. Slowly, almost uncomprehendingly, he swung his red-rimmed eyes to the north.

The cutter was about two miles away, its mainsail boomed out as it ran east into the mouth of the Elbe. With despairing recognition he took it for the Dutch customs cruiser. Only after a few minutes did he realize the cutter had no lee boards, that the stem was ramrod straight, not curved, and the long running bowsprit was of an unmistakably English rig. He had been deceived! The foreshortened mainsail had given the impression of having the short narrow head of Dutch fashion, but this was no Netherlander, this was a British naval cutter, and now he could see the blue ensign at her peak as she passed on her way upstream toward Cuxhaven.

Hope beat again in his breast.

*

'They haven't gone up river yet, then,' said O'Neal, standing beside the two men leaning on the *Alert*'s tiller and nodding at the three ships anchored in Neuwerk Road.

'No,' said Frey, 'and that bodes no good for Captain Drinkwater.'

It was common knowledge at Helgoland, now that Littlewood had brought back the *Ocean* and the *Galliwasp* and Frey and his men had arrived in a stolen sailing barge, that a grand deception had been carried out against the French. It had never been Drinkwater's intention that all the ships of the abandoned convoy should be used to deceive the enemy. Under the terms of the agreement with Thiebault, they were to have gone only as far as Neuwerk, there to await the release of *Ocean* and *Galliwasp*, a tempting surety for the good behaviour of the French.

Drinkwater's failure to appear; the complications arising from the appearance of *Tracker*'s survivors and unbeknown to Nicholas, Hamilton and Littlewood at Helgoland, the temporary interdiction on trade imposed by Thiebault as a result of Davout's arrival, meant that the ships had remained anchored off Neuwerk under enemy guns.

O'Neal studied them through his glass. 'The Yankee colours are all flying hauled close-up,' he observed, the precaution of having them fly their American colours on slack halliards having been adopted as a secret signal that things were not well on board.

A tiny puff of white smoke appeared on the island and a ball plunged into the sea two cables on their starboard bow. The ritual shot had been fired at them every time they sailed into the estuary, but providing the cutter's reconnoitring sorties did no more than establish the emptiness of the river, they were otherwise unopposed. After an hour when they were well within sight of the Kugel beacon and the lighthouse at Cuxhaven, O'Neal shook his head. 'Damn all!'

'Aye . . .'

O'Neal raised his voice. 'Stand by to put about! Heads'l sheets there! Mainsheet! Bosun, stand by the running back-stays!' He waited for his crew to run to their stations, then ordered, 'Down helm.'

With a brief thunder of flogging canvas the *Alert* came round to larboard, passed her bowsprit through the wind and paid off on the starboard tack.

'Now she'll feel the wind,' said O'Neal as the course was steadied and the sheets were hove down hard. Regular showers of spray rose over the weather bow and O'Neal studied a shore transit he had noted.

'She's lee bowing it,' he remarked, 'ebb's away already.'

Drinkwater never took his eyes off the distant cutter and the moment he saw her turn he descended to the platform from the upper part of the beacon from which he had been watching her. Ignoring Castenada's half-witted protests Drinkwater gathered up the blankets. He wished he had the means of making a fire, but all thought of coaxing a spark from the sodden horse pistol lock was, he knew, a waste of time.

Laboriously climbing the beacon he sat and joined the blankets, corner to corner, then streamed the improvised flag from as high as he could reach, managing to catch a knotted corner of his extempore hoist in a crack in the timber topmark. The distress signal flew out to leeward, a stained patchwork of irregular shape.

Drinkwater leaned his hot and aching head on the weathered oak of the Scharhorn beacon, closed his eyes and hoped.

Frey saw the signal, staring at the beacon for a few seconds before he realized the distortion to its topmark. His heart skipped as he raised the glass and caught in its leaping lens the flutter of the blankets.

'D'ye see there?' he pointed. 'Distress signal! Port Beam!'

'Down helm! Luff her, haul the stays'l sheet a'weather!' O'Neal responded instantly to Frey's shout. 'Where away?' he asked, as soon as the *Alert* had come up into the wind, lost way and fallen off again, neatly hove-to and edging slowly to leeward.

'There, sir! On that damned beacon!'

'Very well. Get the stern boat away. You take her Frey, and mind the ebb o' the tide over that bank!'

Drinkwater saw the boat bobbing across the water towards the beacon. For a moment he stood stupidly inactive, his eyes misting with relief. With an effort he pulled himself together and stiffly descended again to the platform dragging the lowered blankets after him.

He tried waking the others but his throat was swollen and the noise he made was no more than an ineffectual croak. His head hurt and he found he could do little except watch the boat approach, his body wracked by shuddering sobs.

He had mastered his nervous reaction by the time Frey reached him, but it took him some time to recognize his former midshipman.

'Mr Frey? Is that you? You succeeded then, eh?' Drinkwater's voice was barely more than a whisper.

'Are you all right, sir?' Frey asked, his face showing deep concern at Captain Drinkwater's appearance. He waved for reinforcements from the boat and by degrees Quilhampton was lowered into it, bruised by further buffeting to his battered frame. Awkward and stumbling, Castenada and Drinkwater finally succeeded in getting aboard, and they began the journey back to the cutter.

The sea ran smooth over the bank, but where the retreating tide flowed into the channel a line of vicious little breakers briefly threatened them. At Frey's order the oarsmen doubled their efforts and they broke through the barrier to the open water beyond. Shortly afterwards they bumped alongside *Alert*'s black tumble-home. Hands reached down and dragged Drinkwater and Castenada up on to the cutter's neatly ordered deck. A strange officer confronted Drinkwater, his hand to the forecock of his bicorne hat.

''Tis good to be seein' you at last, sir,' he said smiling. 'We've been beatin' up and down for days now, lookin' for you. O'Neal's the name, sir.'

'I'm very much obliged to you, Mr O'Neal, very much

obliged,' Drinkwater croaked. 'Mr Quilhampton here needs a masthead whip to get him aboard . . .'

Drinkwater could remember nothing after that, nothing at least beyond slaking his inordinate thirst and finally sinking into the sleep of utter exhaustion.

Lieutenant James Quilhampton woke to the sound of the wind. Above his head he could see exposed rafters and the underside of rattling tiles. The wind played among the cobwebs that strung about the rough, worm-eaten timbers, giving them a dolourous life of their own, an effect heightened by the leaping shadows thrown by a pair of candles that guttered somewhere in the room.

Quilhampton shifted his head. The walls were whitewashed, or had been a long time ago. Now flakes of the distemper curled from the damp walls and patches of grey mould disfigured the crude attempt at disguising the stone masonry. He located the candles on a table at the foot of his narrow bed. A man was asleep at it, head on hands, his face turned away. A long queue lay over the arm upon which his head rested. The hair was dark brown, shot with grey, and tied with a black ribbon.

Quilhampton frowned. 'Sir? Is that you?'

Drinkwater stirred and looked up, his face gaunt, the old scar and the powder burns about his left eye prominent against the pale skin.

'Aye, it's me.' Drinkwater smiled, yawned, stretched and hauled himself to his feet. He kicked back his chair and came and stood beside Quilhampton.

'More to the point, James, is that you?'

'I'm sorry . . . ?' Quilhampton frowned.

'You've been talking a lot of drivel these last few days, I wondered – we all wondered – whether you were lost to us.'

'Where am I?' Quilhampton's eyes roved about the room again.

'Safe. You're on Helgoland, in the old Danish barracks . . . No, no, don't fret yourself, they ain't Danish anymore. They're the property of His Majesty King George . . .'

'King George . . . yes, yes, of course, foolish of me.'

'And you ain't to worry about that court martial, my dear fellow. I've been taking sworn affidavits from Frey and your people.'

Quilhampton nodded. 'That's most kind of you, sir.' He managed a wan smile. 'It's a pity you made me write to Mistress MacEwan pressing my suit.'

'Why?'

'I'll have to write again . . . she'll not want a man who hasn't – '

'I can't answer for Mistress MacEwan, James,' Drinkwater broke in, unwilling to allow his friend to subject himself to such morbid thoughts, 'but I'm damned if I'll have you considerin' such things until you're up and about. Castenada said if you got over the secondary fever, you had a fair chance of walking within a month. We'll make all our decisions then, eh?'

'You'll stay here for a month, sir?'

'Just at the moment, James. There's a March gale roaring its confounded head off out there, so we have precious little choice!'

Hearing the reassuring words, Quilhampton nodded and closed his eyes. He did not hear the note of impatience in Drinkwater's voice.

'I do not think I shall have any difficulty in persuading the Governor, my dear sir,' said Nicholas smiling at Drinkwater, 'none at all.'

'Very well. We need to conclude the matter, and as long as those three ships lie in limbo off Neuwerk . . .'

'Quite so, quite so,' Nicholas eyed the glass and its contents before passing Drinkwater the glass of oporto. 'Despatched by the Marquis of Wellesley, Canning's replacement at the Foreign Department,' he said with evident satisfaction, 'doubtless a tribute to his brother's successes in the peninsula . . .'

'And of his approbation at your, or am I permitted to say *our*, little achievement?' asked Drinkwater, raising the glass.

'Ah, sir, you mock me.'

'A little, perhaps.'

'Your good health, Captain.'

'And yours, Mr Nicholas.'

They sipped the port in unembarrassed silence, Drinkwater still studying the chart spread out before them, and in particular the Scharhorn Sand surrounding the island of Neuwerk. He wanted to return, to lay the ghosts of the Elbe that still haunted his dreams and to release the three transports from their anchorage under the French guns before Davout's proposed absence from Hamburg encouraged M. Thiebault to order them up the Elbe.

They were the ships that were to have stood surety for Thiebault's bond, the guarantee that he and Gilham and Littlewood would retire downstream, paid and unmolested. They and their crews had waited patiently until Drinkwater's release, expecting their 'recapture' daily, but a series of strong westerly winds and vicious gales had postponed the operation until the end of March.

'Of course you may not find things as easy as you assume, Captain,' Nicholas said guardedly.

'What d'you mean, sir?'

'While you were ill, two boats got off. One brought a secret despatch from Liepmann. He had it on good authority . . .'

'Thiebault?' enquired Drinkwater quickly.

Nicholas shrugged. 'Presumably, but there were what he called *inexplicable* rumours of a rift between Paris and Petersburg that were of a sufficiently serious nature as to suggest war was being contemplated, at least in Paris.'

'Good Lord! Then we succeeded better than I imagined; but how does this affect the meditated attack?' He flipped the back of his hand on the chart.

'It is also reported, Captain, that reinforcements have arrived in Hamburg, to wit, Molitor's Division, about nine thousand strong. Cuxhaven has received a reinforcement, so has Brunsbuttel . . .'

'The westerlies will have kept reinforcements from Neuwerk as surely as they have mewed us up here, I'm sure of it.'

'I trust you are correct, Captain, but I would be guilty of a dereliction of duty if I did not appraise you of the facts.' Nicholas held out the decanter. 'Another glass, and then we'll go and see Colonel Hamilton.'

'Very well, Mr O'Neal,' Drinkwater called to the dark figure looming expectantly at the *Alert*'s taffrail, 'you may cast us off!'

The huge, quadrilateral mainsail of the cutter, black against the first light of the April dawn, began to diminish in size as the *Alert* drew away from the four boats she had been towing. They bobbed in her wake while their crews settled themselves at their pulling stations.

'Mr Browne?' Drinkwater called.

'All ready, sir,' replied the old harbour-master.

'Mr McCullock?'

'Ready, sir,' the transport officer called back.

'Mr Frey?'

'Ready, sir.'

'Line ahead, give way in order of sailing.' Drinkwater nodded to the midshipman beside him. 'Very well, Mr Martin, give way.'

'Give way toooo-gether!'

The oar looms came forward and then strong arms tugged at them; the blades bit the water, lifted clear, flew forward and dipped again. Soon the rhythmic knocking of the oars in the pins grew steady and hypnotic.

Involuntarily Drinkwater shivered. He would never again watch men pulling an oar without the return of that nightmare of pain and cold, of ceaseless leaning and pulling, leaning and pulling. He recalled very little detail of their flight down the Elbe, almost nothing of the desperate skirmish with Dieudonné on the ice or the struggle to get Quilhampton into the comparative shelter of the Scharhorn beacon. What was indelibly etched into his memory was his remorseless task at the oars, which culminated in his stupidly losing one and nearly rendering all their efforts useless.

He kept telling himself the nightmare was over now, that

he had paid off the debt he owed fate and that he had received a private absolution in receiving Quilhampton back from the grave. But he could not throw off the final shadows of his megrims until he had released the three transports and all their people were safely back in an English anchorage.

He turned and looked astern. In the growing light he could see the other three boats. Two – McCullock's and Browne's – were the large harbour barges, one of which had welcomed them to Helgoland when *Galliwasp* had run on the reef, the third was the *Alert*'s longboat and the fourth a boat supplied by the merchant traders, commanded by Frey and manned by the vengeful remnants of *Tracker*'s crew. A handful of volunteers from the Royal Veterans commanded by Lieutenant Dowling were deployed among the boats.

Drinkwater led the column in *Alert*'s longboat. Wrapped in his cloak, Drinkwater stared ahead, leaving the business of working inshore to Mr Midshipman Martin, a young protégé of Lieutenant O'Neal's. He was aware of O'Neal's anger at being displaced from the chief command of the boat expedition, pleading that the matter was not properly the duty of a post-captain. But Drinkwater had silenced the Orangeman with a curt order that his talents were better employed standing off and on in support.

'You can run up the channel in our wake, Mr O'Neal, and blood your guns, provided you fire over our heads and distract the enemy from our intentions,' he said. Remembering this conversation he turned again. The big cutter had gone about and was now working round from the position at which she let go the boats and ran up towards Cuxhaven. O'Neal had brought her back downstream and would soon shift his sheets and scandalize his mainsail, ready to creep up in the wake of the boats, into the anchorage off Neuwerk.

'See 'em ahead, sir!'

The lookout reported the sighting from the longboat's bow in a low voice and Drinkwater nodded as Martin repeated the report.

He could see them himself now, their masts and yards clear against the pale yellow sky. They lay at anchor in line.

'Lay us alongside the headmost ship, Mr Martin if you please.'

'Aye, aye, sir.'

Drinkwater felt a worm of fear writhe in his belly. He was almost glad to feel again the qualms that beset every man before action, the fear of death and loneliness, no matter what his situation, how exalted his rank, or how many of his confederates crowded about him. It was a familiar feeling and brought a curious, lop-sided contentment, infinitely preferable to the anxieties of a spy. He eased his shoulders under the cloak and plain, borrowed coat. He was still not in uniform, but there was no longer any doubt about who and what he was.

They were seen by an alert guard aboard the transport *Anne*, a French guard put aboard by order from Hamburg with the object of securing the defecting British ships against the moment when Marshal Davout either relaxed his embargo on trade or decided to inspect a distant corps. His shout stirred an already wakening anchorage and the bugler on Neuwerk, about to sound reveille, blew instead the sharp notes of the alarm.

'Put your backs into it!' roared Drinkwater, exhorting his men; they might yet arrive with some of the advantage of surprise. He swung round at Martin as the midshipman put his tiller over to take a wide sweep around the *Anne*. 'Keep straight on, damn it!'

They heeled as Martin corrected his course and pulled past the first of the anchored ships. A single musket ball struck the boat's gunwhale, but they were past before the sentry had a chance to reload.

There was more activity aboard the *Hannah* but she too was astern before damage could be done to them. The *Delia* lay ahead now, already swinging to the wind as the flood tide that had brought them reached the brief hiatus of high water.

Suddenly pinpoints of yellow fire sparkled along the *Delia*'s rail. Musket balls struck the longboat and sent up the spurts of near misses all about them. In the centre of the boat a man was struck in the chest. He let go his oar and upset the stroke.

His convulsion of agony came with gasps of pain and with thrashing legs he fell from his thwart. There was a moment's confusion as his trailing oar was disentangled, then order was restored.

'A steady pull, lads,' called Drinkwater, relieved now the action had started. 'Five more good strokes and we'll be alongside.'

With the exception of the centre thwart where the mortally wounded man lay cradled in his mate's arms, the men plied their oars vigorously, knowing they had a few seconds before the French reloaded.

'Stand-by forrard!' shouted Midshipman Martin. 'Hook on!'

The *Alert*'s longboat bumped against the side of the transport *Delia*.

'Boarders away!' Drinkwater bawled, standing in the wildly rocking boat as most of her crew leapt up and reached for the main chains. He heaved himself up with cracking arm muscles, kicked his feet until he found a foothold, then drew himself up on to the platform of the chainwhale. He saw the dull gleam of a bayonet, got one foot on to the *Delia*'s rail and drew the hanger Hamilton had lent him. The infantry officer's weapon was light as a foil, but the clash with the heavy bayonet jarred him. He was clutching a shroud with his left hand and he let his body swing, absorbing the impact of the sentry's lunge. Disengaging his blade, he jabbed at the man's face. Instinctively the soldier drew back and Drinkwater flung himself over the rail and down on to the deck.

He was still weak from the ague he had succumbed to after the rigours of his escape and he landed awkwardly, his legs buckling beneath him, but others were about him now and the guard retreated aft, looking round for support from his confederates who were tumbling up from below in disordered dress. There were less than a dozen of them, but they were led by an officer, an elderly man with a bayonet scar sliced deep into his cheek. He gave a curt order and the muskets came up to the present.

'Charge!' Drinkwater bellowed, recovering his footing and running aft amid the fire of muskets and pistols. As his men came over the rail they discharged their firearms simultaneously with the enemy. There was a moment of flashes, cracks and buzzing, the cries of wounded men and then the two sides clashed together in hand-to-hand fighting.

The grizzled infantry lieutenant shuffled forward with the cautious confidence of the old warrior. He feinted with his heavy sword and Drinkwater felt the weight of it with a foolish, unnecessary parry. The Frenchman whipped his blade away, cut over Drinkwater's sword and lunged, at the same time slicing the blade of his weapon.

Had Drinkwater not held Hamilton's hanger his recovery would have been too late, but he was cool now, he had passed through the veil of fighting madness that had drawn from him the superfluous parry. He half turned, cannoned into another body, and in the second's respite had shortened his sword arm and jabbed the hanger with all his strength.

The French officer fell against him with a terrible gasp and Drinkwater recoiled, the man's body smell, mixed with the warm reek of blood, filling his nostrils. The French officer's sword clattered to the deck, the man dropped to his knees, then fell full length. Hamilton's hanger blade snapped off and Drinkwater was left stupidly holding the hilt and three inches of the *forte*.

Somebody lurched into him, he swung, confronted Martin and realized the thing was accomplished. The handful of Frenchmen remaining on their feet threw their muskets on the deck in token of surrender. Five of their fellow infantrymen lay dead or severely wounded, sprawled across the hatch and deck, and although one of their attackers writhed in noisy agony and three lay dead from their first volley, it was the death of their officer which persuaded them that further resistance was useless.

'Where are the crew?' Drinkwater snarled. '*Ou est les matelots Americaines?*' The Frenchmen pointed at the gratings covering the after hatchway.

'Get 'em out, Mr Martin!'

One of the sentries stepped forward and began to speak rapidly. Drinkwater could not understand a word but the meaning of the man's request was clear: to be left on Neuwerk, not taken prisoner.

'Put 'em under guard, Mr Martin!' He turned to the men scrambling out of the 'tween deck. 'Where's the master?'

'He's hostage ashore, sir.'

'God's bones! What about the mate?'

'Here, sir!'

'Get her under way. Cut your cable and make sail, the tide's just on the turn and the *Alert* cutter is in the offing! Mr Martin, get those prisoners in the boat, then –'

Drinkwater's order was lost in the boom of a cannon and a crash amidships where the ball struck home. Drinkwater ran to the rail, raised his hands and shouted at the adjacent vessel, '*Hannah* ahoy! Have you taken the ship?'

'Aye, sir, an' we've eight prisoners!' That was Browne's voice.

'Send 'em over in your boat, d'ye hear?'

A second and third crash came from the battery ashore but Drinkwater doggedly continued his conversation. 'Have you word from the *Anne*?'

'A moment, Cap'n!'

Browne turned away so that Drinkwater could not hear what he said, but a faint call from the farthest ship was, he thought, Frey's voice. It was almost full daylight now and he could see a man standing in the *Anne*'s rigging.

'That you there, sir?' Browne too was visible at the *Hannah*'s rail.

'Aye?'

'She's taken. They've eight men too.'

'Where's McCullock's boat?'

'Here sir, just come from the *Anne* to confirm Browne's report. We've the three o' them in the bag, sir.'

'Not yet we haven't. I'm not leavin' those Masters ashore. Do you pick up all the prisoners and follow me. All your men load their pieces. I'm going in to parley.' He turned and shouted orders at Martin then, seeing the mate of the *Delia* had a man hacking at the anchor cable with an axe and had the transport's main topsail in its clewlines he scrambled after

Martin down into the longboat. A ball plunged into the water close to Browne's barge into which his prisoners were being forced and which still lay alongside the *Hannah*.

In the longboat, facing the downcast French guard from the *Delia* with musket and fixed bayonet, sat a private of the Royal Veterans.

'Be so kind as to lend me your ramrod,' Drinkwater requested, holding out his hand, fishing with the other beneath his own coat-tails. Drawing a white handkerchief from his pocket, Drinkwater knotted it about the private's ramrod.

Having gathered together the three boats loaded with the disarmed French, Drinkwater waved his improvised flag of truce and ordered Martin to pull inshore. From a low breastwork the flash and smoke of cannon fire continued, the scream of the shot passing overhead was followed by the thunder of the discharge rolling across the water. The noise of the shots hitting or falling short came from astern, only to be answered by the crack of *Alert*'s light six-pounders.

Drinkwater turned in alarm. O'Neal had worked his little ship well into the anchorage and already the *Anne* had escaped [illegible] which was drawing up towards the *Hannah* and the *Delia*. Both vessels had hoisted their false, American colours, a shrewd though quite useless attempt to deter the artillerymen ashore. But Drinkwater had observed from the fall of O'Neal's shot that having mistaken their purpose, that zealous officer was directing his own cannon at the three boats pulling quickly towards the island.

'God's bones!' Drinkwater blasphemed, turning to Martin, 'Stand up, man, he might recognize you if he's looking, and wave this damned flag!'

The next moment the three boats were lost amongst a welter of splashes as shot from both sides plunged into the sea around them. An oar was shivered with an explosion of splinters and then, as if comprehension dawned simultaneously upon the opposing gunners, fire ceased and the boats emerged, miraculously unscathed, except for the loss of the single oar.

A few moments later, as with canvas flogging O'Neal tacked

the *Alert* and stood slowly seaward again, Drinkwater's boat led close inshore.

'Here,' he said, seizing the flag of truce from the shaken Martin, 'I'll take that now.'

Drinkwater stood up and braced himself. 'Very well, Mr Martin, that'll do.'

'Oars!' ordered the midshipman. The tired seamen brought their oars horizontal and bent over the looms, leaning on their arms and gasping for breath. The other boats followed suit and the three of them glided closer to the beach. Drinkwater could see the shakoed heads of artillerymen above the island's defences.

'*Messieurs*,' Drinkwater cried in his appalling French, '*donnez moi les maitres des vaisseaux Americaines. J'ai votre soldats . . . votre amis pour* . . .' he faltered, and added 'exchange!'

A discontented murmur rose momentarily among the prisoners before Drinkwater snuffed it out with a harsh, 'Silence!' For a minute nothing happened, then an officer scrambled over the low parapet of the breastwork. They watched him walk, ungainly and bowlegged, through the sand of the foreshore towards the tideline.

Drinkwater nodded at the man who had disclosed the whereabouts of the *Delia*'s crew. '*Vous parlez, m'sieur* . . .' he commanded.

After a few moments of animated conversation between the two men, in which several other prisoners attempted to intervene until Martin suppressed them, the officer tramped back up the beach, leaning in through an embrasure. A further wait ensued. Looking seawards, Drinkwater saw that O'Neal had brought the *Alert* round and the cutter's large bowsprit again pointed at Neuwerk as she stood inshore once more.

'I hope Mr O'Neal has a man in the chains, Mr Martin,' Drinkwater observed, indicating the approaching cutter, 'we can't afford to have him aground now the tide's fallin'.'

Martin screwed up his eyes and stared at his ship. 'I can see a leadsman, sir.'

Drinkwater grunted. 'Your eyes are better than mine.' He turned his attention back to the beach; the artillery officer was returning. At the water's edge he stopped and nodded, the plume of his shako bobbing.

'*D'accord . . .*'

'Run her ashore, Mr Martin,' Drinkwater said, sitting down as he saw the first of the British masters emerging through the embrasure. 'Not a bad morning's work, eh? Squares our account, in a manner of speakin'.'

CHAPTER 20 April–August 1810

# Outrageous Fortune

'So,' said Lord Dungarth, drawing the stoppers, 'we somewhat gilded the lily did we not? Oporto or Madeira?'

Drinkwater poured the *bual* and passed the decanters to Solomon. The Jew gracefully declined and returned them to their host.

'Insofar as my sojourn amongst the stews of Wapping was concerned,' said Drinkwater, pausing to sip the rich amber wine, 'yes.'

'It was essential to contact Fagan,' Dungarth said, 'though your interview with Marshal Davout clinched the matter. There was no harm in dissembling at the lowest level . . .'

'It was without doubt the very nadir of my self-esteem, my Lord. I'd be obliged if future commissions were of a less clandestine nature. A ship, perhaps . . .' Drinkwater deliberately left the sentence unfinished.

'A ship you shall have, my dear fellow, without a doubt, but first a month or two of the furlough you have undoubtedly earned by your exertions.'

'I shall hold you to that, my Lord, with Mr Solomon here as witness.'

They smiled and Dungarth sent the Madeira round again. 'I have taught you the business of intrigue too well.'

'It is not a type of service I warm to,' Drinkwater said pointedly. 'However, from what Nicholas reported was said at Hamburg, we succeeded.'

'Oh, *you* succeeded, Nathaniel, beyond my wildest hopes.' Dungarth's hazel eyes twinkled in the candlelight and it was clear he was withholding something. Drinkwater felt mildly irritated by his Lordship's condescension. He was not sure he had endured the ice of the Elbe to be toyed with, cat and mouse.

'May I enquire how, my Lord?' he asked drily. 'I presume from the papers Madame Santhonax . . .'

'I shall come to those in a moment. But now we have heard your story there is much we have to relate to you. Pray be patient, my dear fellow.' Dungarth's arch tone was full of wry amusement and Drinkwater, made indulgent by a third glass of *bual*, submitted resignedly.

'Your chief and most immediate success,' Dungarth resumed, 'lies with Fagan. His office as a go-between was discovered by Napoleon and used to compromise Fouché. The ignoble Duke of Otranto, by his bold initiative in raising an army to confront us on the Scheldt, has ably demonstrated that the French Empire may easily be usurped. Alarmed, his Imperial Majesty, having discovered Fouché had sent an agent to London, took Draconian action. The agent was Fagan. He arrived here last week. Before the week was out Fouché had been dismissed!'

'A malicious and fitting move by the Emperor,' said Solomon raising his eyebrows and nodding slowly. 'Almost proof that Bonaparte knew it was Fagan who first reported a trade opening between London and St Petersburg.'

Dungarth barked a short laugh. 'An engaging fancy,' he said, 'and knowing Nathaniel has a misplaced belief in these things, there is something else I should tell him, something more closely concerning his person.'

'My Lord . . . ?'

'You mentioned the widow Santhonax . . .' Dungarth said pausing, 'and Isaac says you spoke of her at his house, intimating she might be behind my, er, accident . . .'

'*Dux femina facti*,' prompted Solomon.

'What of her, my Lord?' Drinkwater asked impatiently, suddenly uncomfortable at this mention of Hortense. 'I have related all that passed between us at Hamburg and Altona. Whether or not she finally informed on me, I have no way of knowing. Why else was Dieudonné so placed to intercept us?' He sighed. 'But I am also of the opinion that she gave me what she considered was time enough to make good my escape.'

'I incline to your conjoint theory, Nathaniel,' Dungarth said, suddenly serious, his bantering tone dismissed. 'It is almost certain that she now enjoys some measure of the Emperor's favour, perhaps because Napoleon has divorced Josephine and married the Austrian Archduchess Marie-Louise. Doubtless he wishes pliable Frenchwomen to surround the new Empress, for the beautiful widow has been appointed to the Empress's household.'

'No doubt Talleyrand approves of the arrangement,' Drinkwater observed, 'but what of the papers she passed to me? If we are correct she took an enormous risk. Were they false?'

'Not at all! She is a bold woman and clearly placed great reliance on your own character. In fact they were proposals from Talleyrand himself, concerning the future constitution and government of France, proposals that he wishes me to lay before the cabinet *and* M'sieur Le Comte de Provence,* on the assumption that the days of Napoleon are numbered . . .'

'And that if Fouché can achieve what almost amounts to a *coup d'etat*, then others can too.' Drinkwater completed Dungarth's exposition.

Dungarth smiled. 'Yes. Either with an assassin's dagger or another campaign.'

'A Russian campaign, for instance,' added Solomon, drawing a folded and sealed paper from his breast.

It surprised Captain Drinkwater that St Peter's church was so full. The good people of Petersfield had certainly turned out *en masse* for the occasion. They shuffled and stared at him as he led Elizabeth and their children up the aisle.

Pausing to usher his children into the pew he cast his eyes over the congregation. Curious faces disappeared behind

* Later Louis XVIII after the Bourbon restoration and at this time resident in England.

unstudied prayer books and mouths gossiped in whispers under the tilted brims of Sunday bonnets. He suppressed a smile. Many of the assembly had come out of devotion to his wife and her friend, Louise Quilhampton, whose efforts in starting a school for the children of the townsfolk and farm labourers had finally earned the formal approval of the Church of England.

Drinkwater nodded at the gentry settled on their rented benches and followed young Richard into the pew. A woman opposite in an extravagant hat smiled amiably at him and, after a moment, he recalled her as the bride's aunt with whom he had once shared a journey in a mail coach. Richard, the down of adolescence forming on his upper lip, wriggled beside him and he put a restraining hand on the boy's knee. His son looked up and smiled. He had forgotten Richard had Elizabeth's eyes. Beyond him, Charlotte Amelia was nudging her brother, handing him a hymn book in which she indicated the number of the first hymn.

'I know,' the boy whispered, picking up his own copy. Drinkwater looked over their heads and caught his wife's eye. She looked radiantly happy, smiling at him, her eyes misty.

He smiled back, his mind suddenly – disloyally – filled with a vision of Hortense looking at him in the intimacy of Herr Liepmann's withdrawing room. Was he the same man? Had that event *really* occurred? He could no longer be sure, knowing only that he had thought of her intermittently ever since the conversation at Lord Dungarth's when his lordship had imparted the knowledge that the widow Santhonax was a lady-in-waiting to the Empress Marie-Louise. Nor did circumstances allow him to forget her, for had not the newspapers made much of the fire at the Austrian Ambassador's grand ball? Held by Prince Schwarzenberg in honour of the Imperial wedding, the festivities had been ruined by a disastrous fire in which the prince had lost his sister-in-law and others had been killed or maimed.

He found himself unable to shake off the conviction that Hortense had had some part to play in the dreadful event.

He was rudely recalled to the present by the viols and the

cello screeching and groaning at one another as the orchestra tuned up. Then the general muttering swelled and heads turned as the groom and best man marched in. A satisfied murmur greeted Quilhampton and Frey who were resplendent in the blue, white and gold of full dress and strode in step, the muted click of sword hangings accompanying their progress to the chancel. The left cuff of Quilhampton's dress coat was stitched across his breast. He exchanged glances with his mother, Louise, who sniffled worthily into a cambric handkerchief. Drinkwater thought of tying a white handkerchief to a ramrod and waving it above his head.

The rector made his appearance and slowly the noise from the congregation subsided as they waited for the bride.

Quilhampton looked back towards the porch and Drinkwater marked the pallor of his face. He still bore the marks of his ordeal and appeared as drawn as he had during his court martial. Mercifully, it had been a brief affair held aboard the *Royal William* at Portsmouth. Drinkwater had occupied his time on Helgoland in securing sworn statements about the handling of His Majesty's brig *Tracker* and had drawn up a defence for the judge-advocate to read to the court. He had prevailed too, upon Lord Dungarth, to minute the Admiralty to note on the court's papers that the brig had been employed upon a 'special service'.

Quilhampton's surrendered sword had been returned to him with the court's warmest approbation, but James's smile of relief had been wan, as though other matters weighed more heavily upon his mind. Perhaps it was the verdict of his bride he most dreaded, Drinkwater thought, watching him turn anxiously towards the porch.

Catriona MacEwan entered on the arm of her uncle. She was a tall, striking young woman with a mane of red-gold hair piled under her flat bonnet and a dusting of not unbecoming freckles over her nose. The necks of the congregation craned as one, and the sigh of satisfaction was audible as she caught sight of the thin, awkward man at the far end of the aisle and smiled.

The orchestra sawed its way into sudden life, joined by the

congregation. 'Rejoice, the Lord is King . . .' they boomed, 'Your Lord and King adore . . . !'

'Dearly beloved,' the rector intoned, 'we are gathered together in the sight of God, and in the face of this congregation, to join together this man and this woman in Holy Matrimony . . .'

'I hope they will be happy.'

'Yes.'

'They deserve it, after so long a time.'

'Yes.'

'It has been a long time for us too, my dear, far too long.'

'I know . . . I . . .' Drinkwater faltered, looking at Elizabeth as she sat on her side of the bed. She waited for him to finish his sentence, but he shook his head. He had been home a week but they were finding great difficulty in renewing their intimacy; both of them were guarded and uncertain, wrapped in their own diverse worlds and avoiding each other by pleading the unspoken excuse of preparations for Quilhampton's wedding. There was so much to say that Drinkwater felt the task quite beyond him.

'I keep thinking we are different people now.' she whispered, holding out her hand to him and drawing him down beside her.

'Yes, I know. So do I . . .'

Perhaps that was a starting point; they had that much in common . . .

He *had* to tell her, had to tell her everything; about all that had happened in the forests of Borneo; of his dark forebodings and the impossibility of seeing her when he had returned from the Indies; about the pathetic eagerness with which he had embraced Dungarth's secret mission and how it had misfired; how the *Tracker* was surrendered and Quilhampton lost his arm; of the whore Zenobia and the Jews, Liepmann and Solomon. He wanted to tell her of the meeting with Davout and the execution of Johannes; but most of all he wanted to tell her about Hortense . . .

Long after they had found each other again he lay awake

while Elizabeth slept beside him. He knew he could never share all of these things, that they were his own soul's burden and that he must bear them silently until his death.

Listening to his wife's gentle breathing, he thought perhaps it did not greatly matter. In time, providence balanced all accounts.

Tomorrow he could share with her what he knew would please her. It struck him as perversely ridiculous that he had delayed telling her, but the moment had never seemed right. Besides, it had taken him some time to grasp the significance of the contents of Isaac Solomon's document, the paper passed to him after dinner the night he and the Jewish merchant had dined with Lord Dungarth.

It was an outrageous quirk of fortune that the gold should have realized so much. Sold and shrewdly invested by Solomon in a mysterious speculation, it had realized almost three thousand pounds. He had become, if not a rich man, a person of some independence.

The strange parcel arrived by the hand of an Admiralty messenger. Drinkwater thought at first it was a chart and, for fear of upsetting Elizabeth with so early a receipt of orders, took it aside and opened it privately. The oiled wrapping peeled back to reveal a familiar roll of canvas, the edges of which were frayed. He recognized it instantly. With a beating heart he unrolled it. The paint crackled and flakes lifted from its abused surface.

Its appearance shocked him from a far greater disfigurement than mere neglect: down the side of the painted cheek, from ear to chin, the beautiful face was ruined by a deliberately applied brown stain.

With a shaking hand Drinkwater picked up a small sheet of paper that fell from the centre of the roll. It was in Lord Dungarth's hand and was undated.

*My Dear Nathaniel,*

*The Enclosed comes from Paris via Fagan. It seems the Lady*

*was Disfigured in the Fire at the Austrian Ambassador's Rout. He was Asked to Ensure you Received it.*
*Dungarth*

Drinkwater stared at the smeared mark. It was dried blood.

'God's bones,' he whispered, placing the roll of canvas in the grate. Fetching flint and steel he lit a candle and, squatting down, applied the flame to the corner of the portrait. The oil locked in the paint ignited and crackled with a volley of tiny explosions as the flames licked up the frayed strands, laying a smear of soot over the poor, ruined face. Standing, Drinkwater watched it burn until only a charred heap of ash lay at his feet.

# Author's Note

The years 1809–1811 mark the turning point in what, until 1914, was called the Great War. Trafalgar and Austerlitz matched the sea power of Great Britain against the land power of the Napoleonic French Empire. With Russia allied to France and the Continental System in place, Napoleon was in a commanding position. By 1809 Britain had begun the long slog of the Peninsular War in support of the Spanish insurrection and was also attempting to liberate Antwerp whose occupation by the French had been the cause of war in 1793. The resulting Walcheren expedition was a disaster: it formed the prime cause of Castlereagh's notorious duel with Canning and brought down the Portland ministry. By 1811, Napoleon's restlessness drove him out of this stalemate. Russia had been disregarding the embargo of trade with Britain, and the Tsar, his country's economy in ruins, finally formalized his intention to leave the Continental System by *ukase* on the last day of 1810. Worse, Napoleon's brother Louis, King of Holland, connived at its evasion and the Emperor annexed his kingdom in mid-1810.

On the other side of the Channel there had been bad harvests in 1809 and 1810, there were numerous bankruptcies and the Luddites were destroying industrial machinery. Both sides suffered from an unprecedented economic crisis in 1811.

However a confident Napoleon, who had secured his succession through his divorce of Josephine and subsequent

Austrian marriage, thought his marshals able to deal with Spain, and had already decided to invade Russia. These events were monitored by the British on Helgoland.

This former Danish island was used as a diplomatic 'listening post' (from which access to Hamburg does not appear to have been difficult). The best known secret mission connected with Helgoland was that of the priest James Robertson whose extrication of Romana's Corps in 1808, left a detachment of sick hospitalized at Altona.

The island was also stuffed with British traders who bombarded the Foreign Office with petitions to build warehouses there. A number of facts suggest a secret mission had been under way at the time of Drinkwater's arrival and ended in failure. Captain Gilham and the *Ocean* were part of a convoy destined for a 'secret service' and the ships lay in Helgoland Road for months until the Ordnance Board wrote off their cargoes of military stores to Canning's Secret Service budget. The final fate of these ships is vague; they were either lost at sea 'or captured by the French near Calais'.

There are several intriguing references to the fact that the Grand Army, or part of it, supposedly marched to Moscow in Northampton boots, and it is highly likely that consignments of this nature passed through Hamburg or into Hanover, from whence came recruits for the King's German Legion.

Like Gilham, Colonel Hamilton and Edward Nicholas lived, and there is evidence that their relationship was sometimes strained. Reinke's charts still exist and McCullock, Browne and O'Neal are based on real people. At this time too, a report on the inadequacy of the Helgoland lighthouse was forwarded to London.

Fagan was an agent of Fouché's and a known go-between. Dieudonné of the *Chasseurs-à-Cheval*, provided the artist Gericault with a model for his spirited painting of *An Officer of the Imperial Guard*. He was destined to die in the Russian Campaign.

The rumours that passed through Helgoland in the winter of 1809, especially the news of Benjamin Bathurst, are all a matter of fact, as are the gale at the end of September, the west winds in the following March and the attack on Neuwerk in April 1810, when 'several American vessels were taken'.

Marshal Davout arrived at Hamburg in command of the Army of Germany in January 1810 and shortly afterwards shot a young man for the illegal possession of sugar loaves. The occupying forces were increased in March by stationing Molitor's Division in the outlying villages. This failed to stem the influx of imports and a furious Napoleon ordered the burning of all British goods discovered in the Hanse towns. The wily Hamburgers took to carrying luxuries past their guards in coffins. Herr Liepmann is my own invention but Nicholas refers to an influential person 'well-disposed to us', resident in, or near Hamburg, with whom a regular communication was maintained.

The fragility of Napoleon's Empire, exposed by Fouché's bold action in deploying an army to oppose the British invasion of Walcheren, was even more dramatically exploited by the republican General Malet who briefly took over the government in Paris during the Emperor's absence in Russia.

Lord Dungarth was not alone in perceiving it was the opposing might of the Russian army that was required to break the land power of Napoleon. Talleyrand had whispered as much to the Tsar at Erfurt.

It was Napoleon's claim that Tsar Alexander failed to exclude British trade which provided him with his excuse to invade Russia in 1812. He had long harboured the idea. The 'inexplicable rumour' of intended war between France and Russia reached Helgoland on 19 February 1810 and was reported to London by Edward Nicholas. Since the new ministry might consider Nicholas had exceeded his instructions, is it to be wondered at if he expressed an official doubt as to its truth and concealed his own part in its origin?